The Book of Famous Iowans

A NOVEL

DOUGLAS BAUER

AN OWL BOOK

HENRY HOLT AND COMPANY

NEW YORK

Henry Holt and Company, Inc.
Publishers since 1866
115 West 18th Street
New York, New York 10011

Henry Holt® is a registered trademark
of Henry Holt and Company, Inc.

Library of Congress Cataloging-in-Publication Data
Bauer, Douglas.
The book of famous Iowans: a novel / Douglas Bauer.
p.   cm.
ISBN 0-8050-6002-2
I. Title.
PS3552.A8358B66   1997   97-2228
813'.54—dc21   CIP

Henry Holt books are available for special promotions and
premiums. For details contact: Director, Special Markets.

First published in hardcover in 1997 by
Henry Holt and Company, Inc.

First Owl Books Edition 1998

Designed by Jessica Shatan

Printed in the United States of America
All first editions are printed on acid-free paper.∞

3   5   7   9   10   8   6   4   2

This book is for my parents,
Maudie Evans Bauer and Kenneth Bauer.

Acknowledgments

I'd like to thank the Reverend Sheldon Starkenburg for a delightful conversation and for his information regarding the practices of the Christian Reformed Church, past and present. I'm also indebted to Jim Shepard for sharing with me his knowledge of World War II bombers, especially as depicted in his fine novel, *Paper Doll*. Too, I'm grateful in the extreme to Al Lowman and Allen Peacock, champions. Finally and most of all, my thanks and my love to Sue Miller.

FAME: 1. That which people say; public report, common talk; a rumour. 2. Reputation. Usu. in good sense. 3. The condition of being much talked about. Chiefly in good sense: Celebrity, honour, renown. 4. Evil repute.

—*Oxford English Dictionary*

The Book of
Famous Iowans

1

I have kept three photographs of my mother, Leanne McQueen Vaughn, and anybody who sees one of them invariably asks me who the beautiful young woman in the picture is. No one recognizes a trace of her in me, since I grew, against her certain prediction, to resemble my father. I have his fair coloring; his stocky build; his wide, square face.

It would be easy to think that the photos had been taken, not over a decade, but within a span of a few weeks. For her face in the first, when she was fifteen, appears remarkably the same as in the last, that of a woman whose sophisticated beauty has matured just moments before the picture was snapped. Her expression, too, is closely repeated and seems to me one of cool epiphany. It's conveyed by a watchful gleam in her eyes and in the way she holds her head, gracefully extending her neck so that she looks to be peering out over the heads of a crowd. I know well how it felt to be within its range (and it often felt powerfully confidential and secure). But thinking now of her actions, the choices she made, and how they permanently changed us all, I see her expression as suggesting that she has raised her eyes to look past the distractions of hope and innocence, in order to see what she needed to see.

The first picture shows her standing with her aunt, Marla Jo McQueen, in the backyard of their apartment at 2008 Van Lennen Street in Cheyenne, Wyoming. The year is 1940. The yard looks to be a tiny plot, a forlorn stand of scrubby vegetation bent and leafless against a length of cross-lathed wooden fence. Marla Jo, who raised my mother from the age of ten, is wearing her cafe waitress uniform. My mother's light wool dress is belted at the waist and a row of buttons runs from its neck to its hem. She and her aunt are standing erect with their arms around each other's waists, and their resemblance is unsettling. Both of them have the tall, thin bodies, long necks, and sharp features apparently characteristic of the McQueens. But Marla Jo is a plain, homely woman, her thinness bony and awkward; her long neck disproportionate; her sharply pointed nose warring as a hawk's. In my mother, these same qualities are softened in an utterly feminine way.

She's twenty years old in the second photo, leaning against a 1940 Chevrolet, wearing a loose, floral-patterned short-sleeved dress. Two suitcases stand next to her. The look of the trees behind her and the season of her dress and the Chevrolet make it certain that the time is early spring, and, seeing the suitcases, I assume this to be the very moment of my parents' departure from Cheyenne for Iowa: the Chevrolet weighted down, the punitively barren breadth of Nebraska awaiting them. If so, her look of questing poise is especially impressive here. For she surely knew at least the essence of what awaited her once the secret in this photo—that her pregnancy was "early," as the term of the times politely spoke of it—was revealed to the eight hundred people of New Holland, my father's hometown, where he was taking her to begin their married life.

In the last of the three pictures, she and I are sitting on the back steps of the farmhouse porch in fading summer sunlight. I'm five or six, hinge-boned as a foal. With her arm around me, she's looking into the camera, the young mother in a light cotton dress, and the nature of her beauty appears so apart from her surroundings as to make her presence in the photo inapt. It's as though someone had posed a fashion model of the era with some gangly child, the two of them improbably plunked down on a sagging wooden stoop in the middle of the prairie.

2

The tractor I drove when I helped my father farm was the same one that killed my grandfather Vaughn. It was a lumbering, burnt-red Case, massive as a house within my child's sense of scale and more than a decade old when I began to use it. In order to reach its seat I had to step from the ground to its wagon hitch, then pause to plan my footholds like a climber on a rock face before swinging myself up into place.

I operated the tractor with three simple levers: the first moved in a left-to-right arc and governed the speed; just below it was the gear shift; the third, a hand clutch on my right, sprouted vertically from the innards of the Case. This clutch, as I employed it, was the tractor's vital instrument. Throwing it all the way forward locked it in place, taking the Case out of gear and bringing it to a halt. Conversely, pulling the clutch back toward me caused the tractor to ease into action with the unexcitable obedience of an ancient dray horse.

From the high seat of the Case, I, not yet a teenager, blithely navigated my father's fields while my mind left the task and drifted off into dreams. As I drove I might pretend that I was once again steering my way to victory in the International Speed Disking Championships, a tightly contested competition as I imagined it, held each year in one of our loamy and ideally gradient fields. As the name makes clear, it drew talented young farmers from many countries, but my strongest rival was a fellow Iowan named Telfer, a relentless contestant, alas, forever doomed to be judged the world's second-fastest disker.

At other times, when I should have been paying close attention to whatever implement I was pulling—to the depth at which the disk's blades were working, to the precision of the path I was drawing with a harrow—I might instead be singing happily above the engine noise, making up lyrics or rehearsing other songs I'd perform later that day on my nationally televised *Will Vaughn Show*, a popular hour of music and guests which, in one of my more embellished fantasies, was shot in various locations around our farm, the show's informal tone modeled after that of Perry Como's.

I paid close attention to Como's television style, for he was a favorite of both my mother and my widowed grandmother, Dorothy Vaughn, who lived with us in an upstairs apartment of the huge and eccentrically gabled old house she'd shared with her husband.

Neither my mother nor my grandmother thought much of Perry Como's voice but they enjoyed his casual and self-mocking manner. In my mother's case, there was an ingredient of the professional's empathy in her interest. For she herself had been a nightclub singer, a seventeen-year-old girl whose sophisticated beauty had let her lie about her age in order to perform at the Valencia Lounge in Cheyenne.

As she watched Perry Como forget a line, then laugh and ask the orchestra to start the song again, my mother would smile and shake her head and say, "He fumbles the words and just makes it part of the act." She was a student in general of the styles of popular singers and television hostesses. She especially scrutinized their entrances. "Hurry smoothly" was the ultimate refinement of her theory and her frequent advice to me when she served as the studio audience at the *Will Vaughn Show*.

My grandmother's way of admiring Como was to say that he wasn't "trying to act like a big shot." This was the most damning charge she could think to bring against someone, and, as it happened, she thought to bring it frequently. As my grandmother viewed life, it required you to strive for distinction beyond your Iowa circumstances, then offer something close to regret and apology if you should happen to achieve it. For her, ambition was a measure of vision and resolve, while riding it successfully made you deeply suspect. She held this perception all her life, apparently blind to its essential contradiction. Especially, as I said, she tracked the lives of famous Iowans and had even at some point begun to keep a scrapbook which she filled with clippings from papers and magazines. This was her evolving record of local celebrities and how they'd distinguished our state with their humility or caused it embarrassment by trying to be a big shot.

As a boy, I naturally thought nothing of the fact that I, the only child of a grain farmer, would have my early notions shaped less by him than by these two strong women, both fantasists, who paid a great deal of attention to the idea of—what?—well, of fame, I suppose. For in their separate ways, each obsessively considered what fame was and how it should behave, watching those who had it and whether they carried it with prideful inelegance or diffidence or style.

I'm sure, in contrast, I sensed my father's world, his work, to be one of narrow and local ritual, an infinitely literal life that was not what my mother, or my grandmother either, hinted to me was the life of notice; one that was elsewhere; one that was away. Now, forty years later, I wonder at times what I didn't wonder then: how a man on a tractor is able to engage the unaltering earth as it passes beneath his wheels. Whether he must be able to imagine nothing. Or, rather, to imagine everything. And when I ask myself this, I can only say it seems that a farmer at his task must inhabit one of these states of mind or the other. Which one, I don't know, although it seems to me they would be equally impossible to achieve.

Still, thinking back on those days, I see myself atop the Case, a boy and dreaming-ignorant, happy to be mimicking my father's work. I hear the boom of the tractor's engine on ignition. I feel the waking tug of its hibernative strength. And I'm sure I recall these features so well because some part of me was vividly fixed as I drove on knowing, as I said, it was the tractor that killed my grandfather.

———

The Iowa winter of 1945 began in late November with its usual ferocity. In New Holland, there was a Thanksgiving blizzard and another in December, glazing a surface of snow that, it seemed, would be the season's lasting coat. But early in February the cold suddenly broke and days of blessed weather followed one after another. The temperature reached sixty, then seventy degrees, the air as benign as the soft heat of June. The snow melted quickly and the ice broke on the rivers and the rivers spilled out over the silty bottom land. For more than three weeks, the warmth was unremitting, a torrential storm of ideal sun, and people tried to recall a comparable time.

My grandfather, Henry Vaughn, had observed the first week of heat with a farmer's avid interest in weather, any weather. But he was an energetic man and, with no necessary chores, his fields gleaned and at rest, he began to suffer through the second week. Increasingly he paced. After feeding his chickens, his only livestock at the time, he hurried to the barn and looked around in vain and returned, forlorn and taskless, to the house.

Then the third week began and by that time it must have felt to my grandfather as if the weather were mocking him. On Wednesday morning of that week, leaving my grandmother sleeping, he rose as always to supervise the daybreak and walked out to the porch to drink his first cup of coffee. As he sat there the dawn's warmth reached him and he saw the sun glinting off the ponds of melted snow that now covered the acreage. Everywhere he looked there was mud, like troweled manure.

What happened next has been deduced and refined to the family's official account of that morning. At some point he got up and pulled on his boots and left the porch and walked through puddles toward the shed where all his machinery was kept through the winter. Inside, he climbed up into the seat of the burnt-red Case, which he'd purchased at the end of the previous season. He set its levers and climbed down, slid the crank in and turned it through many tries until the engine sparked. He let it idle for a bit, winter leaving it in gasps and shudders, then scampered around and remounted and backed the Case out into the morning light.

He'd driven no more than twenty feet into the barnyard when the tractor sank in mud. Again he jumped down, hurried to a nearby woodpile, and brought back some pieces of old barn siding. Believing he had a better chance of backing up than moving forward, he wedged the boards as far beneath the tires as possible.

And then he let impatience have him. Still standing just behind the Case, he reached up until he grasped the hand clutch, then drew it partially back, letting the tractor creep slowly in reverse. In this way he could keep the boards in place while the tractor traversed them; he could do two things at once. And when one of the boards slid from underneath a tire, he reached with his foot to kick it back into alignment and slipped in the mud and fell beneath the wheels. In falling, he instinctively held the clutch for support, which locked the Case in gear, and it continued back, rolling effortlessly up and over him, the right rear tire responding to the sudden traction of his body and gaining speed as it crushed his thigh and his pelvis and his chest, before his head, and his arms, which he'd thrown up to protect himself, freakishly provided enough resistance. The Case came to a stop and its cold engine died.

When my grandmother discovered him an hour later, she refused to make sense of what she saw. Her thought was that he'd grown so desperate in his boredom that he'd staged this elaborate and dangerous hoax. From twenty feet away, she called to him. Her voice was frightened and shrilly reproachful; she was appalled by the lengths to which he'd gone to play this joke—lying in the mud, filthy with its spatters, theatrically sprawled against the wheel of a tractor.

Reaching him then and bending down to meet his opened eyes, she read his expression as one of embarrassment. There was no indication on his face of any pain and he looked as though he were about to speak, expressing apology for his own foolishness. He appeared so at ease that she may have even waited to hear him admit the desperation of his prank. Then, finally recognizing the path the wheel had taken, she asked herself how she could get her husband free without causing him any further injury. She looked down at him and said, "This isn't funny, Hal. Help me here. Tell me what to do." All the while the tractor waited like an incurious horse standing over its thrown rider.

No amount of speculation could answer what my grandfather had had in mind that morning. Why he'd started the Case and backed it out of the shed. What task he might have possibly thought he could get done with the spring mud laking everywhere.

What my grandmother always said, in answer to the mystery, was something beautifully uncomplicated. She believed that the considerable part of my grandfather's personality that was forever a boy's had simply surrendered to the perfection of the day and he'd decided to take his new tractor for a drive.

My father, Lewis Vaughn, was drafted two weeks to the day after he'd turned twenty-one. He was sent from New Holland to basic training in Des Moines and then to Fort Francis E. Warren outside Cheyenne. There, as a mechanic, he fit 50-caliber Browning machine guns into the turrets of B17 Flying Fortresses. And it was there that he met and fell in love with Leanne McQueen, the beautiful young singer at the Valencia Lounge, a bar popular with soldiers. When, after two years of courtship, they learned Leanne was pregnant, they married and moved into a first-floor room on Evans Avenue, in the shadow of the state capitol building. My mother had just turned twenty.

On February 25, 1945, my father was fetally curled in the swinging seat of a ball turret, testing the smoothness and extension of its turns, when he was summoned to his captain's office and given word of his father's death.

Numb and frantic after receiving the news, he caught a base bus back into Cheyenne and ran home to his and my mother's new apartment, where she was getting ready to go to work at the Valencia. After much discussion that night and the next day, and against her wishes to be with him, he decided to return alone to New Holland. Perhaps he was thinking that he couldn't know for sure how long he'd have to stay. And maybe he felt too that the surprise of their marriage and the revelation of his new wife's pregnancy might create a social awkwardness that would be unfair to his mother; that her only concern should be to host and to exemplify the mourning.

My father spent two days in New Holland, presiding over the funeral and assisting his mother in all her legal matters. When he returned to Cheyenne he somehow found the words to tell my mother that he'd been made to realize he had no option but to accept an early discharge. They'd be going back to Iowa, to the farm outside New Holland, and that was where they would take up their new life.

I've often wondered whether that decision would have held if my mother *had* gone with him to New Holland for the funeral, where she'd have at least glimpsed a place where all but a few families—my father's among them—followed the tenets of the Dutch Christian Reformed Church, a congregation which did not permit drinking or smoking or any games of cards or chance, did not allow its members to go to movies or watch television shows or attend dances.

If she had stepped into that world of powerful austerity, if she'd glimpsed enough to sense the life of the farm, seen the fertile distances and heard the earth's keen silence, might she have feared that it was not a place where they could dream the dreams my father had said they would be dreaming? Or was she too young, at twenty, or too used to adventure, so that everything and every place looked only to hold more?

However resistant she was, however accepting, when she heard where she'd be living she consulted a map. My mother had not been east of Wyoming and she brought a western sensibility to the notion of geography. She'd assumed, having heard my father speak of the great dissimilarities between Cheyenne and New Holland, that most of America lay between the two places. But looking at the map for the first time, she saw that only one state, Nebraska, separated them and decided that Iowa could not be so different from Wyoming.

Next she noticed that the mere stretch of Illinois—its northern breadth on the map cinched like a corseted waist—was all that lay between her new home and Chicago, where the country's most famous dance bands played in the ballroom atop the Edgewater Beach Hotel. All in all, it appeared to her that these new distances were no greater than those that westerners were used to traveling; no greater than a span of Colorado, a length of

Utah. So she grew excited at the idea of driving regularly to Chicago to listen to the bands at the Edgewater Beach. And she thought, perhaps, as their fortunes improved, she and my father could keep a small apartment there and travel freely back and forth.

More than once I heard her describe her skewed anticipation of what life was going to be in Iowa; how she'd gone to the map and had taken note of the easy-seeming distances. And it occurs that, like me atop the massive Case, she was then already using the plain plot of the farm as the world from which to launch her daydreams of escape.

When she spoke of that time, as they prepared to leave Cheyenne, she usually added that she suspected her fantasies were in part a rallying reaction to my father's disappointment. She said their life's sudden turn had made him so unhappy that she'd wanted to provide the light and hope for both of them. And it's true, as I remember, that there was always amusement in her voice when she talked about her expectations of their coming to New Holland, asking her listener to agree with her that no one had ever been quite so naive.

She especially favored the word *naive*, which she always mispronounced, with loving emphasis, "nah-ehv," as if to make it clear that though she'd ended up in Iowa she certainly recognized and could pronounce a word from French.

3

One night early in the summer of this story, my mother returned home to start supper, having been away from the farm all afternoon, supposedly to town to shop and run some other errands. A flirtatious energy propelled her as she hurried about the kitchen, and all the while she chattered nonsensically, asking me what I'd been doing that day and then a minute later asking me again. She seemed a little out of breath. Her voice rose a few times, its timbre eager and careless.

Of course I didn't know that she'd just come from seeing her lover, Bobby Markum, but I did recognize that her mood was extreme, threatening to reach a pitch of pure emotion which might, I had learned, prove dangerous for us all. And yet, as was also usually true, her mood that night was compelling, seeming to hold at the same time all that was possible and all that was unpredictable.

I've said that she studied the timing and style of the way performers came onstage. And looking back, I realize that she herself was someone who came into rooms and conversations and people's lives with an unaccountable poise. Even her moods seemed impressively *entered*. If not in control of them, she seemed to subside with enthusiasm into them. There was the sense that she concentrated, giving her disposition of the moment everything she had, whether she was angry or joyous—or merely reflective. Indeed, she was a woman of whom you could say that she was ferociously contemplating something. And always, her moods were the medium of my days, like weather, like a climate with its shiftings and its seasons.

At one point that evening she looked up from the stove and, suddenly breaking off her monologue, said to me, sitting at the table, "You are so *pretty*, Will! I forget just how *pretty* you are."

I was three months shy of twelve that June, and naturally horrified to hear this. *Girls* were told they were pretty, so what I heard her saying was that I looked like a girl. But when I shouted my protest, she simply laughed and waved it away. "Some day," she said, "you'll be glad you're pretty. *Handsome* men are a dime a dozen, but there aren't many pretty ones, and girls appreciate the difference." I felt no wish to have this distinction clarified and was grateful she seemed finished with the subject as she continued in the kitchen, glancing now and then through the window to the fields.

She could see my father out there on his tractor, a distant speck, drawing a progress in the earth that appeared at any chosen instant as undetectable as a minute hand's. And over the next hour, as though his effort were the measuring of her spirit, she began to fall from her giddiness at the same slow steady pace of his path across the horizon. The look of lovely foolishness gradually left her face and her normal voice resumed. The nature of her distraction became introverted until her attention seemed to leave the kitchen altogether.

Then she suddenly came up out of herself again and when she spoke to me her voice was alert and she asked what all I'd done that day. I couldn't believe it. I started to say she'd already asked me that three or four times. But then somehow it seemed she hadn't, not this person who was asking now. So I described once more the chores and solitary games that had occupied me. We were setting the table for supper while I talked and her sudden intense interest began to feel like scrutiny. In an effort to break it, I confessed something to her. I liked to detail some small misbehavior for my mother, often exaggerating it, because she rarely tried to hide her delight in hearing it and I placed enormous stock in delighting her.

So I told her that, while gathering the eggs that afternoon, I'd been seized with the need to practice my pitching delivery and had wound up and hurled an egg the length of the chicken coop.

She smiled, then threw back her head and laughed. "Just one?" she asked.

"Well, three," I said. "Well, actually, five. Six. But I cleaned everything up."

She laughed again and said that by all rights she should tell my father. She reminded me of the lecture I'd gotten from him the previous week when I'd made up a new sport, riding my bicycle wildly among the chickens in the barnyard, frightening them so badly they'd stopped laying for two days. She'd asked what possessed me to do these things and I'd told her the game was called "hen slalom"—I'd just watched some skiing championships on television—as if giving my mischief a name would justify it.

I was pleased my story of pitching the eggs had worked, that I'd gotten her light humor back. I went on, explaining that as I'd stepped into the day-gloom of the chicken coop, I'd been recalling some advice that Bobby Markum had given me. And then I confided to her that I thought almost constantly about certain things Bobby had been telling me. This was some weeks before I learned of my mother's affair with Bobby, so to me he was still just the pitcher on our fine New Holland town team and someone I, the team's batboy, worshiped to distraction.

My mother listened to me describe Bobby's instructions and after a silence said, "Well, you know . . . you don't have to do everything someone tells you." Her voice was stretched tight as skin over her words. She'd paused at the table, setting down some water glasses, and she gave me a look that was resonant with conflict; conspiracy and sadness were surely in it, and there could well have been a thread of detached amusement, too.

I said, "What are you talking about?"

She dipped her head and said nothing, watching her hands arrange the knives and forks.

"Bobby's a great pitcher," I persisted.

"So you've said."

"We just talk about baseball."

"That's good," she nearly whispered.

"So why are you making such a big deal of it?"

After another silence, she said, "I'm glad he's helping you."

She was weak-voiced and distant while we ate that night. Both my father and I glanced over at her from time to time. Whatever he was thinking, or fearing or suspecting, I've come to regard her behavior that evening as the first evidence of her affair. But at the time, as the minutes passed while we ate supper, I began instead to wonder if I was responsible for the way she was acting. And soon enough it seemed to me I was, that she must be struggling to keep my secret of the broken eggs.

After I'd finished eating I went outside to play, increasingly troubled as night came on by the idea that I had put her in the position of lying for me with her silence. From where I stood at the end of the yard, I looked back toward the house, then glanced up to see what lights were on in my grandmother's upstairs apartment. Her kitchen was lit, though I saw no sign of her at her table by the window. I felt the urge to hurry in and climb the stairs and ask her if I should admit to my father that I'd broken a few eggs. I'd say I didn't see why it mattered to my mother so much, but it seemed my telling him might relieve her burden.

I often retreated to the sanctum of my grandmother's rooms, often in order to get her advice. I adored my grandmother but, besides that, I asked for her help because her answers were always so satisfying; they came swiftly and decisively and with a bracing clarity, rising as they did from her entirely private logic. She would listen to me in the same way she received the news of the world in general—with a kind of unimpressed equanimity that made me feel, not that my questions were new or valid, but that they were no more foolish than anyone else's. Yet this message, as it came from her, was somehow an encouraging one, or at least not discouraging, in part I suppose because she made it plain that whatever she might think of my concerns was separate from what she thought of me.

That night, standing in our yard, I'd just decided to go in and talk to her when I heard my parents speaking and realized they'd come out from the kitchen and were sitting on the screened porch. Their voices reached me faintly and I thought I could hear a quality of complaint in both of them.

I began again to think about what I'd done that afternoon. How I'd moved down the row of cubby holes in the chicken coop and reached in and lifted two or three eggs from a nest. The usual dabs of shit had dried on them, pasting strands of nesting straw to the shells. I deposited all but one egg in my bucket, and when I began to turn it this way and that, it became a baseball. So I assumed Bobby Markum's pitching stance of lordly poise, held the egg behind my back, and peered through the dimness to the far wall, where New Holland's catcher, Burl Starkenburg, squatted waiting for my pitch. A few chickens hunkered close to me, offering up their drawls of matchless ignorance. I nodded, having gotten Burl's sign, and, remembering to arch my back as

Bobby told me, I pitched the egg and watched it splatter against the wall. I reached into the bucket for another and threw it too, and another, and another, until I'd thrown six. Then something told me I could risk no more. As I hurried to clean up the dripping mess, I made a sound in the back of my throat—that long, wind-tunnel exhale denoting a crowd's wild approval.

Now I could no longer see my parents' silhouettes on the porch—the darkness had become full—but I continued to get the weak breeze of their voices. I could hear that my mother was doing more of the talking. It sounded as though they were speaking more calmly. I took this to mean that things had relaxed and that I'd escaped, thanks to her. Relieved, I again began to practice my windup, with Bobby's classic delivery in my mind. Weight on the front foot. Transfer it back as the motion starts. Weight forward again as you lift your arms.

Then my father's voice was a sudden shard of anger, and I recoiled and froze, even as I realized he wasn't calling out to me. My mother's voice immediately rose to his and it seemed to me I had no choice but to go to the porch and tell him what I'd done. I stood immobile for some seconds, then decided I should pray. I was praying prodigally at this time, testing various ideas of God, and the notion of Him as an unpredictable celestial bully was the one that most impelled me. If He did not answer your prayer, it was not that He was off tending to someone else's, but rather that He'd heard yours perfectly and just decided to ignore it. So my own prayers contained concrete requests and precise quantities that let me know instantly if He was looking favorably on me.

I proposed to God that if the thing for me to do was confess, He should show me by making one of my parents speak with anger again before I'd counted to ten. I hadn't reached "three" before I heard them trade another sharp exchange. I turned and started toward the house.

As I walked up the lawn, I was thinking that if I'd broken only one or two eggs, my mother might not have felt such pressure to protect me. I asked myself why I hadn't been able to stop at two. Or at least admitted only that many to her? If I'd said I'd broken two, would my lie, I wondered, have been offset by its saving her this trouble? And what was the number that took you uncontestedly into the realm of sin? Four or five? Perhaps as few as three? Why, then, had I broken so many? On the other hand, what had told me I should stop at six?

I knew they couldn't see me approaching in the darkness and when I was close enough to hear their words, I realized they were speaking, not of eggs, but of Cheyenne.

I stopped to listen. It was my mother's voice, edgy and defensive, and she was remembering the Valencia Lounge. Listening hard, I could hear her speaking of the players in her band—she referred to them as that, as the players in *her* band—and she began to praise its leader, a young man nicknamed Specs who played trombone.

"You know, he *was* the best I ever sang with, Lewis."

There was, in my father's laugh, a harsh, cornered meanness of response.

"Laugh all you want," she said icily. "Specs was very good."

"The best you ever sang with?" my father said. "Well, that might be true, Leanne. It probably is. But it isn't saying a whole lot, is it?"

My mother could finely modulate what she wanted in her voice: gravity, sarcasm, disappointment—the coloring technique of a singer of ballads. It's perhaps the best evidence I have that she did in fact have talent. She said, "Well, my, my, Lewis, it always surprises me. I forget how much you know about music."

I imagined him wearily shaking his head before he said, "Oh, Leanne, why? Just . . . *why?*" He said nothing more and neither did my mother. Finally he got up and disappeared into the house.

I knew they'd been arguing heatedly for weeks, though I don't recall a time besides this night when I heard them fighting about Cheyenne. But my memory of our days that spring and early summer is that we were all living in a uniquely troubled atmosphere, one alive with a tension far beyond the more familiar ones brought on by my mother's moods. I'm not sure if I perceived this then or if my thoughts are prejudiced by what I know now. So I'll say that, as I believe I felt it, there was a sense of something new and oblique in the air during that time, something which moved like an angry draft that stayed low to the floors at the edges of the rooms, or which murmured from just beyond wherever I was at the moment; from the kitchen if I were in the living room, from the porch if I were in the kitchen. And then these murmurings might all at once grow harsh and reach my ears as spits of sibilance made by my parents' effort to avoid an outburst.

I don't know how directly, by this time in early June, their gathering unhappiness had to do with Bobby Markum. That is, as I said, I've no idea if my father suspected anything; if my mother's behavior when they were alone betrayed her confusion, gave away at least that much.

After my father left the porch, I stayed standing as quietly as possible, less than thirty feet away. I couldn't see my mother, but because I knew where she was I had a voyeur's sense of power, a power I didn't want, for it left me feeling awkward and ignorant of what to do. My eyes were briefly diverted by my grandmother's kitchen light going out upstairs. I imagined her moving into her living room to read the paper and wait for the television news, which she watched every night with an overseer's interest, as if she'd given the world its assignments that morning and was sitting down to learn how they'd been carried out.

Then I saw a match flare in the darkness of the porch and watched my mother's cigarette pulse red as she drew on it.

After a further stillness, she suddenly began to hum. Her voice was aimless at first, but quickly gained interest until she'd moved fully inside a song, not giving it words but applying a subtle and respectful inflection. I didn't recognize what she was humming, probably something she'd sung at the Valencia, a ballad from among those she'd been thinking about moments before. Whatever it was, she continued the song, stopping twice to take a drag from her cigarette, through all its verses and choruses, prolonging its last note, her voice ascending and holding and very slowly fading.

There was a pause. And then she began another song, humming it as well in that same quiet and completely crafted fashion, as though she were closing her second set.

This was all strangely beautiful to me: the sound of her voice coming out of the dark, the thrilling sense of catching her in a moment so unguarded, and the soft concern with which she offered the songs, making it seem as if she felt she must whisper her indulgence through the monitoring Iowa night and all it was made of that didn't—couldn't—understand.

When she'd ended again, she put out her cigarette and lit another and was quiet.

I waited a bit longer until it was clear she was finished, then coughed loudly to announce that I was near. I walked on up to the porch, having decided to say I'd just come from the far reaches of the acreage. I pretended to be panting, as though I'd been running all the way.

"Mom?" I called.

"Hi, honey," she said.

"I was out in the barnyard," I said. I opened the door and stepped into the porch.

"What were you doing out there?" she asked.

"Oh, nothing," I said. "Just playing." I plopped down next to her and sighed theatrically to show her my exhaustion. "What're *you* doing?"

"Oh, nothing," she said. Her voice was smiling. She smoked and said, "Just listening to the crickets."

I paused to listen too because I hadn't noticed any crickets. And now, concentrating, I heard that there were none.

She said, "It's so still, isn't it, without any breeze. I'll bet you could hear the tiniest sound somebody made out there in the yard tonight. Even just their *regular* breathing."

In my instant fear, I started to speak some foolish lie about a game I'd been playing, but she interrupted me to say, "It's late, Will. You should get to bed."

———

I remember her often singing as she moved about the house, but singing really to herself in a private, offhand fashion. And I remember her singing spiritedly along with the radio. Maybe, for my father, in their happiest times, she sang songs from those years to take the two of them back. I'd like to think she did. I'd like to think he asked her to.

But I will always think of her that summer evening as wanting me to know she was singing just to me. And I can't remember another instance that catches her warring nature more fully, for I have to believe she wished that night to give me something of her truest self, but she needed just as much to let me know I hadn't fooled her. I feel there was, besides her double cross, a generosity and a desire for alliance in my mother's impulse to sing me safely in, back in from where I stood, out there in the darkness.

I said that her moods were the climate I lived in. And by extension, I felt susceptible to the weather of my parents' marriage generally, with its periods of calm and incidents of turbulence. But I know this is true for every child, though perhaps especially an only child. Besides, until the change that began that spring, I'd surely gotten comfortable with their patterns, thought them unremarkable, and understood that, also like weather, the life their marriage made was always simply there, was the thing we breathed no matter what.

I imagine the Valencia band. It has played a few opening numbers, then moved into a song which Specs can have his way with—"I'll Get By" or "Moonglow" or "I'll Never Smile Again." After completing a first pass of melody, Specs is standing and leaning into the microphone and forcing his words into an awkward verse-like meter: "Won't you greet *our* canary queen, the lov-uh-ly, the tal-en-ted Miss Lee-*anne* McQueen."

And now my mother, already a close student of the show business entrance, having learned to wait one count, then a second, then a third—a delay designed to lace the audience's response with a subtle rush of relief when she appears—is at last walking out to the Valencia's applause.

Tall and slender and resplendently sequined, she's moving left to right beneath the shaft of spotlight. As she crosses, she's looking out into the smoky darkness to offer the room the contradiction of her unaffected smile and a cool, monarchal wave.

My father is sitting at a table watching her move within the circle of cheap spotlight, its harshness punishing the mere hint of a flaw and beneath which she appears utterly flawless. In the dingy and promiscuous air of the Valencia, she is offering a pure sexual power and he's accepting it with the unchecked eagerness of someone who, at twenty-one, has just been formally made a man and is equally thrilled and terrified to be one.

The sense that passed between them through those nights in the Valencia was surely more than enough of whatever it is— energy, intrigue, lust's sweet unease—that people believe is the stuff that makes a life. But maybe this is easy for me to imagine because of all the times I heard their voices *lift* on a memory of Cheyenne and become fresh and simple with the air of youth once more.

4

Until the age of ten, my mother was raised, with a negligence more ignorant than malign, by her father, Dean McQueen, who mined quartz when he was sober in various lode camps around Leadville, Colorado. These circumstances are quite at odds with my mother's patrician features and her inherent social grace.

She provided only glimpses of her growing up in a handful of treasured anecdotes. From what she did say, I know that her father was a tall, skinny, spider-limbed man. I know that his long, thin face was an intricate network of deep seams and that over the years he acquired a look characteristic of drunks who spend the day outdoors: chronically malnourished and with his skin leathered by the sun and the wind, he gave an appearance of tanned emaciation.

Her describing him so closely was by way of explaining that her name, Leanne, was her father's little joke; that his lanky body in combination with the rhyme his names made had led to his being called Lean Dean, Lean Dean McQueen, or most often simply Lean by those who worked and drank with him. Apparently he was proud of his nickname and considered it a term of affection he'd been awarded for his companionable life among unusually thirsty men. So *Leanne* was his idea of making it feminine, his clever way of calling his daughter *Junior*.

I suspect my mother hoped this story, like the few others she'd kept, would make it clear that she was different from the cautious people and the orderly lives she had come to be surrounded by in New Holland; that her father, the boozy glint-eyed mineral miner, was some renegade eccentric unique to the frontier; and that, by extension, she was too.

But there were things and people she never used in order to emphasize her separateness. Most obviously, it was somehow made plain that the subject of her mother was never to be raised, and, with the exception of a single hysterical instance, I don't remember that it was.

But how does such a rule get laid down and understood? I've wondered if perhaps I once asked about the woman, my other grandmother after all, and received some kind of reprimand that I've suppressed. Though that seems unlikely, I have no better explanation. I don't recall ever being told that a discussion was forbidden, or that it seemed the least strange there never was one.

What I've come to learn about her, from my father and Grandmother Vaughn, is mostly a matter of their impressions and conjecture. So she remains a stock suggestion of a life lived, nothing more. But as much as I can piece together her story, she met Lean Dean where everyone else met him: in a bar in or near Leadville, Colorado, then a mining settlement northeast of Aspen and in those days a place of notable squalor.

She was a local girl. When she met Dean McQueen she might have been as young as fifteen. Her father was a merchant, a grocer, my grandmother thought, and no one knows of any brothers or sisters. Having doubtless seen men like Dean

McQueen from the time she could remember, she could not have held any illusions about the nature of his life. In any case, she started spending her hours with Lean in the Leadville bars. Though she was underage, the attitude in mining towns was casual on this issue.

However much time passed from their meeting to her pregnancy to the hastily arranged marriage, my mother was born in June of 1927, and less than a year later *her* mother was gone, not actually gone from Leadville, but gone from Lean Dean and from wherever the three of them had begun their meager domesticity. Having loved her hours in the local saloons, she likely took up a life in them, and that's the last of anything remotely factual that survives her.

———

Just how my mother was raised until the age of ten is a question she gave conflicting answers to. Sometimes she claimed that Lean Dean took her with him from camp to camp, the two of them living in tents or lean-tos, or stealing nights in abandoned cabins, and that she whimsically visited whatever school was near.

She made oblique references at other times to quite different histories. She occasionally recited the names of a few men— Sam was one, and Bo, and someone nicknamed "Action Jack"— who were chiefly responsible for her, implying that she was being raised communally. She depicted the world of the mining camps as law abiding and domestically unremarkable.

But her story of getting to Cheyenne, when she had just turned eleven, was one she told with consistency, and maybe its details indicate its invention—her having thought through in such careful miniature the account of her traveling by train with her father for Thanksgiving Day with her Aunt Marla Jo.

It was apparently the custom for the two of them to spend

holidays with her aunt. And on this one, customarily, Lean was drunk by one o'clock, at which time he rose unsteadily from the table and said he was going out for some fresh air. He paused at the door and said, "I'll be right back."

Two weeks later, Leanne and Marla Jo received a letter from him, postmarked Colorado Springs, in which he apologized for having been out of touch. He explained that he'd fully intended to return that Thanksgiving afternoon, but he'd met someone while on his walk (which meant he'd found a bar that was open), a man who was also spending the holiday with relatives in Cheyenne and who spoke of needing someone to work for him in his feed and grain store in Colorado Springs. On the spur of the moment he'd offered Lean the job of general clerk. Lean wrote that this had sounded like a very good idea—steady work indoors through the winter—and that the man, whose name was Lucius, said he was leaving in five minutes and that Lean could ride with him, and *should* if he wanted the job.

Unmentioned in all of this was any notion that he might have telephoned or sent a telegram immediately from Colorado Springs, or insisted, before he left Cheyenne, that they stop briefly to explain things to his daughter. Instead, he said he'd been very busy at the feed and grain store, and that it had taken some time to find a decent room to rent. He said the unfortunate aspect of Colorado Springs was all the Mexicans, but on the other hand all the Mexicans meant there were lots of places that served great green chili. He ended by saying that as soon as things were settled, he'd get up to Cheyenne to bring Leanne back.

They heard from him again just before Christmas in a brief note saying he'd be there for the holiday.

He arrived looking drawn. His normally ruddy skin was the shade of jaundice. Thinking back, my mother attributed his appearance to the pressure of having to stay sober in the feed store, then fitting a whole day's drinking into the hours after work before he fell into bed.

She was excited to see him and sensed that he was glad to see her too, though she remembered the visit as passing somberly, Lean's day-long arc of drunkenness a ceremonious one.

If Lean and Marla Jo had talked of what to do about Leanne, there was no word when he was ready to leave the next morning of her going with him. He said good-bye and kissed her and told her he'd see her soon, managing to make his parting seem as though it were a ritual already long established.

Lean continued to visit on holidays and, now and then, as an unannounced surprise. But more and more often he failed to appear when he'd said he would, though whenever he hadn't come, a letter of explanation would arrive two or three weeks later. The first of these were tedious in their outpouring of details. But over time they became more lively, their tales inventive and labyrinthine. It was as though Lean had accidentally discovered a pleasure and a talent, for there was a sense of real application in the letters that suggested he was entertaining himself as he wrote.

And perhaps inevitably—at least that was the word my mother used in her telling—she began to hope that Lean wouldn't come when he'd promised he would because his letters afterward, so warm and imaginative, were far more loving than he ever was in person.

———

My mother had a friend in New Holland, her only truly close friend there, a woman named Eleanor Beal, Nell Beal. She was a year or two younger than my mother, though, in her late twenties, she'd already begun to age in a way that marked those farm women who were virtually equal participants in the work with their husbands. She was growing ever more muscular and weathered. A row of thread-thin vertical lines, like a tribal tattoo, ran parallel between her nose and upper lip. She had been born in New Holland and had married Carl Beal, her classmate since kindergarten, a month after they'd graduated from high school. They had two baby girls and owned the farm adjoining ours. From our kitchen windows you could look uninterruptedly to the east across the fields to their house and their buildings clustered half a mile away.

I suppose Nell's interest in my mother was in part idolatrous, she having come to New Holland from such a distance and such a life. And I suspect my mother enjoyed and encouraged the worshipful nature of Nell's regard. But she genuinely liked Nell for good reasons beyond that. Nell was spirited and funny and able to observe life in New Holland from a shrewd remove, even if she'd not drawn a breath away from it.

Nell was amazed by my mother's childhood and now and then she asked to hear again some portion of the saga of Lean and Cheyenne. The last time I remember my mother telling Nell the story, they were sitting at our kitchen table watching a hard late-morning rain. Nell's baby girls were playing at her feet. Because of the weather, I was roaming about the house, in and out of the kitchen, listening idly.

My mother seemed that morning to be giving the story new thought. Nell was watching her tell it, and something in the air made me pause and do the same.

She said, "Mostly, I felt lucky to be with Marla Jo, to have *any* place to be. But I suppose I was afraid that if I asked what was going on, it'd be in a way like reminding them of something that had slipped their minds and then I'd have to go live with Lean again." She smiled. "And then sometimes, with my aunt, when it seemed it was going to be permanent, I'd get scared of *that*. Not of her, she was fine. Just something in the idea of it."

She paused and reached for a cigarette and, after lighting it, appeared to grow deeply interested in the rain against the window. Then she said, "But overall, I think I felt it wasn't so strange to be living day to day."

———

So far as I know, the last word my mother had about her father was a letter from Marla Jo, some months before the summer of this story, in which she mentioned that *she*, Marla Jo, hadn't been in touch with him for more than a year. I was sitting with my parents at the supper table when my mother told my father she'd heard from her aunt. I remember the moment mostly because Marla Jo rarely wrote and yet this letter had come just days after my mother had returned from her second long visit to Cheyenne.

I know now what I didn't then: that my mother had not gone to Cheyenne, but to Des Moines to look for singing jobs. Having for years discouraged her wish to sing in bars again, concerned with what their narrowly Christian neighbors might think of such a thing, my father must have finally relented, and my mother had packed a suitcase and taken the bus to Des Moines, sixty miles away. There she rented a room in a boardinghouse on High Street and set out in search of a club, a lounge, where she could once again get work. I've no idea how many places in Des Moines featured music of the sort my mother had sung; whether two dozen, whether half or twice that many. I know the Val-Air was still a popular ballroom at that time, but it featured well-known touring bands—Glenn Miller's, Bob Crosby's, Tommy Dorsey's—moving west to east across the great heart of the country.

I don't know if she managed to get auditions, was politely listened to and thanked for coming in, or perhaps won a few nights of work somewhere. But because everything about her going was unclear, she and my father told me, as they told everyone else, that she was visiting her Aunt Marla Jo, who was ill. She was gone more than two weeks, during which time I missed her desperately, until the morning my father and I drove to Marshalltown to meet the bus that returned her, *from Cheyenne.*

For some weeks after that, if I'm right in recalling it, there was an almost obeisant energy in her manner, as if to suggest how grateful she was to have been rescued from the antic haplessness of her history.

———

I learned about my mother's search for work not from her or my father, but from my grandmother one evening as the two of us sat in her upstairs kitchen. I remember that the heat in her apartment that night was a stunning, sodden thing. I remember we had, my grandmother and I, tried and failed to eat our supper, so she'd made us ice cream floats to fill our stomachs.

Before she told me my mother's secret, she'd recalled my parents' arriving from Cheyenne and how, with a determined buoyancy, she and my mother had spent several days complimenting and deferring to one another while at the same time each was taking the other's measure. She said, "The first thing you noticed, of course, was her looks. I said to your father, 'How did you manage *this*? You're a handsome boy, honey, but the two of you together, it looks like the princess hasn't got around to kissing the frog!' "

But, she said, while my mother's beauty was something to admire, what there was to *like* was her intelligence; that she was smart enough to know she should be scared to death and strong enough to do all she could to hide her fear. Still, my grandmother said, when she looked back, she wished my mother *had* been able to say she was frightened; perhaps then she wouldn't have felt "she had to have her dukes up all the time."

Much as she'd liked my mother's savvy right away, she hadn't liked my father in the moment they all met. She had come down the sidewalk from the porch to greet them, having seen their

Chevrolet moving slowly up the drive, the car so crammed it might have belonged to Dust Bowl Okies. My father and mother had opened their doors, and my grandmother had given my father a hard hug, then broken their embrace to welcome my mother. My father had said, "Mom, this is Leanne," then stepped behind my mother and placed his hands on her shoulders. And as my grandmother opened her arms, she also caught the look on my father's face, which was almost a smirk, a boy's expression of self-satisfied pleasure as he waits for your praise of his great cleverness. *Look what I've pulled off here,* his expression said. *She's every bit your match, Mom. In fact, she's just like you.*

My grandmother knew my father was mostly just imagining how well the two of them would get along, and she thought he may have also held a sentiment of which he was unaware: that his choosing Leanne McQueen was a compliment to his mother. Still, he conveyed in that moment, and in the first days afterward, the sense that he'd returned with a prize, perhaps one he'd not been thought capable of winning. And this was why my grandmother was disappointed in him—for his regarding his wife as in any way a trophy and for his being fool enough to think that she was anything like her. Although in some ways, my grandmother said, she supposed both mistakes were understandable.

My grandmother was a large, heavy-bosomed woman. When she sighed, she sighed deeply and the room she was occupying seemed to sigh as well. She was only sixty in the summer of 1957, but, typical of the times and certainly the place, she looked and dressed and often spoke of herself as old. Her gray hair looked finespun in lamplight and her weak eyes behind her glasses appeared deep-socketed as a ghoul's when she was tired.

That evening in her kitchen, as I remember, was a few weeks after my parents had argued on the porch. And I know my grandmother was by then exhausted from the turmoil of their marriage and from what had erupted since that night. So, though candor was her custom, her words in her kitchen were unusually plain, even for her.

She sighed, and the kitchen sighed, and as she continued to speak, her recollective voice had turned soft, less complaining, nearly slipping into the cadence of a bedtime story. And as I listened, it seemed impossible that the characters in her tale were my parents and herself. It was especially hard to picture my mother and my grandmother circling one another diffidently.

We sat in her kitchen and let the country's quiet come in, and then my grandmother spoke of her guilt all these years, knowing her need was my parents' reason for returning to the farm. She said she wished they had lived as adults before the war, so my mother in particular could have known that the permission of those times had not been real life and would not be.

5

My father died in May 1995, and it was after the week that my wife, Anna, and I spent in New Holland for his funeral that I found myself wanting to write these memories. Not because there was anything revelatory about the days devoted to my father's burial. I learned nothing I hadn't known about his and my mother's life; nothing factual, anyway. But perhaps inevitably, almost as soon as we'd arrived, I began to think of him, a young newlywed not even half my age, returning from Cheyenne to help bury *his* father. Deepening the coincidence, my own marriage—my second, to Anna—was new and she was visiting New Holland for the first time. So from that easy comparison of my life with my parents', I asked myself again what might have happened if my mother had come with him and sensed the verdant isolation of the farm and its surroundings. I wondered, as I've said, whether she would have been capable of viewing things there with any dispassion. She was newly pregnant and, more newly still, a bride. (I smile as I think that, whatever else, these were conditions that would have made for an extraordinary *entrance*.) Besides, since she would have been meeting my grandmother and the place under the most strained circumstances, it might have been impossible for her to envision the nature of life there. But maybe not.

And so I wondered whether my father could have heard my mother if she'd said she wasn't sure their returning would be wise. Or if she'd said she understood why he felt he must come back, but he should not make up his mind until it had calmed. Or if she'd said, as Anna said to me as we talked late into the night after the funeral, "I think you'd have to love more than the work to live here happily." She thought, then added, "Or maybe you'd have to love the work more than anyone outside it could understand." If my mother had said something like that to my father, might he have asked himself if he could love more than the work; or thought he could love the work enough? Or heard what she surely would also have been saying: that she needed his help to see how this new life would give them enough of what they already had.

After that week in New Holland, I began to gather some first thoughts by finding what I could remember without trying; that is, what came unbidden when I summoned an hour, an event, in the hope that I would hear my mother or my father. At the start, what I heard was not so much their words as simply the varying tones of their voices. And it seemed I understood a lot by listening to the way they'd sounded when they were living, or remembering, a moment in their lives.

This didn't surprise me in the case of my mother. But it was also true, if more narrowly, for my father. I realized, for instance, that whenever he talked about Cheyenne, a quite particular quality distinguished his voice. There was nothing of nostalgia's ghostly longing in it, but rather an energy that was almost the opposite. His Cheyenne tone was youthful. It sounded deeply thrilled, as though he were thinking of times that had urged him to live permissively, almost illicitly, compared to what his life had been and once again became. And I suspect he was, in part, able to feel such unhesitant affection for those years because he was looking back on them from so secure a distance.

When he spoke the word itself, *Cheyenne*, he was usually referring not to the place but to the span of his experience there. He would say, "I have never known sand and wind like Cheyenne. One day, we'd finished a shift and walked out of the hangar. We knew there'd come up a terrible sandstorm. We'd heard it while we were inside and saw it blowing in around the doors. And when we walked outside, the sand had completely stripped the paint off of every car."

And he would say, "Cheyenne, I'd watch the B17s touch down and that was the world's most beautiful sight to me. It seemed a miracle, something that huge, able to fly so light and fine. They were prettier by a mile, the B17s, than those boxy B24s and I was always glad I worked on the 17s instead. Until Cheyenne, I'd never seen anything bigger than some piddly little single prop a fellow over by Coon Rapids had."

Some time before he died, when his mind was fully occupied with remembering and forgetting, he said to me, "One day when our shift was over, I was working, I remember, connecting the hydraulics hoses in the top turret, and I climbed into the sling seat where the gunner sat. I just sat up there real quiet, looking down on everybody leaving the hangar and I tried to imagine what it would be like to sit there really, with your head poking up into the sky and Messerschmitts coming at you from every direction. I swiveled back and forth, sighting down the barrel, and I don't know how long I'd sat there, the hangar was filling up with the next shift, when some old boy spotted me and shouted, 'What are you doing up there, Lew, playing war?' And then he laughed, but I felt pretty foolish, like a kid who'd got caught, because that *is* what I'd been doing. Rocking back and forth like some kid in a swing, pretending machine-gun fire."

In the language of his memories, events were ultimate and nature was extreme. Cheyenne sat more than a mile above the sea. Its air was so rare that when he arrived his ears popped continuously and the sound was like a rifle going off inside his head. Unused to the air's thinness, he drank strong beer one night at a downtown lounge and the alcohol got to him so quickly that when he tried to turn around he fell off his bar stool. The wind was so fierce and unrelenting that at times the town ran waist-high ropes along the sidewalks so you could pull yourself forward into its teeth. The air was so dry that if you didn't keep salve on your lips they'd crack and bleed until you looked as if you'd been in a fight. When it was time to harvest the surrounding fields of sugar beets, there were suddenly Mexicans, thick as sparrows, in the streets. And out by the airport where the conversion hangars sat, there was so much tumbleweed it sometimes looked as if God were carelessly baling the desert. There were herds of jackrabbits, their ears as tall as an Indian's war feathers. And the sandstorms stripped the paint off your cars. And the slow descent of a B17—its massive grace perhaps like the anomaly of a fat man gliding lightly over a dance floor—was the world's most beautiful sight. And he was happier . . . and it is here that imagery failed him. He was simply happier than he had been in his life.

———

He first saw my mother, though only later would he realize it, the night he fell off the bar stool. He was drinking with a new army friend, Henry Brock, in the Valencia Lounge and he was already drunk when she came out onto the stage and began to sing with the small house band. He remembered saying to the bartender, a stylistically irascible woman named Pearl, that he'd just recently reported and was bewildered by the speed with which Wyoming beer affected a person. Pearl asked my father where he'd just recently reported *from*, and when he said Iowa, she said that that explained it, since he was now living more than a mile higher in the air than he had been.

Then Henry Brock nudged my father and said, "Lewis, look. Look at this."

"Look at what?" my father said.

"This," said Henry Brock, who'd turned toward the stage. "This over there. The singer."

And when my father had spun around to see what Henry Brock was talking about, he'd fallen off the bar stool and cracked his head on the brass foot railing.

So while my mother, a seventeen-year-old girl with a strong alto voice and a glibness of delivery studiously modeled after that of Dinah Shore, while she sang the final words of "The Nearness of You," my father was being helped up and led out of the Valencia, bleeding inordinately from the small cut on his head.

She was riding a green horse down Capitol Avenue when he saw her again two weeks later. She wore a filigreed satin western shirt and loosely tied neck scarf and an enormous Stetson hat radically perched on the back of her head, all of it—the painted horse and her apparel—to represent the Valencia Lounge in the parade that opened Cheyenne's annual rodeo, Frontier Days.

It had been the owner of the Valencia's idea to have the horse join the procession, signs hanging from its neck and its tail, reading, in front, "Come to the Valencia Lounge! Corner of Capitol and Eighteenth," and in back, "It's a horse of a different color!"

She was one among dozens of riders moving down Capitol Avenue, all the rest of whom were striving for a look of Old West authenticity. So her luminous horse—its streaked-on color was a remarkable chartreuse—appeared to be half again as large as any of the others and to be floating just above the street, or threatening to.

My father liked to say that Frontier Days was mostly an

excuse to wear cowboy boots and sit on a curb and drink beer until you couldn't. And that's what he was doing, sitting on a curb and drinking beer and watching the parade with Henry Brock, when he saw the horse and its sign. Turning to Brock, he said, "Isn't that the same place where I fell off the stool?"

Henry Brock said, "Yeah. And that's the same girl I was telling you to look at when you did."

And so, after the distractions of, first, sudden drunkenness and then a chartreuse horse, my father at last looked up and took in Leanne McQueen.

She was smiling as she waved to spectators lining both sides of the street. People were pointing and laughing at the horse and then its signs, yet she rode with a dignity that, with her cool beauty, must have seemed an intentional spoof, like a clown in polka dots sipping tea with drawing-room formality.

After watching her pass, Henry Brock turned to my father and said, "Was that girl riding something? Maybe some kind of horse?"

My father smiled and, in a voice that aped Brock's lovesick witlessness, replied, "The girl was all I saw. I don't remember nothin' about no horse."

VERSE:
Up in the the sky, in the clouds above the roar,
A pilot dreams of finding love, what else would he look for?
My heart doesn't need wings to make it soar,
When I think of you, that's all I need, I need no more.

CHORUS:
You send me high into the air, no doubt!
You thrill me, I float up there, a care without,
I'm like the pilot, high up in the blue,
Yet there's a place more heavenly,
It's down on earth with you.

In Cheyenne, when he was twenty-one years old, my father wrote these lyrics as a gift for my mother. I imagine him working on them with a humorless concentration, lying in his bunk, his body curled around his notebook to hide it from the others in the barracks, protective as a mother of his risky endeavor. I think of him moving through a B17, inspecting the Browning assemblies and crawling along the catwalk above the bomb bay, all the while writing and rewriting phrases in his head.

For a short time, Henry Brock and my father went together to the Valencia to listen to my mother. I see my father in his barracks dressing and preening, and, out of the corner of his eye, watching Henry Brock do the same. I imagine him calling, as though just struck with the idea, "Hey, Brock, I thought I might go into town."

And Henry Brock replying, just as falsely, "Into town? Sure, why not?"

Picturing this, I wonder, is my father not yet able to admit to himself just what it is that's going on among the three of them? Or does he call to Brock because, in the confusion of his passion for Leanne McQueen, he sees him at that instant as his friend, not his competitor, and he needs the support of Henry Brock in his effort against his rival, Henry Brock?

I've assumed, with no knowledge, that Henry Brock was a daunting opponent, conducting *his* courtship of Leanne McQueen with a discernible ease and confidence as he sat with her and held her hand; that he had the words and the way to tell her how beautiful she was.

My father, on the other hand, inexpert and amazed, would not have been capable of smoothly offering his interest. I think of his expressing his desire for my mother as a kind of ardent physical labor, apparent on him like a sweat. If this was so and if she recognized it, she may also have sensed the accompanying strength of his steadfastness, a quality she'd not known in her vagabond childhood. So that all her ideas of sophistication—those elements of cool artifice that she believed made the ballad singer's style so grand—would have met their challenge in my father's earnestness.

Which is why his writing the lyrics seems so wonderful to me, showing that if doggedness characterized his courting of her, its substance was still that great bold foolishness that is always at the heart of an opening love.

I suppose in part it's the lyrics that have made me think of Brock as a smoothly formidable rival. I take them as evidence that my father sensed he must simulate Brock's style, no matter how unnatural, in order to beat him at his own game. And that writing the words to a love song was the surest way to win a woman who sang love songs.

And I'm sure the lyrics worked, that they helped to win my mother's heart. Not because she thought they were good, but because she saw instantly they were terrible and, so, felt the seriousness of my father's will to have her.

I imagine he was curious about everything in her life. That he learned the manager of the Valencia, an acquaintance of her aunt's, had hired her thinking she was Marla Jo's twenty-five-year-old younger sister. My father often said he was charmed by Marla Jo, a sarcastic flint-hard woman who defined a mothering of sour loyalty. And that he was taken with the idea of the two women's life in a tiny apartment on a busy small-city street, for he had not known anyone, until Cheyenne, who lived in something less than an entire house surrounded by a less than generous lawn. He was apparently fascinated by the very notion of Lean Dean, who'd not been heard from for some time, but whose absence, or whose remote threat of an appearance, he regarded as a tantalizing specter in her life.

Of my father, she doubtless learned that he'd farmed with his father only when his help was truly needed and had worked as a mechanic in a garage in New Holland. She'd have learned that, unlike some of his friends, he'd made no attempt to say that his work as a farmer was essential to the war. He hadn't done so, not just because it would have been a lie, though it would have been; he simply felt that to declare himself a farmer, one whose work was vital, bore no relation to how he saw himself.

I suspect she heard him say how grateful he was, not only to have found her, but to have found the place and the direction of their future. That he wanted his work after the war to continue to have to do with airplanes. It was clear to him that such a life, their life, would unfold somewhere in the West, where the airplanes would be built and the new money would be and the same buoyant spirit then carrying them would continue.

———

Describing his dreams for their future, I think of the day I went with my mother and him to celebrate his thirtieth birthday. This was three years before the summer of her affair, and my father had decided to mark his "turning into an old fart" by driving to Des Moines to eat a special Sunday dinner at the restaurant atop the municipal airport.

I would have then been eight, and to me everything about the day—the long drive, the Sunday visit to an elegant restaurant— seemed a dazzling indulgence. I suspect it seemed something close to that to my father as well, especially the place, whose high windows allowed us to watch the airplanes taking off or landing. Neither happened too frequently in Des Moines in those days, so to observe an arrival or a departure was to follow the arc of a full narrative.

Which is just what my father did. While we ordered and waited for our food, he scanned the runways surrounding us to identify the planes and describe their features. And then, as if he sensed he'd lose his audience with all his technical information, my father looked down to a man boarding a plane and began to invent his résumé and his reason for flying in an airplane that Sunday afternoon.

I don't remember what he said about the passenger. Let's say he decided he was a businessman going to Chicago for a job interview and wishing to arrive one day early so he'd be rested and quick-witted in the morning. Whatever he said is unimportant; what I remember is my father's pleasure in the game.

To my delight, he continued for some time to offer up his plots, warming to them and eventually giving both my mother and me fantasies that fit with those we generally carried. He told my mother he was sure the woman walking down the ramp was the singer Peggy Lee come to give a concert. Acknowledging, in her absence, my grandmother's interest in the lives of famous Iowans, he said that the older woman behind Peggy Lee was Mamie Eisenhower, who'd be driven up to her childhood home in Boone. For me, at that age a worshiper of cowboys, he offered the secret information that the tall man just then boarding was actually Roy Rogers, disguised in a business suit and sneaking out of town.

Laughing—we were all laughing—I asked him why Roy Rogers needed a disguise. Because, he said, winking, he wouldn't want Dale to know why he'd been in Des Moines, if I got his drift. He laughed and winked again and the silliness slowly left his face until it came to rest as a satiated smile.

We all were quiet for a moment, sipping our coffee. (With my mother's permission, my grandmother had recently started serving me coffee, believing that it quickened intelligence and sharpened memory.) But I wasn't ready for my father's play to end and I asked him, "So, who are *you*, Dad?"

He looked at me, puzzled, and I tried to say what I only partially grasped at the time: that he'd chosen a traveler for the rest of us, but not yet anyone to represent *his* dreams.

He smiled again and I saw that I'd explained myself at least well enough. "Oh," he said, "I'm already on the plane."

"How come?" I asked.

His expression became comically bug-eyed and demonic as he gripped an imaginary steering wheel. "Because I'm *driving!*" he said, looking at me. "I'm the *pilot* of that there plane."

———

As I've said, my own fantasies by that time had already become braided with those of the women who supervised my days: my mother's memories and her study of style; my grandmother's wildly imaginative theories, her sweeping and wholly arbitrary verdicts. So I especially loved listening to my father that day, a man whose inner life I saw as dwelling in the instance, whose memories, I assumed, were dreamlessly complete.

And while I may have recognized, even as he spoke, that such fancies were something I rarely got from him, I doubt I understood that he was revealing how *he* dreamed and what he dreamed of still.

Now I wonder if my mother understood anything of what he was offering us that day. All I recall is our general high spirits, but perhaps my mother's, within them, were in some way contrasting. I don't remember turning to her and catching her expression; if I did, I don't remember what it was. Perhaps if I had, and could summon what I saw, I'd have a few more answers about my parents.

I do think, as my father's reminiscences of Cheyenne make clear, that he very much needed to remember the past. But perhaps, once he'd left, he tried more and more to use his memory as a kind of marvelous reserve. And I suspect my parents' troubles began whenever it was that my mother concluded he was asking her to use their past in the same way; that he wanted her to assure him he *had* lived those years, while at the same time asking her to let them be no more than memory. Who knows if she was right? Who knows how their life might have been different if he'd been able to show, as he did on his birthday, that there were things he'd yearned for and given up perhaps too easily. If she'd been able to see that he still dreamed.

———

They were married in Cheyenne's City Hall on January 21st, 1945. She had celebrated her twentieth birthday two months earlier. He was twenty-three. Her maid of honor was Marge Rafanelli, a friend from the Valencia. Intriguingly, Henry Brock was my father's best man.

I don't know how or when or even what my grandparents learned of these events. But they were not present for the ceremony. It's true that there are many reasons why this might have been so—the distance, the expense, the entrapping winter weather, the rarer notion then of long-distance travel generally. Still, I have no memory of any conversation that helps to explain their absence.

Not surprisingly, Lean Dean was not there either.

Aunt Marla Jo attended, of course. If there were a picture of the wedding party—I've never seen one—she would be standing next to my mother. I see her frowning into the camera, dressed in a severely tailored suit and a hat that looks like a collapsed soufflé, appearing like some haggard transvestite cowboy. Marge Rafanelli, small and dark, would flank my mother on her other side. She's dressed in a suit as well, one she's bought for the occasion and in which she knows she looks extremely smart. She gives her face to the camera at an odd three-quarter-profile angle, wishing to appear a bit unaffected by the event, as though she's happy enough that my mother has asked her, but also feels that her future is waiting for the photographer to finish.

My father and Henry Brock are trig as silent film stars in their dress uniforms, looking too perfectly soldierly to be soldiers. My father's jacket flares stylishly at the waist. His smiling face is broad and new as hope. Brock affects a parade-rest stance. His cap rests under his arm. His thick wavy hair is like a brillian-tined crop.

I can conjure them all, their manners and their costumes, except for my mother, who stubbornly resists my picturing her on her wedding day. Pregnant with the life that I would become, she stands serene and admired, perfect as a doll, only and utterly the radiant child bride.

———

I found the lyrics my father wrote for her as I was going through his things after his funeral. They were written on a simple sheet of lined paper, folded twice and wedged between the back panel and the bottom of a desk drawer. At the top of the page, he'd written, "These are for you, Leanne. This is truly how I feel. I love you, Lewis." And at the bottom, below the lyrics, he'd added, "Maybe you, or you and Specs, can think of some music to go with them?"

I read them through several times, trying to get some idea of the rhythm he could have had in mind. I even played around with some melodies for his chorus, quietly humming a few dif-ferent starts, one close to "You'll Never Know," another, remem-bering my mother's fondness for Dinah Shore, sounding like "The Gypsy." As I did, an ache of complicated pleasure grew. I felt proud of my father in the way that a parent responds to some show of his child's brave failure. It was as if I'd found a piece of a son's juvenilia—a rhyme laboriously printed on a handmade birthday card or a homesick letter from camp.

As I began to refold the paper I noticed a different hand-writing on the other side of the page. The os and as were perfect Palmer ovals. Its style was fastidious and fascinating to me as the origin of what would become my mother's wildly looping hand.

Seeing it, I was sure I understood then why he'd kept the lyrics—not for what he'd written, but for what she had.

> Dearest Lewis,
> It's you I love, it's you,
> Now and always,
> Leanne.
> P.S. It's *you*.

———

I don't believe my mother was thinking of these lyrics when she said, the night they argued in the darkness of the porch, "I forget how much you know about music." It's true she paused until she had the retaliatory tone she wanted, but her mind had to have been too preoccupied, too hectic with the thrill of all that was enfolding her, to be able to retrieve such a cruelly appropriate piece of their past.

But when I remember his response, the instant of charged silence and then his leaving the porch without a further word, I fear *he* thought she had the lyrics very much in mind. And if he suspected at all that she was having an affair, did a part of him remember that he wrote them to persuade her that she should love him, him and not another man; a thing he'd then assumed he would have to do just once?

6

You could say that, thanks to my father's thoughtfulness, I introduced my mother to Bobby Markum a year before they began their affair. For it was then that my father, having noticed my growing love of baseball, asked some of the men on the town team if I could serve as the batboy for their home games. But because he worked in the fields till dark, the task of driving me into town fell to my mother.

I said that her affair with Bobby did not begin until the following spring, which is what I've always told myself and others. I'm not sure why I've assumed that to be true, since I really don't know when my mother and Bobby became aware of one another. What I *do* recall in the beginning is her anger at having to drive me back and forth to the games. Indeed, I remember that at first it seemed each time would be the occasion for an argument between us.

Typically, after changing into my uniform I would seek her out and announce that it was time for us to go. In response she would say she'd be ready in a second, but after five or ten or fifteen minutes had passed, her dallying became unfathomable to me, seeming suspiciously deliberate. So I'd begin to nag her until she snapped at me, saying that I might be surprised to know that the world did not revolve entirely around me. After that, I'd leave the house for the car, growing wild with the fear that I'd be late and my job would be given to someone else. Finally she'd appear, rushing now herself, looking frazzled and put upon as she hurried down the walk.

In the car, tearing into town, she'd sometimes wonder aloud how she was going to pass the "hours" before the game began without dying of boredom. I was too preoccupied to be as troubled by her complaints as I might otherwise have been. I'd also begun to learn that there was nothing anyone could say to her when she fell into such committed petulance. So I tried to let it pass, watching the speedometer climb, grateful at least that she was driving so fast.

But over the weeks she grew gradually more relaxed about driving me to the games. I realize it was shortly after that season that she would leave us for two weeks. So her restlessness must have been moving strongly in her by then. And if it was, it would make sense that her interest in Bobby began that first summer. Thinking of her at those games, sitting in the bleachers bored and sulking, I can imagine her taking sudden notice of him and fixing on a moment of his considerable grace: the way he drew his right foot back and forth through the dirt between pitches, the toe of his shoe pointing balletically as it raked the mound; his habit, after striking a batter out, of lightly touching the bill of his cap with the fingers of his pitching hand, a nuance of salute that seemed to recognize the hitter. I can easily believe that some such gesture, a pause, a preening instant, even the theatrical eruption of his temper, might well have caught her eye, not because she cared anything for sports, but because she admired the performer's stylishness.

She had to have known who Bobby was. In New Holland it was impossible not to know who people were, their names at least and a sketch of how they'd gotten there. I've wondered when they first spoke. Who turned to whom, and under what clumsy pretext? I hear her using me: "I'm Will Vaughn's mother." I hear him replying, "*Sister*, maybe. That I'd believe."

Did she sleep with him then, a kind of prelude, her way of saying, You should know that I may wish—I may need—to do this? And if she did, why do I resist even so the idea that they continued through the ensuing fall and winter? Or that he came to her during the time she was living in the rooming house and trying again to be a singer? Maybe because I remember how it felt to wait a year to begin an affair.

———

I met my first wife, Melissa, in college at the state university in Iowa City. After graduating we moved to rural Door County, Wisconsin, because she'd summered as a child on its bay shores and had always dreamed of living there. She found a teaching job in an elementary school, I got work as a reporter for the area's only daily newspaper, and we were married on a deck overlooking a pristine harbor. And after a couple of years I came to hate it all: the foolish tedium of my job, the quaint clean beauty of the place. But mostly I hated the idea that I'd come there because of Melissa, whom I'd been eager to please and was now resentful of pleasing. At that age, not yet thirty, that was the sort of person I was, desperate to please a woman I wanted and hating the weakness of my desperation.

For her part, Melissa showed me she was grateful I'd come with her. And with everything else, I began to resent *that*: her evenness and her daily generosity, feeling them the symptoms of a dull imagination. For that was also the kind of person I was then. So I argued more and more for leaving and finally she said she would. I applied for a job with the Associated Press and we moved to Springfield, Illinois, where I covered the state's raucous politics for its capitol bureau.

One of my colleagues was Ellen Rose, a reporter for the *Chicago Tribune* who'd been transferred downstate the year before. I was soon finding reasons to spend time with Ellen, weeks and months leading up to a night in a bar across the street from the capitol. I had drunk enough to confess what she already knew: that my marriage was failing and that I'd fallen in love with her.

When I finished saying these things, she smiled. It wasn't until after we were together that I sometimes saw her smile as unspeakably sad, her eyes becoming heavy-lidded, her expression somehow bereft, even as her mouth lifted. One of our early fights began with my urging her to tell me what was wrong, why she was sad, and her saying *nothing* was wrong, she *wasn't* sad, to which I replied that no one could manage such a face as she'd just shown me unless she was feeling deeply sad.

In the bar, she smiled and said she loved me. She moved her hair, draping blackly, away from her face. She said it would be a mistake for us to start right then. She said that if things were as I'd described them, I'd leave Melissa and get divorced. And then I'd feel horrible for a long time, who knew how long. What she *did* know was that it would be disastrous for us to be together while I felt like that.

After leaving Melissa, I waited, a kind of feverish celibate, roughly a year, and I remember the time as one of the most thrilling of my life. I saw Ellen every day and often in the evening in the company of others. And I felt each conversation and every encounter to be both what they were and something much more—absurdly freighted with the promise of what I couldn't yet have. There were times when I felt a sensitivity to her presence that I eagerly melodramatized. I remember working in the pressroom while she was interviewing someone on the phone, and the tone of her voice sounding to me as if it were figured with a resonance that was more than I could bear.

In the meantime, as she'd said, I was also living through fits of guilt and twice, maybe three times, over the course of those months I called Melissa, who'd gone back to Wisconsin, and begged her to return. The last time I called she asked me bitterly why I wanted her back.

Because I did, I said. It was as simple as that.

But she said she knew I didn't. That I was only waiting to hear her say she didn't want to come back so I could tell myself what I'd done was all right. Then she said she was sorry to admit that she *did* want to return. But she wasn't going to, and what I'd done was *not* all right and I would just have to live with that.

I was leaving a crowded Christmas party in the house speaker's chambers when Ellen walked up to me and smiled, I thought not sadly, and said that I seemed sane. That I'd seemed so for a while. I asked her if that was a compliment or an insult and she smiled again and said it was a necessary fact.

———

If my mother and Bobby did begin, or promise to, that previous summer, wouldn't they have endured at least a version of my wait for Ellen? And what would the terms of *their* wait have been? What would have been its reasons? Fear? Unsureness? Or something simply practical: the need to think through where and how they'd meet? And in the meantime, while they waited, did they see each other on the square, in the grocery, and did my mother find these meetings almost laughably enriched? Did her blood race a little when his car passed hers, if she ever noticed it? If, in any sense, they waited?

———

Whatever my mother noticed or did not, whatever happened or didn't between them that first summer, there was a moment during one of the first games I worked when, for me, Bobby became someone separate from his teammates. He was leaving the mound after a terrible first inning. I'd already witnessed his explosive temper and had learned in studying his actions on the mound that it was usually signaled by the flick of his glove against his left thigh. Having spotted this gesture—minute, a tiny trembling—after he'd walked his second batter in the inning just completed, I now waited for him to kick out at something or fire his glove against the fence behind the bench. Instead he sat down, turned his back to the field, took a tube of airplane glue from his jacket, and with the purpose of a surgeon applied a line of it to the inside of his index finger. It was then that I noticed that the finger itself was shorter than it should have been.

In the second inning, his curve ball began to break more effectively and by the fourth or fifth inning it was unhittable, snapping harshly down at angles of disdain.

Bobby was bent over on the bench changing back into his street shoes when I approached him after the game. I cleared my throat and asked him why he'd put the glue on his finger. Still bent over, he said, "You saw that, did you?" He looked up at me and grinned. "You're not gonna report me, are you?"

I said I wouldn't know who to report him to or what I'd be reporting.

He laughed and sat up and held his shortened index finger out to me. I could see then that it was severed just below the first joint. "You know what this is, don't you?" he said. He spoke this casually, and it seemed to me he was brandishing its blunted length. I couldn't imagine what he was asking me.

"It's my advantage," he said. "Before I lopped the end off, I wasn't but an average pitcher." The way he said this made me think he might have done it deliberately to make himself better. I was lately being haunted by something I'd heard on a radio Western: the generic scene of the wounded cowboy taking a swig of whiskey while his friend with a Bowie knife says, "This is gonna hurt," and then digs a bullet from his leg. That moment and Bobby's, as I suddenly pictured it, seemed made of the same superb barbarism, the shock and rationale of frontier pain.

Bobby said, "The way it lays next to the regular finger, the two of them together, it concentrates the pressure so when I snap my wrist I get a hellish movement on the ball."

I imagined this spinning magic coating the ball like a finish. Then I said, "So what'd you get, a blister?"

He looked at me, puzzled.

I said, "Did you glue down a flap of skin?"

He understood then and laughed. "Some games," he said, "no matter what, your ball just won't do what it's supposed to, and the glue, it's still sticky when it dries, holds it on your finger just a hair longer to give you the spin you need."

I paused before asking, "Is that fair?"

When he answered me his voice was amused. "There's maybe one game in ten, your curve won't break for you even when you're doing everything right. That always seemed to me like the *ball* wasn't being fair. When that happens, like I started out tonight, you ought to be able to get things back to even, don't you think?"

I frowned and shrugged.

He looked me up and down. "What's your name again?"

"Will Vaughn."

"That's right. Lewis Vaughn's kid. How old are you?"

"Almost eleven."

"Almost eleven. Well, here's the thing, Will Vaughn. I want you to do me a favor. I want you to come and see me in ten, fifteen years, and tell me then if you think it's fair or not to use a little glue when things aren't working like they should. Okay?"

When I saw him next a few nights later, Bobby nodded and moved quickly past me to start warming up with his catcher, Burl Starkenburg. And for several games after that he hardly spoke to me. Then one night, before walking out to the mound, he looked over in the direction of the other team's first batter and asked, "What should I throw him, Will Vaughn?" as if I'd been his consultant all along.

By then some weeks had passed since our ethical discussion and it seemed to me miraculous he'd remembered my name. But this was his pattern throughout that first summer—long periods of barely noticing me, broken all at once by a warm exchange. And I ask myself if that was some of what made up the fine elaborate coyness between my mother and Bobby. Now, thinking back, remembering nothing, I see it might have been.

7

As for me, I remember seeing Bobby only from a distance after the end of that first season. I spotted him a few times driving slowly in town in his 1949 maroon Ford coupe, which he kept buffed to a high shine even in winter. I watched the Ford pass and pictured myself sitting next to him, the two of us assessing the completed season and wondering how we'd do come the following spring. I heard myself saying that I hadn't yet decided how I felt about his using the glue on his finger. I understood his point about the ball misbehaving, but still it didn't seem to me quite fair.

Once, clustered with some classmates in a booth in the Hungry Dutchman diner, I saw him at the counter. He was drinking coffee with three or four other men, but I was too shy to seek his attention, fearing he'd ignore me in front of my friends.

The second season of my knowing him began pretty much the way the first had ended—there were times when he spoke to me, even teased me some, followed by stretches when he ignored me completely. But unlike the year before, there were also moments when he'd pull me aside to coach my swing or pitching motion, and it was these rare instances that I came to live for.

Then one Friday night after a game he walked up to me as I was getting ready to put away the bats and balls. To my surprise, he picked up the large canvas equipment bag and gave it to me to hold, then bent down and began to collect some of the bats. Dropping them one at a time into the bag, he said, "I hear you like wrestling."

"Wrestling?" I thought briefly that he was asking me to wrestle.

"Yeah, wrestling."

"Who told you that?"

He smiled. "A little bird." He said, "I thought we might drive into Des Moines tomorrow and watch the wrestling." He wiped his forehead with the sleeve of his sweatshirt. He'd enjoyed an easy game, not asking much of his arm, slowly pitching himself into shape for the long season.

I stood there, blinking dumbly at him. Finally, I said, "I'll . . . I'll have to ask my mom and dad." I turned and searched the emptying bleachers for my mother.

"Sure," he said. "But I bet it'll be okay." He handed me a bat. "Be ready around ten—if they say you can." He took off my cap and rubbed the top of my head. Then he replaced it, taking care to adjust the way it sat, and turned to leave.

I watched his back for another stunned moment before I called to him. "Do you know where we live?"

He turned around again and gave me a quick smile. I remember a line of slyness in it. "I'll find it," he said. Thinking now of that moment, I add to it the idea of my mother somewhere near and watching, her smile a duplicate of his.

For a couple of years my grandmother and I were devoted to the Saturday night wrestling matches televised from the Marigold Amphitheater in Chicago. Both of us especially loved the great Vern Gagne. My grandmother loved him because he'd been an All-American football player at Minnesota. Minnesota, of course, borders Iowa to the north and this was enough for her to claim that Gagne had actually been born in Iowa and moved with his parents to Minnesota as a child.

I loved Gagne because he'd invented the extraordinary sleeper hold, a maneuver in which he appeared to apply a precise pressure to his opponent's neck, sending him immediately into a peaceful coma. Then, with the match won, Gagne would kneel down and seem to reverse the hold's effect and his victim would awaken, confused as a newborn.

But I'd pretty much lost my interest in wrestling. Baseball and Bobby and God and Perry Como, plus the time required to stage the many fantasies of myself as grandly famous—all these diversions had come to have stronger claims on my imagination. Still, I did watch the matches now and then with my grandmother, whose enthusiasm, or at least her habit of viewing, remained high. My guess is that my mother had heard her telling me of a professional tour coming to Des Moines and assumed I was still the fan I'd been. And standing by our bench that night, watching Bobby leave and thinking of the chance to spend such a day with him, I *was*, immediately, a fan of wrestling again.

However long their affair had been going on by then, I take Bobby's invitation as a sign that my mother had begun to tinker in her thoughts, moved by that anarchic spirit of new lust and unconsciously beginning to work her way toward the edge of what she could get away with.

I imagine her lying beside Bobby in his bed after they've made love, idly gazing at the room's time-pocked linoleum floor, motes whorling in the buttress of sun slanting in from a front window. Surely they were never so foolish as to climb his outside stairs in the light of day, and yet that is how I see them: sunlit in his room, their slender bodies matched as twins'.

I don't know, he says. You really think he'd want to?

He'd be thrilled, she whispers. He adores you, you know.

Whatever else inspired her, she knew very well how I felt about her lover.

―――――

I recall that my parents reacted to Bobby's asking me in ways I'd come to see as typical of each of them: my mother, in the car on the drive back to the farm, smiling and wondering who might have told him I liked wrestling, and saying it sounded like a lot of fun; my father, at home, frowning and bemused, saying he didn't know if it was a very good idea. If my memory is right, if that is how they separately responded, my mother would not have needed to work very hard to hide her duplicity from me behind her delight. And as for my father, it seems at least possible that his hesitation at that point had mostly to do with the local sense of Bobby as a loner and a drinker, and someone about whom— amazingly in New Holland—not much else was known.

After my father voiced his skepticism about my going, my mother turned to me and asked me to get ready for bed. In my room, I could faintly hear them. Their voices were an instance of those murmurous drafts I've described. A few times the talk burred harshly without the clarity of words, and I wonder if she tried to offer my father the same surprise she'd shown me, or whether she admitted suggesting the idea to Bobby, saying she'd seen how much I idolized him.

I got into bed, turned out the light, and waited. Not too much later my mother appeared at my door, then stepped into the darkness and walked over to me. She sat on the edge of my bed and told me she'd explained to my father how much the wres- tling matches meant to me. Her voice was a strained lilt that sounded as if it were on the verge of moving into something she couldn't control. In the darkness I could barely see her, or she me, for she fumbled for my hand and squeezed it very tightly. Then she leaned down and kissed me and said she knew I'd have a great time.

After she left I lay awake, trying to picture the thing I'd dreamed of doing—riding with Bobby in his wondrous Ford. But suddenly the notion was too enormous. The drive would take more than an hour, a lifetime, several lifetimes, as I thought of trying to fill it. We would talk about baseball, but what else?

Then I imagined our conversation turning naturally enough to wrestling—his asking me who I liked and didn't like—and I realized I would be exposed as a fraud. As I lay there, I felt a shiver of the great humiliation that would be coming tomorrow. In my panic it seemed my only hope was to go upstairs and ask my grandmother to bring me up to date.

She was sitting at her card table, placed in front of her best armchair. Her gray head was bent over the task spread out before her, which I could see was that scrapbook of famous Iowans she'd begun, I believe, a few months before. Long columns of newspaper clippings, ordered as playing cards arranged for solitaire, flanked both sides of the large black ring-bound book.

From her doorway I watched as she cut something from the newspaper, then put down the scissors, massaged her hand, and flexed her fingers. Only when she lifted her coffee cup to her lips did she see me standing there.

She took a sip and said, "What are you doing still up?"

I walked into the room and climbed up on her couch. "I couldn't sleep," I said.

She pushed the huge scrapbook forward and shut it, a book-keeper closing her ledger. I was trying to imagine how to ask her about wrestling. I was concerned she'd be jealous when I told her I was going.

"What'd you cut out?" I asked. "Something about Vern Gagne?"

She gave me a quick scowl, of which there were a dozen shadings, including a few of approbation. She pointed to the longest row of clippings on the table, to which she'd just added. "Jean Seberg's motion picture, every one of them."

For weeks she'd been particularly attentive to the story of Seberg, then just seventeen years old, who'd been chosen from thousands of applicants to play Joan of Arc in Otto Preminger's film *Saint Joan*. As I've said, my grandmother's claim that a famous person had an Iowa history could be dubious at times, even patently false. And while this became increasingly true as she got older, she was already capable of outrageous assertions. She insisted for instance that the singer Eddie Fisher had been born not far from New Holland. She told my mother, who hated Eddie Fisher, that he was a member of the family that owned the Fisher Company in Marshalltown, a large manufacturer of engine governors.

"That's crazy," I remember my mother saying. "Eddie Fisher's Jewish, and the Marshalltown Fishers aren't. I don't think Fisher is even his real name."

And my grandmother replying brusquely, "I don't know where you get your information."

To which my mother, to her credit, did not ask my grandmother where she got *hers*. She was mostly amused by my grandmother's claims and knew they were founded on her being arbitrarily drawn to certain famous people. In this case it was to Fisher's daytime television show. "He's a polite young man," she would say while watching it, "and really very shy, you can tell."

"A voice like that," my mother said, "he *should* be shy."

But there was no disputing that Jean Seberg had been born and raised in Marshalltown, which made Otto Preminger's announcement of her selection on the *Ed Sullivan Show* extraordinary news in Iowa. For the past few months, Seberg's life had been worshipfully documented in the newspapers and my grandmother, in a fever of scholarship, had read and analyzed all the stories she could find.

She picked up the latest clipping and squinted at it. "It says while they were making the motion picture, she worked every day with some Englishman, what I guess they call a voice coach, to—here's her talking—'to remove my obviously midwestern Americanisms.'" She read these last words with slow sarcasm and I suspect she sensed that Seberg was already close to thinking herself a big shot. My grandmother looked at me and smiled. "My question is, if she was supposed to sound like an Englishman, why'd they pick somebody from Marshalltown in the first place?"

Over the years I've thought often of my grandmother, assiduously combing magazines and papers, adding to and taking from her book of Iowa lives. As I said, I believe she worked at it off and on for the rest of her life, more than twenty years. And I know for sure that in her last coherent months she attended to the book with great enthusiasm.

As a child, I viewed her keeping the scrapbook as a simple reflection of who she was, just another medium for her lively judgments, another way of documenting her opinionated mind. But I've long since come to see it as bizarre, if not the impulse, then certainly the humorlessness of her devotion at the start. And I wonder if my parents, my father especially, worried that she was becoming more than eccentric. Which would have been hard to determine. Because indeed she was eccentric, genuinely, but also delightedly and self-consciously so. She was someone who used, I would say relied on, New Holland in order to see herself in contrast to it.

Unlike my grandfather, and his father, she was not well loved in New Holland. Her family had been farmers outside a neighboring hamlet, but, still, she'd married a Vaughn, one of New Holland's founding families, and that fact alone might have been nearly enough had so many people not been put off by her candor, her conversational outlandishness.

No doubt she knew all this, and recognized too that for the sake of being regarded as the spirited misfit, there was no better place for her than New Holland. The social price she paid was an isolation, in part chosen I suspect, in part the verdict of the culture. And while it's true that her isolation had lately been increasing—she'd stopped driving, for instance, just the winter before, explaining that her eyesight made her dangerous at the wheel—I imagine it had begun in earnest the day her husband died.

Sitting in her armchair, she leaned forward and, to my dismay, began to read another newspaper story, this one recounting the Paris premiere of Jean Seberg's film, which was held in the city's fabled opera house. "They did it for some charity," my grandmother said. "The Union of Polio Sufferers of France. It stands to reason they'd have worse polio over there, crammed together like they are in those filthy old cities with the plumbing and sanitation what they must be."

"Gram," I said, "I need—"

"It says Bob Hope was there, at the premiere."

"Gram."

"Also, that bald Yul Brynner. Lord, *his* accent, he should be the one with the voice coach." Then she put the clipping down and looked up at me. "What?" she asked. "What do you need?"

"I need to ask you about wrestling."

"Wrestling?" she said. "What about it? It's two fellows in their underwear trying to hug each other to death." She laughed at her joke and pushed her glasses higher up on the bridge of her nose.

Then I told her about Bobby's invitation and, as I'd feared, her surprise seemed initially a pout. She raised her eyebrows and said, "You don't even care about wrestling. You barely watch the matches anymore."

"I do too care," I said.

"Oh really?"

"Yes."

"Who's the world champion?"

I paused. "Vern Gagne."

She snorted. "Pat O'Connor beat Vern Gagne for the championship, it was at least six, eight months ago."

I shrugged and she smiled, apparently pleased she'd won her point. Then her face began to soften as she looked at me. "I don't mean to be a grouch," she said. "It sounds like fun is all. I wish I was going."

I said, "I wish you were too."

She continued to look at me, but her mind seemed elsewhere. Finally she said, "Who'd you say again was taking you?"

When I repeated Bobby's name, she nodded and said, "That baseball player you think's so great." Some weeks before, I'd shown her the sports page of the Marshalltown paper, featuring Bobby in a forecast of the league New Holland played in. She'd looked at his picture and said simply, "Good-looking man. Skinny fellow." Then I suggested she put the story in her scrapbook and she immediately shook her head, explaining that she was only interested in celebrities whose recognition was truly national and preferably gained in some way, some place, outside of Iowa. She didn't add that this made it almost impossible for a famous Iowan to be presently living in Iowa.

At her card table, she smiled again and said, "If you're going with him, you certainly do *not* wish I was going too."

I looked away. We were silent for a few moments, and I could almost feel her mind considering what I'd told her. Then she asked me if I was excited. I said, as casually as I could, not wanting to make her feel worse, that I guessed I was.

She gave one of her room-filling sighs and fussed with the collar of her print housedress. And whether she thought it odd or suspicious that Bobby had asked me, it was clear she understood why I'd come to her and what I saw as my dilemma. For when she spoke again, her nonchalance was complicitous.

She began by idly wondering if all the wrestlers who'd been advertised as part of the tour would actually be there. Trying to match her supposedly casual tone, I said I wondered too.

She said she hoped for my sake that Pat O'Connor would be there—since of course he'd been promised—and how disappointing it was that Vern Gagne wouldn't be. And then she proceeded for fifteen or twenty minutes through a full roll call of all the names and all the genres I should expect to see the next day—midget and mixed tag teams, ladies, Gorgeous George—and after that she went on to describe half a dozen currently popular wrestlers whose names I'd never heard.

She said people at the moment seemed to favor most of all the barefooted, high-flying style of Argentino Rocca. "First he knocks you down with this kick to the head, then he gets you in a leg lock and the match is over"—she snapped her fingers—"just like that."

I sat, trying to take all this in, and when she'd finished she drained her coffee cup and looked at me. Her eyes through her glasses were as fiercely beaded as an adder's. "So," she asked, "can you remember all that?"

"I think so," I said.

"Just to make sure," she said, pushing her chair back, "it wouldn't hurt to drink a cup of coffee. I'll get you one."

———

I'd been ready for an hour when Bobby pulled into our driveway, stepped out of the gleaming Ford, and paused to look around the acreage, a pan of slow appraisal, as though he'd come to bid on it. Then he touched the brim of his dress straw hat and seemed to tilt his head to raise his angle of vision. Maybe he was looking to see if he could spot my father in the fields. Maybe he did.

I was watching from a living room window that gave to the driveway and the lawn and fields beyond. When he reached the back-porch door, I could see that he was dressed in a silk short-sleeved shirt buttoned to the collar. Its two shades of brown made a pattern of large blocks. His summer shoes were also two-toned, a cream-colored face, a surrounding chestnut brown shining as brightly as the Ford. (I'd noticed from the first that his black baseball cleats were freshly polished every time he arrived for a game.)

He knocked and I could hear my grandmother, who'd been downstairs keeping me company, mutter something from our kitchen and get up to answer the door. I didn't think much about it at the time, but one of the things that stand out about this day is my mother's absence from the farm when Bobby arrived. I'd come out of my room that morning to find a note from her telling me to have fun, saying she'd had to leave early for a morning of errands in Marshalltown. As I've thought about her choosing to stay away, I've at various times considered it everything from perverse to cowardly to selfless and I could believe there was something of each in her decision.

From the window, I watched my grandmother open the screen door and Bobby take off his straw hat and sweep it through a low formal arc. I heard her rasp of appreciative laughter in response, then her call to me to hurry up and join them.

I came out onto the porch, we all stood smiling awkwardly at each other, and then Bobby said we should probably be going. My grandmother kissed me and told me to be good and to try to get Argentino Rocca's autograph.

—————

On the highway, in his Ford, Bobby said, "What's so great about Cleveland?" He'd just asked me if I had a favorite major league team.

"I like their uniforms," I said.

Bobby nodded.

"Plus, they've got Bob Feller."

I watched his chrome-bright steering knob, mounted at four o'clock, flash in the sun as he slightly moved the wheel. I watched his fingers on the knob, the shortened one seeming to me ingeniously customized.

I looked up at him and waited. He'd taken off his straw hat. It was perhaps the first time I'd seen him bareheaded and I boldly took the chance to study his face. It was long and narrow and symmetrically creviced—places in it whose purpose seemed to be to hold deep and complimentary shadows. His coloring was quite dark, which separated him in yet another way from the blond Dutchmen of New Holland. Not long ago I saw, in a coffee table book on movie stars of the thirties, a pin-up picture of the actor Robert Taylor when he was very young—swarthy and glamorous, dramatically lit—and it struck me that his face was how I remember Bobby's.

Finally he said, "You're too young to know about Feller in his prime."

"He's from Van Meter," I said, as though this were an obvious explanation.

"What's that got to do with anything?" Bobby asked.

"Van *Meter*," I said. *"Iowa."*

"Never heard of it," he said.

As I understood the world, there were few Iowans, and none who followed baseball, who didn't know the great Feller's hometown. But I'd forgotten that Bobby was from Missouri—the little town of West Alton, just above St. Louis, where a long, low tongue of land lies between the Mississippi and the Missouri. He'd found his way to New Holland only a few years before. The company he'd worked for had been hired to build a stand of concrete grain silos for the town cooperative. I would learn that he was younger than my mother—twenty-seven, twenty-eight that summer—but he'd already lived in several places, traveling since high school with one of the company's crews and working for three or four months, six months at most, in small towns in Missouri, Illinois, and Iowa.

I don't know why he chose to stay in ours. But I wouldn't be surprised if it had a lot to do with his seeing how well our town team played and how fervently it was followed. For I believe he thought of himself first of all as a baseball player, who, given the constantly changing seasons of his work, had had no chance to play with one team for any length of time.

I asked him, "Who's *your* team?"

He said, "I used to like the Cardinals."

"I know Stan Musial and Red Schoendienst."

Bobby said, "When I was a kid it was Pepper Martin and Ducky Medwick. And," he added with emphasis, "the great Jay Herman 'Dizzy' Dean."

I knew Dizzy Dean as a television announcer, a colorful braggart whose Arkansas twang, a kind of country iambus, was unaltered by the years he'd lived in other places.

"Was he as good as he says he was?" I asked.

Bobby said, "He was for a fact."

"Really?"

"He was the best."

I hesitated before saying, "My grandmother says he's conceited and thinks he's a big shot." It's true there was something about Dean that especially set her off. If she happened to walk by while I was watching a game, she might stop and speak to him directly, ordering him just to describe the play and quit talking so much about himself.

Bobby had laughed and nodded at hearing my grandmother's opinion. I waited for him to say something but he didn't and I feared I'd insulted him. I asked, "But you don't think he is, right?"

He took his hand from the steering knob and absently stroked his chin. I watched his nailless cinch-seamed finger, marvelous as a blade, graze the line of his jaw. "Sure," he said at last. "I think he thinks he's a big shot."

"And that's okay?"

He smiled. "Not with your grandma, it sounds."

"But you think it is?"

After a moment he said, "I saw him one time, about the third inning he started yelling in to the batters, telling them what he was going to throw, where it was going to be. 'Curve ball, inside.' 'Change up, low and away.' Like that. Then he gave them just exactly what he said he would. And he pitched a shutout."

"Wow."

Bobby looked over at me and winked. "If you could pitch like that, would you think you were a big shot?"

As would often be the case in our conversations, I had no idea how to answer him.

Bobby said, "Maybe there's a difference, saying you're a big shot when you know you are, instead of thinking you are when you're really not." He was smiling all this time. "Maybe the one could be okay and the other one not?"

"I guess," I said.

"I don't know," Bobby said. "You should probably check it out with your grandma."

I sat back in my seat and looked out the window. The fields were closely striped, the crops' beginning green making artful pastel rows against the blackness. In pastures, cattle were settled fixed as boulders. I moved his front winged window back and forth, playing with the pitch of the whooshing air.

———

We approached the outskirts of Des Moines and rode slowly toward the center of town. I could glimpse in the far distance the grand gold dome of the capitol building. Its immensity was a sun's. I watched people moving along the sidewalks at a warm spring weekend pace and I wondered at the ease with which they seemed to know their way.

The Ford paused and surged as it began a long, low hill and then Bobby said it: "You getting excited? Who's your favorite wrestler?"

My heart fell and my mind set to work to bring back everything my grandmother had told me the night before. Finally I managed to say, "I guess it's still Vern Gagne. Too bad he isn't going to be there today. Yeah, I'd say Vern Gagne, even if Pat O'Connor did beat him for the championship." I looked at Bobby and then I frowned, trying to show him I was rummaging through my store of knowledge. "That was about eight months ago by now, wasn't it?"

He smiled and shrugged. "You say so. I wouldn't know the guy—who is it?—from King Kong."

"Vern Gagne," I said. "Really?"

"Really," Bobby said.

"The sleeper hold?" I asked.

"Is that his specialty?" He playfully pronounced it "spesh-ee-al-uh-tee."

"He knows this place on your neck that when he squeezes it, you go to sleep."

"So why's he call it the sleeper hold?"

"Well," I started, "because it—", then watched his smile appear. I hurried to help him laugh at my being such a sucker, but before I could I saw his expression drop.

"Shit!" he said, and then to me, "You didn't hear that."

I looked out and saw smoke rising from beneath the hood.

He pulled to the curb just over the crest of the hill and shut off the engine. Then he got out and so did I and we wordlessly walked around to the front of the Ford. He stepped forward and lifted the hood and I saw cauldron wisps rising from the radiator cap. He looked around for a moment and I could sense his temper rising. The effort of containing it seemed to bloat him briefly and the Ford's vicious hissing was the sound it might have made.

But I was reassured by seeing him like this. Until now, Bobby, in his summer straw and silk shirt and spotless two-toned shoes, a fastidious dandy from an earlier decade, had and had not been the same person who pitched for New Holland's baseball team. Now, in his struggle to keep his anger in, I recognized the player I worshiped.

He took a deep breath and set off on a stroll around the car. I could see him opening the trunk and when he reappeared he held an army blanket. When he met me again at the hood, he said, "Stand back." Holding the blanket, he leaned in, and after a twist of the radiator cap, steam shot up. He jumped back and stood beside me and we waited for the geyser to play itself out. He moved me away from the rivulets of rust water coming toward us. He'd so far managed to keep his cream-faced shoes immaculate.

"I'll be right back," he said and started up the walk of the house we were parked in front of. I watched him knock on the door and when a woman opened it, he turned and pointed to the car, then disappeared inside.

I stood looking at the water pooling beneath the radiator. Cars slowed as they passed, their drivers peering at me, and I began to feel embarrassed, so I picked up the blanket and put it in the back seat, then opened my door and got in.

I looked around the inside of the Ford. In my eyes it had lost none of its sleekness and the lesson of its failing was that, like any piece of machinery—any tractor, any plow—even one as marvelous as Bobby's Ford could at any moment turn on you.

Minutes passed, no more than a few, but I began to wonder how it could be taking Bobby so long. I felt the long looks of the people in their cars and they were making me feel even more self-conscious. Trying to ignore them, I imagined how Perry Como would surely wait through this crisis, seated coolly in the seat, fussing with his collar, smoking a cigarette, and mumbling a song to himself: *You'll see a castle in Spain, through your windowpane, back in—*

Then Bobby emerged carrying a bucket of water. After pouring it in he slammed down the hood, set the bucket on the sidewalk, and hurried around to his side.

He said, starting the car, "I guess there's a garage in a block or two."

———

Three hours later we climbed back into the Ford and pulled away from the gas station, Bobby easing into traffic to return us home, the only outward evidence that we'd even left New Holland two horizontal stains on the thighs of his slacks where he'd leaned against the edge of the station's greasy desk. He'd been rubbing at them all afternoon, making them gradually worse.

After we'd reached the garage and he'd conferred with the mechanic, Bobby had gone to a cooler and removed two bottles of soda, then come over to the bench where I was sitting. After handing me a soda, he'd explained that the radiator was irreparable and we'd have to wait while the station tracked down a used one. Then he'd plopped down on the bench beside me and lapsed into silence.

He seemed so despondent I couldn't look at him. I searched for the way to tell him not to worry, that he hadn't let me down and my heart was not broken, that I didn't even care about wrestling anymore. But as I thought about saying this, the situation grew complicated: if I were to make him feel better, I'd have to offer up a kind of confession.

Remembering that day, it seems clear that Bobby's disappointment was only indirectly on my behalf. Though he'd promised to give me a dazzling afternoon, it was not for my sake, at least not principally. Like all new lovers, he surely wanted to show my mother he was incapable of failure. And what he'd hoped to take back at the end of the day was further proof to her of his perfection. What he had instead to offer was his old car's broken radiator.

After a long silence between us, he raised his head and turned to me. "You know," he said, "it's fixed." His voice was tentative in a way I'd never heard.

I looked up at him, yet again confused by something he'd said. Assuming he meant the Ford, I asked, "Then how come we're still here?"

He said, ignoring the nonsense of my question, "They decide in the dressing room who's going to win. You see some guy getting knocked unconscious? It's all faked." He looked at me and waited. Whatever he saw made him think he could continue. "Those special holds? Like that one you were talking about? They're all fake."

"The sleeper," I said.

"It's fake," Bobby said.

This was apparently his idea of how to ease my dismay. I can't say how much I already knew what he was telling me, or how much I'd been feeling obliged for quite a while to honor what I thought was still my grandmother's belief.

Finally I said, "Yeah, I knew it was."

He said, "You know it's faked?"

"Yeah," I said. "Is that why you don't like to watch it?"

He said, by way of answering, "It's two guys in their underwear pretending to choke each other."

"That's kind of what my grandmother said."

"Yeah?"

"Well, she didn't say 'pretend.'"

We both nodded and were quiet and then I thought to ask, "So why'd you want to come today?"

"Well." He looked at me. A long moment passed. He said, "I figured you'd like to."

"Oh," I said. Then, "Why?"

"Why'd I think you'd like to?" He'd looked away and around the station, studying its grimy walls. "Most kids your age aren't so smart to know it's faked."

I thought about this for a while. It seemed a compliment. Then I said, "It still would have been a lot of fun."

He fell into silence again, and so did I, one that now felt much less awkward to me. But I did continue to think of what he'd said about wrestling and I found I was still reluctant to reject my fascination with the sleeper hold. I wondered if it might be just possible that Vern Gagne himself was honest, even though everything around him was fraudulent. It occurred to me that, maybe, he didn't even know. That he performed in heroic Midwest innocence, privately baffled at how well the sleeper worked.

———

The sun was low and put a gold cast on the land, but we would reach New Holland before it set. I kept trying to estimate how much longer the day would last, fighting like a miser each minute slipping past.

As we rode through the countryside, I reviewed the day and saw the picture of Bobby holding off his tantrum while steam rose from the Ford. I think there was a particular reason why I enjoyed Bobby's temper and was only once frightened by it. It was because its quality seemed to me that of a boy's. I don't mean a young man's; I know he was not yet thirty. I mean a child's. I think, in a way, I felt it was ingenious—a grown man discovering he could still throw quick boy's fits, as if he had found some loophole in the rules.

So I looked over at him and asked, "When the car broke down, how come you didn't want to get mad?"

He thought before answering. "I *was* mad," he said.

"But you didn't throw anything."

He appeared to be meeting my seriousness. "Probably," he said, "I just tried harder today, with you there."

"But I'm at *games*."

He said, "That's different."

"Why?"

"Why's it different? Because ... because this was just a busted radiator."

I nodded, satisfied. It seemed a perfectly reasonable answer. But after some moments, Bobby said, "Because I promised your mom I'd take good care of you."

Whatever inspired him to say this, it was the first time he'd mentioned her to me all day, and I heard nothing odd in it, thinking only that it sounded like a pledge she would insist on. As curious as I was about the details of Bobby's life, I didn't wonder how or when he'd made his promise to her.

———

We were only a few miles from New Holland when it struck me that a great moral crisis awaited me at home. I turned to him and said, "My grandma doesn't know wrestling's crooked."

I watched his face. "Well," he said. I sensed his reluctance to take up so tiresome a subject again. "You think it's crooked? I mean, it's not like they break any laws."

"Okay, *faked* then, like you said."

He was silent and then said, "Maybe it's more they're *actors*. Somebody gets shot on television, they don't expect you to think he's really dead, right? They're just acting."

"But shouldn't I tell her?" I persisted.

He looked at me. "You think she'd feel bad if she knew?"

"Probably," I said.

"So why would you want that?"

"But isn't it a lie if I don't?"

"If you don't, you're not saying *any*thing."

"Then you think I shouldn't."

"All I'm saying, wouldn't you feel lousy if something you told your grandma made her feel bad?"

"Yeah."

He nodded. The subject seemed closed as far as he was concerned. But then he said, "You think you'd feel worse if you thought you were lying?"

I shrugged.

When he spoke again his voice was abruptly livelier, participatory. "Here's something we might do. *You* might do."

"What?"

"I was thinking how your grandma wanted you to get that autograph."

"Argentino Rocca," I said. "He gets your head in some kind of a foot lock, I guess."

"She seemed real excited about it."

I nodded. "She wanted to go herself."

"She's probably waiting to hear all about your big day."

"Yeah," I said. "I know she is."

"What you could do is pretend we went. You could describe the matches and, what I mean, tell her what a great time we had."

There was complicity in his voice, as if he'd suddenly sensed a way out of a dilemma that was more his than mine. And I realize now that's precisely what he sensed.

I said, "Why would I do that?"

"Well, if she's waiting to hear about it, she'll be real let down when she finds out we didn't go."

Looking out I saw that we'd somehow reached the edge of New Holland, which meant that, after a moment, we reached the other edge, where Bobby turned and headed toward our farm.

Then he said, "You know, it could be your mom'll be let down too."

I naturally hadn't thought to bring my mother into it. "Maybe," I said. "Yeah, I guess. But not like my grandma."

"Still," he said, "there they are, the two of them let down. So what you might do is tell them both we went and had a great time."

I hesitated. "I don't know."

"Mmm," Bobby said. "I remember now. You're one of those guys, two wrongs don't make a right."

We rode a couple of miles as I tried to think this through. And Bobby let me, again staying silent. Then I saw out the window on my right the gray line of our field posts and in the distance the white farmhouse rising up tower-tall.

I said, "What if my grandma *really* starts asking me about it? How the wrestlers looked and things. What they wore. When she's interested in something she *really* wants to know about it."

Bobby smiled faintly and said nothing. Then we slowed and he pulled into the driveway, following it along the side of the house. He shut off the engine and rolled down his window. We sat in silence until I finally said, "I'm pretty sure I couldn't fool her. Maybe my mom I could. But Grandma, I don't think I could make enough stuff up."

Bobby nodded a couple of times. I couldn't read his face, but the quiet told me I had let him down terribly.

"It was just an idea," he said. "How you could run a little test before you had to decide. I just thought, if it made them happy, but you still felt lousy, then I guess you'd know you should tell your grandma wrestling's phony. But if it made them happy and you *didn't* feel bad . . ."

"I know," I said. "It's a *great* idea." And I meant it; at that moment the whole of Bobby's plan felt as tangible as a gift.

He reached over and opened the glove compartment and

found a scrap of paper and a pen. I watched as he scribbled on the paper and handed it to me and I read, aloud, "Argentino Rocca." Neither of us knew that he'd misspelled it "Rocka."

He said, "Maybe that would be enough to fool your grandma."

He gave me a small shrug and his eyebrows lifted. I studied the paper, picturing my grandmother's high excitement as I handed it to her. And when I turned to speak to Bobby, to say the autograph was good but I still didn't know, I saw my mother's face leaning into his window.

"Hi, there," she said.

I can see her mouth smiling, her scanning eyes urgent, the lines of her forehead forming yet a third mood.

We each greeted her while I palmed the piece of paper, and she said, "So how was it? Did you have fun?"

Neither of us said anything and I could only look straight ahead. Then I felt Bobby shift in the seat to face her. Whatever his thoughts and feelings, whatever his face showed her, I turned and watched the back of his head as I heard him saying, "You won't believe it, but we never got there." With that he gave a chuckle and shook his head.

I could hear them talking softly as I climbed out of his car. What I felt was a measureless gratitude to Bobby, for the brilliance of his plan and for saving me from it.

8

In the weeks after our ill-fated drive to Des Moines, there were four or five nights when Bobby signaled to me after a game and we got into his Ford for long, gravel-road meanders that eventually delivered me home to the farm. While he drove, he drank several beers and we reviewed the team's performance, our discussions rarely straying beyond baseball. This was fine with me, though I recall being tempted once or twice to ask him what he thought of God. But in such a God-haunted place as New Holland, where Bobby's Christian Reformed Church teammates avoided any tournament that might make them play on Sunday, I saw him as someone standing outside the culture and I feared showing him my own bouts of moral fervor.

So I never told him I'd finally decided it was wrong—because I was convinced God thought it was wrong—for him to use the glue on his pitching index finger. He'd surely forgotten ever posing that question.

It's also true that I really never came to feel at ease with

Bobby, not for any length of time, certainly not enough to raise so intimate a subject as God. I continued to hope such ease would come, and I consciously believed it was what I wanted, though now I see that of course it wasn't; what I really wished to feel toward him was awe.

———

Once our drives began, I waited after every game with my heart in my throat as I put the bats away and tried to catch his eye. I'd watch him zipping his jacket or changing back into his street shoes, and at the same time I'd watch my mother making her way down from the bleachers. I needed in those suspended seconds to get his nod and tell her of it; that or hide my disappointment when he didn't summon me, which meant I'd have to ride home with her—a drive that had become a punishment, one I endured in silence, churlish and near tears.

I believe that Bobby's asking or ignoring me was one way he and my mother spoke to one another, whether or not they thought of it as that. But I suspect she was watching him to see if he would nod, just as he was watching her as she stepped down the bleachers, while I, their go-between, waited for his sign.

On those nights when she and I rode home together, the quiet in the car was as textural as thought. Obviously, it was her silence as much as it was mine, so I imagine her some nights looking over as she drove and seeing me as the surrogate for his rejection, but other times regarding me as the face of whatever she didn't want him to have that night. For my mother was capable of sitting very still while contentment, a thing she sometimes hid and hoarded, moved in her.

And again I picture her lying beside Bobby. I hear her saying, her voice airy with false innocence, *He was really disappointed you didn't let him ride with you last night.*

Or Bobby saying to her, *I looked around for him after the game. I guess you'd gone.*

Or, *He thinks about you all the time, you know?*

And, *The thing I think about all the time is his mother.*

────────

She never asked me what Bobby and I talked about on our drives, though she no doubt learned more than she wanted to know by listening to my tediously true accounts—absent any mention of the sips of beer he gave me.

But my father did ask me, with a growing disapproval that I somehow felt was directed solely at me, for what I alone was negotiating with Bobby; that is, his irritation seemed a focused one, as though he never asked my mother why she'd let me go with Bobby again.

When I think about my father's behavior those several weeks, I sometimes have the feeling he had some notion from the start of the three of us, Bobby and my mother and me, allied against him. But more reasonably I think he worked to deny that his and my mother's unhappiness was something more than a season's. I think he clung to the belief that, if there were rumors, he would hear them.

────────

I remember doing just that when Ellen was leaving me. We'd been together five years, had moved to New York two years before, and her way in the beginning was to offer me excuses, ones which I grasped with relief. I remember her coming home after midnight for the third time in a month and saying she was sorry she hadn't had a chance to call. She was working for the *Times* then and I had begun to write for magazines, so I often traveled for a week or more at a time. As she'd entered our apartment that night it appeared that she paused in the doorway and, as if fixing the tilt of her sun hat or the fall of her skirt, tried to rearrange her mood and her expression, change it from plea-sure to another fatigue. She said she had to finish the story before she came home because the paper wanted to run it the next day. Then she came in and flopped down on the bed. I knew in my mind that she was lying because I knew the clock of the paper's deadlines. And in her mind, Ellen knew very well that I knew.

And what I said was that she must be exhausted.

And she said she was. She really was.

Not long after, I looked at her as we sat at the table and, breaking a deathly calm, said out of nowhere that she was working too hard. She nodded and said yes, she was, I was right. And then, with no prompting from me, she volunteered that that was all it was, just work. That there was nothing going on and I shouldn't be suspicious.

I thought at least she would smile at her accidental confes-sion. I waited for it. But she didn't, not even a smile I could claim was sad. I saw that she had neither the smile nor the sad-ness in her.

———

I wonder what else my father might have thought could be at the heart of my mother's absence and darkness—and also her demonstrative fits of love. For it's true that as much as he and my mother were fighting that summer, her bursts of affection for him, *their* heatedness, too were new.

I recall, for instance, watching one night as my father walked into the kitchen from the fields, covered as always with a full day of dust. Seeing him, my mother immediately left the stove to greet him. She put her arms around him and kissed him and stepped back from the embrace smudged with his dirt and grease. I'd come out of my room and was standing in the door-way. Seeing her face and her dress streaked and smeared, I burst into laughter. My father smiled at her and said, "Look at you." And she said, "We look like Wyoming Mexicans picking sugar beets."

Then he kissed her again and even I could sense that the mood of it was changed. As I stood there watching, they began to rub their faces and their bodies against one another, a kind of escalating dare that became more than merely antic. And when at last he pulled away, a good deal of his grime had come off on her. He held her at arm's length and said, with enigmatic softness, "And don't forget it."

She shook her head. "I never have." She was smiling when she said this, her face hilariously bruised with dirt. Then together they glanced in my direction and my father seemed surprised, as though he'd forgotten I was there. He laughed, embarrassed, and, fingering a dirty sleeve of her dress, said to me, "We look pretty silly, huh?"

"Ah, yes," she said. "Here we are." Her voice was now theatrical, as though she were announcing the two of them to me. "The two silly Vaughns."

I remember feeling awkward and feeling too a leap of happiness, because it seemed so clear that happiness is what they felt. I had the urge to run up and hug them both, to rub against them and get their marvelous dirt all over me. But something kept me from doing it, maybe the way my mother had so grandly announced their exclusivity, that she and my father were the two silly Vaughns. The Two Silly Vaughns. As if, beneath her play, she was desperate to see the two of them as a carefree act, a wacky team.

I realize now that I was also surprised at hearing my mother say she and my father were the fools, the silly pair. For much of her message to me in my young life had made me feel that she and I were the dreamers, conspiring against the caution of the place, a caution I'm sure I thought was my father's as well.

Another night, in my room, I was awakened by them coming

into the kitchen. They were returning from a party at Nell and Carl Beal's. I could hear that they weren't so much angry as agitated. There was an exasperation in my father's voice that sent his words high as a girl's when he asked my mother why she'd said what she said.

"Because," she snapped, "I get sick of listening to these damned farmers talking about the Russians, the bogeymen Commies, when not a single one of them got drafted like you did." She mentioned the names of some young men my father's age, all of whom, I assume, were at the party. She said, "Kenny Van der Meer and Frank Wilson and Tom Terhausen, they all stayed home and grew corn with their daddies."

"Okay, fine," my father said. "But you said I flew B17s."

"Well," she said, "you *made* them."

He said, "That's right, I helped *make* them. I didn't *fly* them."

"God, Lewis," my mother complained, "what's my crime? What difference does it make if I said you flew them?"

I'd crept out of bed and gone to my door and opened it a crack. Listening to my mother, I remembered my father's birthday at the airport restaurant when he proposed a fantasy for each of us and said, for himself, his eyes alive, *I'm the pilot of that there plane.*

Finally, I heard my father say quietly, "There's all the difference."

"Not to them."

"I mean, to *me*."

There was a moment more of silence and when she spoke I could hear to my relief that her voice was calm. "I just wanted to remind you, you were different from them."

My father said wearily, "Oh, God, Leanne. I am not."

She said with renewed urgency, "Yes we are." Then, fumbling to recover, said, "I mean, *you* are. You're diff—" Whatever look he gave her, it stopped her from continuing, until she said, "What is it? What?"

"I don't know," he said. "I don't know what." He waited, then said, "You can't live in your memories."

She said, "You shouldn't live without them."

"Is that what you think I do?" he said.

They exchanged a longer quiet and her next words were once more calm, almost coy. "Come here," she said. And then, "Lewis? . . . Hey, you . . . Come here."

I could hear that she was leading him with her voice, out of the kitchen and onto the porch, saying again, "Come here . . . Yes . . . Yes . . . Come here," until the kitchen door shut, closing off from me the sounds of their voices and those their bodies would begin to make.

Remembering that night, what I hear is my mother's voice, again and always her voice, trying to coax my father's memory— as seductively, as urgently, as she was beckoning his sex—trying to coax it to a place she was sure she could still touch. And I wonder if by then she'd have been satisfied with signs she apparently couldn't see, with the sense that he consulted his memories as needfully as I believe he did?

———

I'd never seen Bobby pitch as well as he did the night of our last drive. He'd taken a no-hitter into the seventh inning, then given up a bunt single and, in the ninth, a lucky ground-ball double over third base.

In the car, his exuberance made him at first goofy and defenseless, all his competitive contempt turned sweet. When I tried to reconstruct some moment of his brilliance he refused to hear it, saying that some nights, if everything is working, "It's not what *you* do, it's just letting the *ball* do what it already has in mind," again speaking of the ball as though it possessed its own considerable will.

He was drinking more than usual and each time he opened a can of beer he gave it to me for "the virgin swig." I made a great show of smacking my lips and emitting a manly "Ahhh," while the sour effervescence of my spoon-sized swallows slid all too slowly down my throat.

Now and then as we drove that night, Bobby turned left where he habitually turned right, right where he turned left, as though to flout the strictness of the landscape's geometry. A sprinkle, hardly more than a mist, had begun and we'd been driving in it for a while, long enough for me to feel that it was past the time when we were normally headed toward the farm. But I wasn't worried, my concern for whatever my parents might say lost in the feeling that, thanks to Bobby's performance, the night had opened out into a celebratory lawlessness.

And so, lost and very happy to be, I was roused by a sudden change in the tone of Bobby's conversation. He drained a can of beer, tossed it out the window into a ditch, and said, "Sometimes this town . . . I don't know, I guess it's got pretty much everything you need." He looked over at me. "What I mean, when you get down to it."

I nodded and tried to appear contemplative, as though I were comparing New Holland with the many other places I had known. I said finally, "I guess. When you get down to it."

He smiled. "Maybe a few *more* Dutchmen than you need, huh?"

My laughter covered his.

He said, "I'd been figuring I'd move, but I don't know. Maybe, maybe not."

"Really?"

He smiled, I'm sure enjoying the sound of my alarm.

"Where would you move?"

He shrugged his shoulders. "I wasn't thinking so much where." He took another beer from the case that sat between us. "How about you?" he asked. "You like it here all right?"

I nodded, eager as a real-estate salesman. "It's got pretty much everything you need."

He reached for the opener on his dashboard and handed it and the can to me. "Do the honors," he said.

I managed to puncture the holes in the can without spilling too much beer. I raised it to my lips, then gave it back to him. He took a long swallow and didn't show me he'd noticed how little I'd drunk.

After a short silence, he asked, "So you . . . you and your mom—and your *dad*, too—you all like living here?"

"I think so," I said. "As far as I know." I tried to think of something more intelligent to say. "My dad's from here," I said. "So, yeah, I guess."

"But," he persisted, "your *mom*. How about your mom?"

"No," I said.

"*No?*" His voice rose. "You know that for sure?"

"Yeah," I said. "She's from Cheyenne, Wyoming. They met when my dad—"

"What I meant," he interrupted, "does *she* like it here, too?" There was a sloppy crossness in his voice, the first clear sign of the beer. I began to babble something, saying I hadn't really thought much about it.

Bobby was quiet, letting me prattle on until he lost patience and began to speak over my words. "You figure, I mean a place where they think a good time is an extra hour of church . . ." He shook his head. "Ah. How the world turns out."

I watched him continue to shake his head slowly. It was the first time I'd sensed him as other than invulnerable. I asked, "So why do you live here if you don't like it?"

He said nothing. He turned the windshield wipers on for the first time and after we'd driven in quiet a short while longer he slowed the Ford and eased it to the side of the road. We came to a stop and he shut off the engine and continued to sit silently, tapping the top of the can. The sound was a metallic scratch and then a light dull thump, the peg-legged gait of his nailless finger. He took a last swallow, rolled down the window, and flung the can across the road into the ditch. He left the window open and looked back at me. At last he said, "You got a ball?"

I reached down to the floor where I'd put my glove. I took my baseball from its pocket and handed it to him. He gripped it and showed it to me. " 'Cause of this," he said. When I frowned he held the ball closer to me and said, "This is why. You asked me how come I stayed here."

I had no idea what he was talking about. I said, "So you could pitch for the team?"

His eyebrows arched, then he laughed bitterly and shook his head. "No," he said. "I'm talking about how this looked to certain people when I hold the ball, with my finger."

He leaned against his door and looked out at the soft rain. "Two, three years ago, *three*, it was three, this guy comes up to me after a game. I was *on* that night like I was tonight. I struck out fourteen."

"Wow," I said.

"So this guy comes up and introduces himself. He says he's a scout for the Cubs and I'm a hell of a pitcher and I should come to a tryout they're holding in a couple of weeks where they're gonna be looking to sign players."

Bobby glanced at me as if for my reaction, but I was already too rapt to show him one.

He said, "When the guy's leaving he says, 'Between you and me, I'd say you got a shot.' He says to me, 'Your curve ball, that son of a bitch just drops off the table, don't it.' " Bobby gave a kind of snort at this memory and reached into the case of beer. "He says, 'I have not seen a ball do what yours does in a *while*. Show me how you hold it.' I told him it was just the way everybody grips a curve, then I showed him and he squints and after a while he says, 'Hmm. I guess it is.' "

Bobby's speech had begun to slur, his enunciation prissy-lipped. But he went on with his story, describing his great impatience for the day to arrive and, in the two weeks he waited, of seeing his life and the town with that heady arrogance—he called it "relief"—of carrying the secret that he'd already left.

He said there were probably a hundred players at the tryout in Des Moines and that a dozen of them, maybe fifteen, were pitchers. He said the day was very hot and dry, ideal pitching weather, the dryness like a gift, in Iowa, in summer. He said he pitched two innings, had rarely thrown better, the movement on his ball "a thing of beauty, truly."

And when he'd finished and was leaving the field, a fat bald man came down from the stands behind home plate and made his way to Bobby. He said hello and told him he was impressed with what he'd seen. Then the man looked down at a sheaf of papers on the clipboard he was carrying. He shuffled them until he found the scout's report on Bobby and after a moment of reading it he asked Bobby to confirm his age.

Twenty-four, Bobby said. Twenty-five in a month.

The man said, "That's right," as if he'd been making sure Bobby knew. Then he looked up at Bobby and asked to see his index finger.

Bobby was taken by surprise, but offered his hand, feeling oddly as though he'd been caught with stolen goods. The man turned the finger this way and that and felt the callus pad of Bobby's release point. All the while he showed no emotion, a dry diagnostician.

Finally he said, "The thing is, almost twenty-five." He swept his arm to take in the whole field. "There's two or three out there, including you, that's over twenty." He shook his head. "But even at your age, I'd be tempted to give you a year in Class D if it wasn't the age on top of your injury there."

Bobby said he'd shown the man—as he'd shown me—how the ball came out of his grip spinning fiercely. That he'd then explained to him that what he saw as an injury was actually an advantage. I remembered that he'd used the same word, "my *advantage*," when he'd explained to me the way his finger helped him pitch. The man listened and said for all he knew that might be true, but considering the length of a professional season, Bobby's finger would be raw, blood and bone, by early June.

Then the man wished Bobby good luck and, moving with a waddle, made his way back up into the stands.

" 'Good luck'?" Bobby said as he sat slumped in his Ford. He made a breathing sound that was disgust and said again, "Good luck."

I was overwhelmed to think that there could be such unfairness in the world. As I sat there I began to imagine some idea of injustice as a scourge, as a germ in the water or in the very air, that struck at random, like polio. It seemed clear to me just then that there was no way to guard against such unfairness. If Bobby had not been able to, how could I, how could anyone?

Finally he reached forward and started the car. "So," he said, "that's why I'm still here. Wasn't that the question?"

He rolled up his window against a now truer rain, then the Ford started away from the side of the road. I watched the bright circles his headlights made on the gravel, lines of rain etching through them.

As we drove the night appeared to deepen even more, that astonishing darkness of a rain-wet countryside that seems to be the world insisting on simplicity. Then Bobby came to the intersection and turned left and it took me a moment to realize that we were driving down the road that passed our house, that we'd been parked, while we were talking, alongside our south field. He'd driven us so circuitously that night, and I had been so caught up in his pleasure at the start, that I'd lost my bearings in the night-infinite landscape and had no sense of where we were when Bobby stopped.

I saw our house up ahead, its gawky gables and lit-up windows making their unmistakable pattern, and I let out a laugh despite the gloom in the car. I said by way of apology, "I saw our house. I didn't know we were here."

He looked over at me and smiled faintly. "I'm full of surprises. You should know that by now." As we neared the house he slowed the Ford more and turned off the headlights. He said, explaining, "I don't want to wake everybody up." But it was clear my parents' bedroom and my grandmother's upstairs lights were lit. We seemed to coast in blacked-out secrecy until he came to a stop where our driveway met the road.

He looked across toward our house. "You're all set?"

I nodded.

"I'm just going to go on," he said.

"Okay."

"Hustle in. It's raining."

I said thanks and got out and watched the Ford drive away, its lights still dark, until it disappeared behind the drape of rainy night. I waited until I couldn't hear him any longer, then hurried up the driveway toward my life.

For all I know, Bobby's stopping beside our field that night was a moment of simple thoughtless chance. But I choose to think it wasn't, that he stopped us there from habit. And I've pictured him, for the time he loved my mother, often driving late at night to the borders of our farm, or in darkness down our road to the edge of the acreage, then parking and watching the tedium of our evening—our kitchen, our bedrooms lighting up and going dark—as if looking, in the movements of our life inside the house, for a signal of what she planned to do.

Does she *like* it here? he'd asked me. Your *mom*. I mean your *mom*.

———

By the time of that drive I'd already begun to add to Bobby's life many details that made it even more exotic. I imagined that as a child he'd been briefly kidnapped. I decided that before coming to New Holland he'd spent time in prison, wrongly convicted of killing a man and serving two years before being set free. (The tip of his finger had been cut off in a jailyard knife fight.) I told Dale Van Zant, my regular playmate who lived on the farm across the road from ours, that Bobby's father was a Negro. Dale said that was a lie and where was my proof? I said Bobby had told me, that it was a secret, and that it explained his unusually dark complexion.

Perhaps this is simply the nature of things, that someone we see as larger than life gives us the urge to set him in ever grander myth. Still, I've wondered if it was in some sense the opposite; if there was something in Bobby's nature that invited me to improve his history. Whether, in my regard for him, I also somehow perceived a frightened young man, one whose life of small frustrations reinforced his belief that the world was designed to keep you down.

But in fact I think such perceptiveness is beyond a child, or at least was beyond me. I say this partly because I didn't hear in Bobby's story the terms and conditions of his failure to escape. I didn't understand that he'd stayed, a captive in New Holland— not so much the place, but captive to such a life as his was, to such a way of regarding the world—because it had once seemed he might be miraculously rescued and then he wasn't, and then his will was done.

In thinking about Bobby I believe I'm really wondering more about my mother than about him or myself. I'm wondering why it was Bobby who wakened her maverick energy. Did she need to invent and shape him for herself, even as I, who worshiped him, needed to? And was there something about him, was it finally what he offered, that told her she could form him however she wished?

Or did his glib bitterness and his easy courage somehow nourish her idea of her own defeat? For I think my mother liked to tell herself that her burden was her vivid imagination. But I've come to believe that what she suffered from was longing.

9

The rain that had fallen while Bobby drove me home continued all the next day and the next, soaking the turned earth and interrupting my father's early summer work. It's my memory that when weather kept him from the fields, he was willing to accept a few hours of relaxation, driving into New Holland for coffee and gossip with other farmers enduring the same idleness. But when that was done and he'd returned from town, he began, in the way his father had, to look for a chore to fill the time, glancing now and then to the skies for assurance that the burdensome gift of rain would end.

So a wet weekend passed, and when he saw that it was still raining Monday morning, he left the house and moved about the acreage gathering the trash, the empty cans and bottles, the heaps of things discarded, become mere shapes veloured with rust, to load into the bed of his pickup for a trip to the huge county dump near Marshalltown.

It was mid-afternoon and the rain had weakened to a drizzle

when he'd fit everything he could into the truck and then he came into the house to look for me. I was in my room reading comic books and brooding. I was dressed in my batboy's uniform. There was a game scheduled for that night and I was hoping against hope that it might still be played.

Seeing me, he understood immediately. "I don't see them playing tonight," he said. "Even if it stops, the ground's three days wet."

I looked at him and, saying nothing, nodded. I regarded his sense of weather and what it did to soil to be infallible.

He said he was sorry, and his smile was particular, as if coming from someone who also knew how it felt when the weather kept him from doing what he loved to do. In light of all that was about to happen, I'm glad to remember his expression in this way, as a sign he *had* come to embrace his life that much.

Standing in my doorway, he asked me if I wanted him to call around and make sure the game was canceled.

"That's okay," I said.

"You feel like riding along to keep me company?"

"Sure," I said. "Okay." I put down my comic book.

He looked at me in my uniform. "You want to change out of that? You might get it muddy."

I shook my head. "It always gets dirty anyway."

———

Leaving the dump an hour later, we were headed back home when my father looked at me and said, "I could eat a piece of pie. What about you?"

I nodded, pleased, knowing this meant we were stopping at his favorite cafe on the highway between New Holland and Marshalltown.

I was feeling better despite the canceled game. I'd always loved riding with my father to the dump, especially during that time I'd recently passed out of when I'd been deeply a cowboy and the cliffs and canyons of its trashed terrain were the mountainous Old West, the country Roy Rogers rode. I'd seen the foraging birds wheeling and diving in the smoky sky and I'd imagined them vultures, those regular horrors of cowboy lore. Indeed, for a couple of years, whenever I made the trip with my father, I first changed into a cowboy shirt and hat and holstered pistols. And once there, while he proceeded with the business of unloading our trash, I pretended to ride over the gouged-out earth, making a rhythmic clicking noise with my tongue against my teeth to simulate the sound of horse hoofs over rock. Craggy, striated, offering up its raw vistas, never mind that they were strewn with refuse, the dump I saw as a child was remarkably exotic, perhaps as much as was *his* version of the West, which my father carried with him all his life.

But I no longer saw the dump through the cowboy's eyes. Instead, I'd worn my uniform and brought my ball and glove with me, as I carried them everywhere. And I wonder if my father had noticed what I was wearing and had viscerally gotten the symbol of it. I wonder if that's why he'd suggested I should change.

———

The cafe was, more accurately, a popular roadhouse which also served suppers and ran a lively bar at night. We parked in the empty driveway and hurried inside through a suddenly resumed rain and my father said hello to a waitress I also recognized. At that hour we were the only customers and he led us to a booth near the huge jukebox. When the waitress came he ordered cherry pie and coffee for himself.

"How 'bout you, honey?" the waitress asked me. Then, seeing me in my uniform, she asked, "Did you win?"

I ordered what my father had and he sat and listened while I explained to the waitress my batboy's role. As she left for the kitchen he winked at me and said, "She's been here forever. They say she's the owner's sister. The owner before the guy who owns it now."

When she brought us the pie and coffee, she said, placing my cup in front of me, "Be careful now. You drink too much of that stuff, honey, it'll stunt your growth."

"No, it won't," I said. "It improves your memory."

"Who says that?" she asked.

"My grandma," I said.

"Well, hey," she said and shrugged her shoulders, "if your grandma says so. I'll have to remember that." Then she cackled. "Hah! You said coffee improves your memory and I said I'll have to remember that."

I watched her walk away again. I asked my father, "Does she know Grandma?" As I'd heard the waitress, it seemed she was saying she knew of my grandmother's knowledge, which only fit my sense of her—someone famed throughout the county, at least by reputation.

My father said he doubted the waitress knew her.

Thinking of my grandmother, I remembered for some reason a nagging problem I still hadn't solved. So I asked my father, "Dad, *you* know wrestling's fake, right?"

He looked at me oddly, as though I'd asked him a trick question. And I see now that in a way I had, for he must have heard in it something of the day Bobby had tried to take me to the matches.

He said, "Why do you ask?"

"Grandma doesn't," I said. "And it seems like it's a lie if I don't tell her."

He appeared to be trying to keep himself calm. But unlike my watching Bobby work to keep his anger in, I couldn't sense what my father had engaged, though perhaps I saw enough to know that his effort was against something more difficult than temper.

When his eyes returned to me, he smiled. "So, if you'd figured it out, about wrestling being rigged, why'd you want to watch that tournament, or whatever it was?" He sounded intrigued, and as though he needed to have what I would say, and this told me I couldn't offer him the truth. I didn't know why, only that his interest was too open and exposed, one of those terrifying times when a child can hear his parents asking a question to which they don't know the answer.

So I said, "I guess I thought Grandma would want me to go." I thought to add, "I figured she'd like it if I got Argentino Rocca's autograph."

He frowned.

"He's her favorite right now," I said.

My father took his last bite of pie and his smile now was closer to his own. "Argentino Rocca." He shook his head. "She must be having a hell of a time figuring out how *he* came from Iowa."

He let us laugh at her expense, which felt surprisingly good to me, the burden of her briefly lightened, and then he said, "I wouldn't worry about your grandmother. She pretty much believes whatever she decides to. If she wants to think wrestling's on the up and up, she has her reasons. I don't think there's much you could tell her."

I understood enough of what my father was saying to think that he was making sense.

And then he said, "I'm not sure your mother knows what's real and what's not, either."

"What do you mean?"

That look of need reappeared and passed like a twitch across his face. He said, "She wanted you to go and watch the thing. You must not have told her you'd figured out it was all faked." He looked at me again, and I felt in my confusion at least the relief that I could tell him the truth.

"No, I *didn't*," I said, though it wasn't clear to me what I was defending her against.

He fell silent then, sipping his coffee and signaling the waitress to bring the pot. She filled both our cups and, smiling, said to me, "You're gonna be so smart, your brain won't fit through the door."

A couple, drenched from the rain, had hurried into the diner some time before and ordered whiskeys to warm themselves up. I'd heard them say something about being caught out in it. Now I watched, over my father's shoulder, as they stood and headed for the jukebox with their arms around each other. Huddled, peering down to read its menu, they picked a slow song and began to dance. They were probably a little drunk, their hair still wet, the woman's in strands, the rain in their clothes making them cling. They swayed very slightly back and forth about the room, stumbling a few times and laughing at themselves.

My father and I turned to watch, smiling at each other like two shy, backcountry bachelors and exchanging exaggerated faces when the woman whispered something in the man's ear that made him laugh. And whatever my father might have got from watching them—the little dance stage, the sound of the jukebox ballad, the couple's unbroken embrace—whatever reminiscent pleasure or longing, he kept a tight false smile on his face until the song ended and the man, with great flourish, bent the woman back in a low and surprisingly graceful dip.

"Hey, how about that?" my father said to me. "That was pretty good." Then he added, his eyebrows lifting, "Maybe you should have them do a dance on the *Will Vaughn Show*."

It was the first time he'd ever directly spoken to me of this fantasy, the one I'd always imagined he thought my most foolish. Whenever I'd seen him approaching while I was singing my theme or pretending to have a conversation with a guest, I quickly shifted my play to something else. Until that moment in the cafe, I'd thought my show the exclusive principality of my mother and me.

Back in the pickup, we drove through sprinkling rain, the day having become hot in spite of it, so that we'd rolled our windows down and let the wet blow in on us. When we left the highway for gravel, five miles from home, my father pulled over to the side of the road. "All that coffee," he said, "gave me an idea I can't put off any longer."

He opened his door and stepped out of the pickup. I could see his broad back framed in the open window, then heard his piss hitting the roadside gravel. As it does, the sound made me need to join him. I got out and walked around to where he stood and, side by side, we aimed toward the ditch. I stared vacantly across it to a fence line, then a pasture. The rain was nearly vaporous, our streams the stronger sounds.

Also looking straight ahead, my father said, "You got your ball and glove?"

"In the truck," I said.

He sighed, finishing, and said, "Feel like playing catch?"

"Now?" I asked.

"Sure."

"Where?"

He nodded toward the pasture.

In synchrony, we shook and flexed our knees and hunched and zipped.

"In the rain?"

"It's just a sprinkle," he said. Then he turned and opened the pickup's door. He leaned across the seat and reemerged, holding my glove and ball. Handing them to me, he said, "Let's go," and nodded again toward the pasture.

We plunged into the ditch, made our way up its bank through wet weeds and climbed the fence to stand in the pasture's high grass.

"Toss it here," my father said and he caught the ball and threw it back. His way of catching was to viciously snatch the ball out of the air, as if it were an insect he was trying to snag. And he threw with a stiff-armed pushing motion that emphasized his strength and his awkwardness.

We'd played catch in the past, when I could coerce him, but not since I'd become enthralled with Bobby Markum. So the gracelessness of my father's form, after watching Bobby, was newly surprising to me and I felt the urge to teach him how to throw and catch a ball. It was an urge I'm glad to say I let pass, for in offering him advice I would have been mimicking the words of the man who was sleeping with his wife, though I don't know if my father would have understood how purely my words of instruction were Bobby's.

We tossed the ball back and forth until he said, "Throw me your glove." I did and he put it on. "Okay," he said. He got down in a catcher's squat and held the glove up as my target. "Pitch to me. Let's see if you can hit it."

The drizzle seemed to stop for a gathering pause and then the rain began again in earnest. I halted my delivery, thinking my father would stand and call me to come with him. But he remained in his squat and said, "Come on, throw it!" so I threw him the ball and he tossed it softly back to me.

"Okay!" he said. I threw again and again he returned it. "Right here now," he said, pounding the pocket of my glove. His insistence was exuberant. He was having some difficulty keeping his balance, frequently touching the wet grass with his free hand for support.

It's been too often described because it is true: the sense that gets spoken when a man and a boy throw a baseball back and forth. And there in the pasture, in a muted sweep of rainlight, with me in my uniform, I pitched to him, the metronome of our motions and our sounds—the steady popping of leather and the rustle of wet grass and my father's enthusiastic commentary—

gradually taking me out of my life. As far, I'm sure, as my teenaged mother was taken out of hers when she stepped into the chords of the Valencia band's refrain; as far as my father was when he sat in a turret after finishing his work and envisioned the assault of Messerschmitts. And maybe as far as my mother was, the night before or after this day, when she lay with Bobby Markum and asked him to ask her what all she was thinking.

I see my father and me in that field, each of us poised between two places in our lives: me leaving one stage of boyhood, when I'd dressed in cowboy clothes, for one in which I'd felt the impulse to teach my father something; and my father also, having moved beyond the point of sensing nothing, now inside the moment of not accepting what he sensed. And the thought of him playing catch with me recalls, of all things, the wonderfully terrible lyrics he wrote for my mother. For here he was again doing badly, clumsily, a thing that the man who was his rival did so well. Though I do wonder who it was he most consciously had in mind; who it was he believed he was performing for that day: for my mother, for me, for Bobby, or himself?

The ball was getting very wet and my next pitch sailed high over his head. My father jumped late and waved my glove at it.

"Don't you want to quit?" I called.

"What for?" he said. As though cued, the rain started falling even harder. "Do *you*?" he asked.

I laughed. "Okay, no."

So we continued, squinting through the downpour, whooping when a gust of it struck us directly. Through the rain, the outline of his body was blurred, his wide white smile the thing I focused on, though I couldn't throw with any accuracy at all.

"You gonna let a little rain spoil your aim?" my father shouted.

I howled in reply.

"Let's go!"

"I'm trying!"

Then I started my windup and slipped and went down. I lay on my back laughing wildly, the rain pelting my face. When I struggled to my feet my uniform was a sodden blanket. This seemed the invitation to abandon all pretense and when I wound up again I whirled my arm through several circles like a character in a cartoon. Releasing the pitch, I made a warpath sound and paid no attention to where the ball was headed. Instead I tumbled forward through a somersault and ended up on my stomach, my face in muddy grass.

I got to my knees, expecting to hear my father's laughter, but saw that he'd stood and was walking toward the road. I assumed he was going after the ball and I scrambled to my feet, waiting for him to turn back to me again. But he continued on, the dark figure of his stocky body barely visible behind the screen of rain. I ran to catch up and nearly had by the time he reached the fence.

"Sorry, Dad," I said. "Did you find it?"

He didn't say anything or turn around, so I bent down and began to search the grass. Then I sensed him moving, he seemed to be walking in place beside me, and I straightened up to see him flinging his arm in the direction of the road. His grunt was simultaneous with the sound of the ball thudding thinly against the side of his pickup. I heard the ball ricochet beneath it and it rolled out and came to a stop in weeds that fringed the ditch.

He turned and looked down at me. The rain had beaten his cap almost flat. Its bill was sloped as a roof, water dripping off it. I could not see his face. He said, "It's fun, isn't it. Just to fall down in the mud and not care if you get dirty."

I had no idea what he meant, if he was scolding me or had understood my clowning. But I was stunned that he'd thrown the ball against his pickup, the sudden violence of it mystifying.

Then he said, "We'd better get going." He reached down and picked me up and clumsily lifted me over the fence.

We moved back through the ditch to the road. I picked up the ball and swept my palm along the side of the truck, feeling for the dent I was sure the ball had made. But I couldn't find it quickly and I knew I couldn't linger.

―――

While my father had quizzed me all along about my rides with Bobby, he never told me I couldn't go. As a father, as a man, he understood, I think, that such a roil of confusion as was building in him can disturb the clarity with which we make our judgments. And I believe he worked to remind himself of that until he realized the ambition of my mother's unhappiness extended beyond some days of early summer; until the night, a few weeks later, when he charged drunkenly onto the baseball field and our altered lives began.

10

I remember my father appearing at my side, pausing for an instant to place his hand on my shoulder, then continuing out onto the infield and making his way unsteadily toward Bobby. And whenever the memory of this moment comes to me, it always begins with the sound of his cry. I hear it as a keening of elaborate grief, as the way he announced himself to Bobby Markum. I hear it coming just as he was stepping past me and even now there are times when it's tempting to think of its signal as gladiatorial.

As he stepped away from me toward Bobby, my father left the smell of whiskey in the air. I saw that his sweat had inked an oval down the back of his denim shirt, the top half of his "uniform," as my mother teasingly called it—a freshly washed denim shirt and khaki pants, which he always changed into after he'd scrubbed himself clean of that day's field dust.

I looked out at Bobby and saw him standing as he always did in the moments between his pitches, his long body posed in hip-thrust nonchalance, his right foot forward and bearing his weight, his right hand holding the ball, resting behind his back at the base of his spine. As he watched my father's approach, Bobby's face held that look of amused contempt which his features settled into as he warmed up on the sidelines.

Then I saw him begin to flick his glove against his left thigh, the indication, as I've said, that he was about to lose his temper. I saw my father weaving as he stepped toward Bobby with that murderous effeminacy of someone drunk and enraged. And I watched Bobby's gesture, his glove slapping his thigh in a way that made it seem a weapon.

I turned to search the crowded bleachers for my mother.

At the same moment some of the players began to move toward my father. The Vanderlinden brothers got up off the bench and started following shyly after him. The batter stood watching, a smirk on his face. One of his teammates called out playfully, "Time out! Farmer on the field!" Burl Starkenburg rose up out of his catcher's crouch and also took a step toward my father.

Again my eyes swept the bleachers and to this day, when I think of all those people watching, I hear the patented sound of crowd-roar in the air, as though everyone were cheering some great play my father was making. But his appearance must have created a stunned silence in the stands, for people would surely have been astonished or embarrassed, taken by the sense that they were watching an episode whose retelling might outlive them. And how many among them were also quieted by the fact that they already knew, as they watched, why my father was drunk and going after Bobby Markum?

Suddenly my father paused and veered to the left and then he charged toward Bobby with surprising speed. Bobby pivoted to avoid his lunge, but my father reached out as he stumbled past and grabbed enough of Bobby's shirt to pull him off balance. Then he gathered himself to lunge again, but before he could a circle of players closed on him. He was very strong, his struggling to escape them was fierce, and they all braced their bodies and leaned in to gain some leverage.

"Whoa now, Lewis!"

"Easy, Lewis!"

"Easy!"

Their voices were impatient and disciplinary, the tone they used when speaking to uncooperative livestock. There was a second skirmishing and more shouting, someone cursed when his foot was stepped on, but I couldn't see my father's fury, only the circle's hasty realignments.

When I looked again at Bobby, he'd moved a few steps away. He brushed at the dirt on his pants, then stood, staring up into the night. He shook his head slowly and lowered it and raked the infield with his cleats. In my memory, he looked sad and weighed down with a sense that life had yet again confirmed his view of it.

My father was by now subdued. The players began to lead him away from Bobby. They were moving in a huddle of gingerly unity, all of them young men he'd grown up with in New Holland. I heard one or two of them speaking softly to him.

My eyes darted wildly from my father to Bobby and back, and they'd nearly gotten him off the field when he raised his head and, looking past me, saw my mother. She was stepping through the gate behind the bench. I'd heard its squeaking hinges and turned to see her. She came forward and bent down next to me and put her arm around my shoulders.

Seeing her, my father paused, then quickened his step, as though intent on charging her as he'd charged Bobby, and the men scrambled to regain their hold on him. One of them said, "Jesus, Lewis!" and another, "You poor bastard," and another, his tone a parent's scolding, "Lewis, that's enough."

They led him past us, their faces dour with their assignment.

My mother stood and we turned to watch them move through the gate and along an aisle of grass between two sets of bleachers. They passed a small group of girls wearing bright summer shorts, their bodies seemingly entirely their stick-thin legs. All these girls were in my class. I watched them watching my father, their hands cupped over their mouths, their giggling escaping fresh and thrilled.

"Come on, Will," my mother whispered. "Let's go home." She placed her hands on my shoulders. I felt greatly relieved, being told what to do. But I was glad not only for her authority. I also felt the gratitude the guilty feel when finally caught—of being freed from their dumb and artless wait for the inevitable. I sensed this deeply, although I had no idea what I was guilty of. "Will," she repeated. "Come on. Let's go," and either in spite or because of my humiliation it took this second urging to get me moving.

Then we left the field, allowing our neighbors in their murmurous excitement to begin to write the history of that night. I believe neither my mother nor I paused to cast a backward glance, not daring, for our separate reasons, to look again at Bobby.

———

As we drove away, I searched the parking lot for my father, but there was no sign of him or his pickup; it was as if the night had taken him in out of the weather of busy shame he'd just created. Turning to my mother, I saw that she was so far inside her mood as to seem almost literally in some other place and sensing this pushed the fury of my fear.

"Where's Dad?" I shouted and gave her no time to answer. "Where is he? What's *wrong* with him? Why did he fight Bobby?"

She'd lit a cigarette with the ashtray lighter and when she leaned over to replace it I could see her tears. She smoked and noisily exhaled before bothering to wipe at their wetness. "He's upset," she said. "He's just upset. I don't know where he is. How could I know where he is?"

"How come he's upset?" I was fighting tears myself. "Why is he mad at Bobby?"

"He's not," she quickly answered.

"Because he gives me rides home?"

"No," she said. "He's not mad at Bobby."

"Why are *you* mad at Dad all the time?"

She looked at me and, sounding startled, said, "Why would you say that?"

"You are. You're always arguing."

She smoked, saying nothing, which I heard as an admission. "Tell me! What's—"

"Will, stop it," she snapped. "Just stop it. We'll talk when we get home. Try to calm down."

I said, more frantic still, "It was my fault wanting to play catch in the rain. It wasn't Dad's idea." This lie seemed worth the risk as I remembered her anger when we'd entered the kitchen, soaked and filthy. She'd ordered me into the mud room to strip off my uniform and from behind its door I'd heard her shouting at my father, asking him what on earth he'd had in mind, asking him what he was trying to prove. And heard him shouting back at her, saying he was sick of her crazy moods, saying he was having some fun with his son, asking her what in God's name she could think was wrong with that.

In the car, she again glanced at me with surprise, as if she'd had no idea I might have overheard their quarrel. And thinking now of her anger as we'd come into the house, I wonder if the sight of us seemed evidence to her that he'd learned what and who her secret was.

"I wasn't mad at him for that." Her voice was staticky with tears.

"Yes, you were. I heard you yelling."

"I said. . . ," she reached for a firmness. "We'll talk when we get home. But not unless you calm yourself down."

"Will Dad be home?"

She said, quite deliberately, "I don't know, Will," each word needing more patience than she had.

I slammed my fist against my door and turned away from her. I began to weep. I looked out to the unanimous blackness of the passing fields and pictured them seamlessly joining the sky, and I imagined myself sliding out the car window and drifting away from my mother and my father and from the sudden despair, black as the night fields, of my life.

━━━━━

At the farm, I ran from the car before my mother shut it off, ignoring her call, ordering me to wait. I burst into the house, calling my father's name. There'd been no sign of his pickup but, crazy as the night had been, I took that to mean nothing. I rushed, panting, from the kitchen to the living room and down the hallway and when I reached the stairs I shouted, "Dad, are you up there? Gram? Is Dad up there?"

I could hear her stirring. She called back weakly, "What?" and I'd started up when I saw through a window the headlights of the pickup as it was pulling in. I turned around on the stairs and ran back through the house out onto the porch. From there I could see my parents, beneath the yard light, standing in the driveway by the pickup. I slammed the screen door behind me and, running toward them, heard my father.

"*I'm* a fool!" he shouted. "You're calling *me* a fool?!"

"Yes!" my mother said. "You made a fool of all of us."

"*All* of us, Leanne?" he sneered. "*All* of us? Who're you thinking when you say '*all* of us'?"

I reached them then and shouted, "Stop it! Stop it!"

My mother turned and reached for me and pulled me to her hip. "Go back in the house, Willie."

"No!"

"Go!" she said. She tried to turn me around and I wiggled free of her.

"Say you'll stop!"

"Willie, *go,*" my father said. "I mean it."

I looked at him and then at her and I remember them peering down at me with an identical wild light in their eyes, as though in this extreme they found the thing they could agree on. I was made more frightened, and angrier, by their cooperation and I turned and raced back up the lawn, listening for their voices as I ran but hearing nothing.

I paused on the porch and looked out. They'd moved from the spot of yard light and had, for the moment, utterly disappeared. The sight of the darkness, the sense of them hiding in it, sent me hurrying back through the house toward the stairs.

Reaching them, I looked up and saw my grandmother standing at the top in her bathrobe and slippers. My eyes were filmed with tears and sweat, blurring her. I said, "Gram," and, scrambling up to her, heard my mother's hurried footfall coming into the kitchen. My grandmother put her arms around me. "What's going on?" she said.

As if to answer her, there was the sound of the screen door slamming again and my father's voice shouted, "I don't care if the whole damn town *was* there. I don't give a shit *what* the town thinks!"

My mother's laughter was thrilled meanness. "Oh, really, Lewis? Since when, if I may ask? That's all you've cared about since the day we got here! So when did you stop giving a shit?"

My grandmother squeezed me. She whispered, "Praise the Lord and pass the ammunition."

There was silence and when my father broke it his voice conveyed a great relief, as if he'd suddenly realized what had all along been obvious. "Well, you're just a whore, Leanne." As if he'd seen that the answer to the riddle of her was so much simpler than he'd made it all these years. "You think you're a great singer stuck out here on a farm, but that's not why you're miserable. You're just a whore who's had a hard time getting any business." I stiffened and I felt my grandmother stiffen, too. And it was then that I heard him, for the one time I remember, make mention of my mother's mother. "It's all in the family, Leanne. You're your mother's daughter. You're just a whore."

She slapped him then; nothing else explains the sound or her shriek accompanying it, and I felt my body become my crazily working heart. There was the scrape of a chair across the floor and a thud that must have been my father bumping into something. I pressed even closer to my grandmother, pushing my head into her heavy bosom, and she squeezed me tightly.

There was a sudden sickly quiet that rose up the stairs. My grandmother turned and guided me from where we stood toward her living room. As we moved away, I heard booming footsteps crossing the kitchen floor again, then another flurry of doors slamming.

We reached her couch and collapsed on it together. She lifted her arm and drew me close to her once more and began to run her fingers through my hair. A more muffled exchange started downstairs, which meant they'd moved into their bedroom. I tried to speak to my grandmother, but there was only sobbing in my throat. What I wanted from her was a confirmation. I needed her to tell me it was as terrible as it sounded. I tried again to speak to her and wept instead.

But in fact she was giving me the answer with her silence, for I'd learned in loving her that only when something surprised or upset her greatly was her response a speechless one. I tried but failed to will all my concentration into the feel of her fingers through my hair.

I awoke the next morning on my grandmother's couch beneath one of her sheets, my baseball uniform in a pile on the floor. Her heavy-bladed turning fan was broadcasting its breeze. I lay still for some minutes while impressions came to me. Through her high east window the sun was full and bleaching. The brightness and the heat and the sound in my mind of my parents' voices from the night before—all these seemed inseparable features of the light.

What had wakened me were the noises coming from my grandmother's tiny kitchen as she slammed her drawers and cupboard doors and cymbaled the lids of her pots and pans. It was not unusual for her to set these sounds loose in early morning and typically, hearing them, my father would raise his eyes to the ceiling as he sat at the table downstairs with his first cup of coffee. "There she goes," he'd say.

And if my mother were sitting with him, she might say, "How does she *do* it?" her voice admiring and impressed with my grandmother's gift for creating an orchestra of sounds from so few instruments. Yet I'm sure they understood that the noises meant she was especially upset. And they must have assumed, as I do now, that the reason was usually some thought of my grandfather, the memory inflicting a vigorous sadness she could only bear by getting up and moving wordlessly about: tossing things, dropping things, letting things collide.

Finally I sat up and wrapped the sheet around me, feeling the breeze of her fan feathering my shoulder blades, and that's when she came into her living room.

"*You're* up bright and early!" she blurted. Her voice was blaring, hoarse and raw, as it often was, and always when she'd been crying.

11

My grandmother and I looked dumbly at each other. "It's going to be a real pistol!" she finally shouted, meaning the heat of the day. "The radio says the humidity's already ninety percent. My dress is soaked through and it's only seven o'clock!" She patted a delta of wetness that had spread across her bosom.

I was used to her speaking in these energetic gusts and I'd recognized her growing inclination to exaggerate. But she sounded that morning especially heedless and extreme, as though her aim was simply to fill the air with noise.

She said, "Put your uniform on and come eat some breakfast. Or just stay in your underwear. It's too hot for wool."

"I'll wear my pants," I said, reaching for them and pulling them on, their flannel on my legs feeling important no matter how hot it was.

I followed after her into the hallway, alert for indicative sounds from below. As I'd lain on the couch listening to my grandmother's kitchen clangor, it had seemed and not seemed that I'd dreamed everything that had happened the night before. I didn't remember my grandmother putting me to bed, only the two of us sitting on her couch while my parents' fighting found a muted range of rage. Somehow they kept it there for quite a while and I heard them through a great dull fear, one I'd come to know well enough to fall asleep with.

As I trailed my grandmother into her kitchen, I realized that it would be typical to hear nothing from downstairs at this early hour. My father would already be outside in the barnyard or the fields; my mother, just stirring, would not yet be in the kitchen. I knew this the way every child knows the clock of his world, learning the lives of those from whom he demands that the world remain utterly predictable. But the silence I heard rising up the stairway that morning seemed a thing that could be touched. No doubt this was what my grandmother's gibberish was trying to cover, that deathly after-quiet that gives the sensation that the very air has been recently ransacked.

In her kitchen, I watched her take a box of cereal down from a shelf. She was drinking a cup of coffee and poured one for me. She continued to talk about the humid heat and her wish that the air would let the moisture go: "We need the rain!"

Then she paused and took a sip of coffee and seemed to fix her eyes on something just behind me, and I felt the certainty that I would spin around to greet my mother in the doorway. When she wasn't there, I quickly turned back, shaken by how much I'd expected to see her.

My grandmother's expression was searching, as though she were trying to remember her lines.

"What?" I asked.

She inhaled and violently cleared her throat and said, "I was thinking about Harris's appendix."

She was referring to the death of her only brother. To the story of his struggling into their house one morning, doubled over with pain in his right side, and calling to my grandmother, then thirteen, four years his younger, who got him into bed and hurried to their well and pumped its icy water to soak some towels for wet packs. But the cold towels only worsened the pain and when their mother came in and felt them, she slapped my grandmother's face and shouted in her panic, "It's *hot* towels that ease a cramp!"

So my grandmother heated some water and within half an hour of the steaming towels' application, her brother's relief was suddenly extraordinary. Of course, as well as relief, there was also infection moving through his body, released from his appendix, which the heat of the towels had burst. Soon his temperature rose alarmingly, his skin paled to the hue of watery milk, and by the time his father neared the house for the noon meal, returning from the neighbor he'd been assisting, Harris was nearly comatose. He died in the back of a long feed wagon as his father hurried the horses to the doctor in Marshalltown.

My grandmother knew this story held a ghoulish power for me, but it seemed inexplicable that she'd mentioned it now. And then she said, "What I mean is, I know you're upset"—my stomach seized—"but I'm going to tell you what's been going on around here. If I didn't, or say I told you something else, it would be the same as putting the wrong towel on your heart. You'd feel better, but only for a little while."

She described for me then the previous night, when our nearest neighbor, Orie Van Zant, crossed the gravel road that separated our farms and walked slowly up our driveway toward my father's shop. No doubt he'd waited until he'd seen my mother and me leave for the game. From his west pasture, where his son, Dale, and I often played, Orie could look directly across and into our barnyard and see that the light in my father's shop was on.

As I recall my grandmother struggling to tell me what had gone on the night before, I picture Orie Van Zant, a man my father's age, made to feel old by his difficult task, walking with an octogenarian stiffness toward the shop. I think of him stepping through the doorway and bidding my father a hesitant hello and informing him that he could not, under his Lord's impatient eye, hold his say for one more day and simply must speak of my mother's adultery. Imagining that moment, I'm certain that Orie did not feel a pulse of superior glee, for his piety was quiet if inexhaustibly alert. Rather, I suspect he believed, from a life in his church, that the most vital chores were the most thankless ones and knew he had no choice but to speak to my father.

Orie had no suggestion, offered no forum, no ritual, for how my mother should confess her newest sins. Since we were not members of the Christian Reformed Church, it wasn't a matter of his asking that she come before its consistory, on which he sat as an elder, to say she'd broken one of God's commandments. But until she'd somehow made it clear that she *had* repented, he hoped my father would understand why they, the Van Zants, could have no contact with us. Which meant, with all else, that he couldn't permit Dale to spend time in my company.

Orie told my father that he would pray for us and he offered to do so then and there. Much as it may have challenged his shyness, he asked my father to join him just this once, in the hope that in prayer they might together glimpse the way toward our family's rescue.

Taken up with Bobby Markum.

That's the phrase my grandmother chose.

At her kitchen table after she'd paused in her account and looked up at the ceiling, she said, "Orie said to your dad that, apparently, your mom's . . . taken up with Bobby Markum."

Everything she told me that morning she had learned from my father very late the night before. After she'd arranged me on her couch, she'd lain in her bed listening. And while I know that children sleep the sleep of the dead, it's hard to believe that I didn't hear my parents' new round of shouting and slamming of doors. But I didn't, I slept, while my grandmother traced the paths of their sounds until it was clear my mother had left.

She descended the stairs then and found my father at the kitchen table. He was barely able to raise his eyelids, his head beginning to throb as his drunkenness was lifting. They talked and he wept fitfully as the sky began to whiten. He told her that after Orie had left, he'd climbed into the pickup and driven back-country roads, his rage growing, until he'd headed into town. And after he'd been escorted from the field, he again drove the back roads, drinking the six-pack he'd bought in the bar.

As I listened to my grandmother's account of all this, I tried to picture my father, the calm and cautious man who checked my mother's flamboyance. But I didn't know the person she was describing, the drunken man I'd watched stumble out toward Bobby Markum.

My grandmother looked at me and said, "At dawn, your dad took off in the pickup again. I'm sure, if I know him, and I do, he'll be back soon." Then, with her apron, she dabbed behind her glasses at the tears in her eyes and when she continued her voice was hoarser. "Like I say, your mom . . . left last night, and I don't know where she went either." She paused again, while I waited for her to tell me that she knew my mother would also be returning any minute. She said instead, "Now you and me, we'll have to wait and see how the day goes, won't we?"

She'd already paid a visit that morning to Orie Van Zant, ignoring the ban and marching into his barn and, finding him there with Dale and Dale's younger sister, Marilyn, telling him in front of his children that if his was the kind of Christian behavior that guaranteed eternal life, she'd take comfort in the idea of him in a heaven surrounded by walleyed Republicans and assorted other idiots.

But for now anyway, she said to me, it was best that I stay on our side of the road.

All that day, I followed almost literally on her heels. As she had announced, the air was sweltering and humid, more typical of August than the middle of June. Both of us were soon sweating freely as we weeded her garden and raked the sticks and small branches from a recent windstorm. Now and then she paused to say that this weather was ideal for her arthritis, that the wet heat traveled deep into her joints.

It was for me as if my movements were taking place outside my body, my limbs not really mine at all. Instead, I was monitoring each passing moment as first it held me and then ended without the reappearance of my mother or my father. Such attentiveness to every second made each one into an hour, made an hour a week, and all the while I was trying to imagine how life would be when it began again.

For I knew, and it was all I knew, that these moments were not life, but some sickening suspension of it. And I saw that it would not, could not, start once more until my parents returned and we all *behaved* again. However upsetting that might prove to be, however fabulous my mother's melodrama, however newly brutish my father's resentment, it didn't matter to me what tone would be sounded as long as it meant that life was resuming. So, for all the things that followed, all that would happen in the next few days, I think this first one, with nothing but the drone of worry filling me, will always be in memory the meanest of them.

The two of us were mostly silent for the first few hours, while my mind was alive with recurrent noise. I heard my mother's shriek as she slapped my father, the flat wet pop of her hand against his face. And mostly I heard, again and again, my father's calling cry, that unearthly wail, as he'd moved past me onto the field toward Bobby. And who can imagine what my grandmother was thinking? What wild concern she was feeling for her son? What vibrant puzzlement toward her daughter-in-law?

Silence then, and the heat and our sweat, until I stood my rake and looked up at her and asked, "What do you *mean*, Mom's 'taken up' with Bobby?" To which my grandmother stopped and absently tapped her fist against her mouth and replied tonelessly, "I mean *that*. Just what I said. Apparently, she's taken up with him."

Not long after that I tried again, and her voice came close to irritation. "Now, Will," she said quickly, "you heard me before."

I suppose my question threatened her confidence that she could lead me through such a discussion—an impossible one, obviously. And maybe by that point her stubbornness had taken hold and she told herself she'd already been handed a responsibility—me, on this day that had no end in sight—so unfair that she was not about to make it even harder for herself. Or maybe she suspected that I *did* understand, at least enough, and so, titillated, wished to make her speak more explicitly. But whatever her reasons she flatly refused to alter or elaborate the way she'd first expressed herself.

Apparently, your mother's taken up with Bobby Markum.

Can we possibly say what we guessed about sex at any certain point of near adolescence? What we knew without knowing and what we'd wildly misconstrued? Besides, whatever I did or didn't sense, how much could any of it have helped me understand that my mother had taken up with Bobby Markum, since clearly I knew nothing, as I approached the age of twelve, of the addictive lure of risk, the stupid daring of desire?

What I *did* know about was my mother's beauty, especially apparent, as I've said, in a culture that takes the youth and the beauty from its women. But beauty is one thing and sex is something it is not, so my best idea of what I might have reasoned was that Bobby wanted to take my mother from my father because she was much more beautiful than any other woman in New Holland. And when I thought of it this way, my father's actions the night before began to make a certain sense to me. They seemed the way a man famed for his bravery would behave: wishing at all cost to keep what was his. But the idea of this, as I moved through the day, made me no less sick with my terror and my sadness.

Sometime that afternoon I walked with my grandmother to the chicken house to get a hen for that night's supper. We stepped inside and she deftly snared one by the neck using a long-handled wire hook. I left the coop and walked ahead of her, holding the axe she always let me carry, and when I reached the stump I waited and handed the axe to her. I watched while she laid the hen on the stump, positioning its head between two long nails. Then I took its legs, pulled on them slightly to stretch the neck, and my eyes followed the axe as it moved through my grandmother's practiced time-grooved arc.

I would then have normally played a sort of tag with the headless hen, trying to dodge it while it careened off trees and fences, its blood fountaining, rising in death to an outrageous show of life. But that day, as the hen's body flapped crazily about, I stared at it unmoving, seeing in its madness something of the way I'd seen my father charging drunkenly, first toward Bobby, then my mother. I looked away and down at the limp head on the stump. For all its unmistakable beak and bead-eye, comb and wattle, it was for a moment the severed tip of Bobby's finger.

———

Two evergreens stood at the edge of our long front lawn where it began its slope toward the roadside ditch. Over the years the trees had become entwined, and I often crawled beneath them into an arborous cave where I could peer out through their ground-sweeping branches and watch the world while feeling hidden from it. Toward the end of that day, spent from waiting and watching and the steady nausea of fear, I found myself there, lying on a floor of pine needles and looking out across the road to the Van Zants' farm.

Orie was working in the field directly across from me, his John Deere tractor mounted with a cultivator that rooted weeds from between new rows of crops. I saw him in the distance, the lowering sun lighting him. He was still far enough away so that his labor made only the slightest noise. He was steering toward me down the half-mile rows of soy beans that would lead him to the edge of his field, just the slender width of road from where I lay.

As he drew ever closer, the tractor's sounds began to become more of his work. Now I could make him out, his head and shoulders smudged inside a soft husk of dust. He wore a high denim cap, like a railroad engineer's. He leaned radically to his right in the tractor's seat, watching the cultivator blades and holding this awkward posture with the rigidity of a trained animal as my father did when he plowed or planted or weeded a field, and as I was not yet strong enough to do.

At last he neared the end of his field—the John Deere now enormous, its implosions like a stammer—and raised a lever to lift the cultivator. There were the squeak and groan of its reluctant mechanics. Spade-shaped blades caught the sunlight as he swung the tractor through its turn, and watching him I suddenly imagined myself hurrying out from beneath the trees and running just across the road to where life was continuing as I'd known life the day before. I was racing into Orie's field and stepping into his path as he was settling in again. I was waving my arms to stop him, then scrambling up onto his seat and shouting frantically above the popping of the engine that he must forgive my mother for taking up with Bobby Markum. He must forgive us all, my mother and my father and my grandmother and me. He had to use his connections with God; he simply had to.

In his field across the road, his back was to me now, the low sunlight distending his shadow across weeded rows. He adjusted the depth of the blades and put the tractor into gear and moved away again toward the opposite horizon. New dust came up behind him and his noise began to fall.

After a minute it was quiet enough to hear the slamming of a door and I looked in its direction to see Dale coming out of their house and running toward the barn. I watched him enter its darkness and stared, waiting for him to come out again. I couldn't believe how free and casual he'd appeared. He'd hurried across his lawn as though nothing had changed since yesterday. I'd expected to see him moping about, resentful of the terms of his father's edict, listless and hunch-shouldered in his sadness at my absence.

I started crying at last. It was the first time that day I'd let my fear come loose completely and once I started I cried harder and harder, rolling in the pine needles and beating my fists into the ground. Then, pushing myself, I cried more wildly still, using my sadness to make me sadder. I paused to breathe, inhaling as deeply as possible and holding the air. I wanted my appendix to burst, wanted to die a shocking and vengeful death beneath the trees. I wanted my parents to find me there and know it had been their shameful recklessness that had caused it.

Then I resumed crying with an energy as desperate as my father's wail, as outraged as my mother's shriek, and continued until my strength began to leave me. Feeling weak at last, I quieted down and was finished. My head rested on my forearm, its skin wet from my tears. I took slow, full breaths and watched ants weaving their way through the pine needles.

The sun was setting. The enclosing shade grew even deeper and quite cool, and I lay there, dumb and stunned, for some while. In thrashing about I'd turned away from the road and, looking toward our house, I heard behind me once again the approaching noise of Orie's tractor. For me there was always a contradiction in this sound, a lulling menace as it grew, like a Grimms' narrative, and I may have started to doze off when my grandmother's voice began calling to me.

Peering through the branches, I could see her coming around

the corner of the house. She stopped and called again and her hand cupped her ear as for her echo.

"Will?" she called, breaking my name into syllables. "Supper's ready."

She walked back and forth along the front of the house where the lawn rose and leveled out again. Her stride was a sentinel's. Her big body dipped with each step she took, which meant her especially arthritic left knee was stiffening in the cooler air.

"Will? Answer me!"

She continued to pace the ridge of lawn, her step quickening, her limp more emphatic, and I knew that I was watching the power of absence, what it does to those who love you or are certain that they do, and need, perhaps too urgently, to know where you have gone.

"I'm going in now. You want to starve to death, that's fine with me."

Behind me, I heard Orie approaching.

"I'm awfully hungry! I'll wait fifteen minutes. If you're not upstairs I might have to eat your food."

The need of a child was in my grandmother's voice and the love I felt for her in hearing it was larger than the world, of which we seemed the lone inhabitants. I lowered my head and rested it on my arm and closed my eyes as she called my name again. She bid me good night. She said she hoped I'd sleep through the heavy rain she could see forming in the western sky. She waited and started to shout still another threat but now her voice was covered by the noise of Orie's tractor as it arrived in order to leave again.

12

After my grandmother went back in, I gave my full attention to Dale Van Zant across the road. He continued to move in and out of his house. Watching him, I began to realize that I was only punishing myself by hiding. So I crawled out, parting branches, and headed up the lawn.

I hurried through the downstairs rooms. Their dusky darkness seemed a taunt. Climbing the stairs into the day's risen heat, I caught the smell of sizzling fat. When I came into my grandmother's kitchen she was seated at the table and her hand was reaching for the fried chicken on my plate.

"Whoa!" she said. "You're a lucky boy. A second later and I'd've snatched your drumstick. I guess you didn't hear me calling you."

"I was riding my bike," I lied.

"Ah." She got up to get me a glass of milk and brought it and a bowl of potato salad to the table. She said, "I'm as hungry as a stevedore tonight." I glanced at her plate but it looked too clean to have held food. She reached for the potato salad and dished an enormous portion onto her plate. "See?" She had no fork or spoon and made no move to get them.

"Who's Steve Adore?" I asked. I nibbled at the chicken and my knotted stomach felt as though it might refuse the tiny bite.

She raised her chin and gave a throaty shout of laughter. "Stevedores? You never heard of stevedores? It's not a person, it's a job. They're those big hairy brutes who load things onto boats."

She leaned back in her chair. "In fact, when I was a girl, this was before I met your grandfather—didn't I ever tell you this?—I almost ran away with a stevedore." She was fluttering her eyes like a damsel about to swoon; it was the way they moved when she was improvising. "The day I met him, he was unloading a big boat docked on the Mississippi, over at Princeton, that little river town where my father took Mother and me for one of our 'excursions,' he liked to call them, which, Princeton, is also the birthplace of John Wayne, whose real name is Marion Morrison, and, Judas priest, he took my breath away. The stevedore, not John Wayne. Or is it Winterset, where John Wayne's from? Yes, it's Winter—"

"Gram, where *are* they?" I blurted. "When are they coming home?"

She immediately leaned forward in her chair.

I said, "You promised this morning they'd be home by now."

Of course this wasn't true; she'd only offered that my father would be back soon. But to my accusation, she whispered, "I know I did."

I asked, "Did Bobby *kidnap* Mom or something?" The words she'd refused to clarify that morning had naturally been sounding in my mind all day.

Her voice was soft. "Why would you think such a crazy thing?"

"You said Bobby 'took her up.' Did he take her somewhere?"

Her face puckered. Laboring, she got up from the table, her stiff leg swinging out like a scythe, and stood at the sink with her back to me. I heard a small, peeping noise, the voice of someone fragile, not my grandmother. Her shoulders lifted and fell as in a pantomime of weeping. I didn't know what to do, what I was capable of doing. She stayed turned away from me and there was something so frightening about the silent violence of her tremoring that I felt held in my chair, but finally I rose and walked up behind her and lifted my arms to reach around her waist.

I felt her body trying to accept my strained embrace and after some moments more she picked up a dish towel and wiped her eyes. "Who's got me?" she said weakly. "Vern Gagne? What's this, some new hold? The hind end paralyzer?" Then she turned and put her arms around me and led me back to my chair. She looked at the indifferent bite I'd taken and at her own untouched plate and said, "The only thing that sounds good to me is a root beer float. What about you?"

I helped her scoop the ice cream into tall glasses and as she poured the root beer into them I got spoons and plastic straws from her drawers. We attacked the floats greedily, relieved to concentrate on them, our appetites at last awakened. For several minutes we said nothing.

When she broke the silence, my grandmother said, "I'm mad at them, Will. I'm completely annoyed at both of them." It was as if she were telling me that I could be too, but my impulse was to think of how I might defend them.

My straw made a croaking sound as it vacuumed my glass and she got up and began to fix me another root beer float. She was clearly distracted, holding a scoop of ice cream over my glass for several seconds before plopping it in.

She sat down again and pushed the filled glass toward me and this was the moment, as I earlier described it, when she began to speak about my parents and their marriage. All the while her focus appeared to recognize me vaguely. More than anything, she seemed to be thinking out loud. Her reckless letting go, I'm now certain, was in some sense involuntary, coming after she had moved through the day, brooding and resentful, while working to keep her feelings from me.

In her kitchen, she paused at last. Her voice, as I've said, had been quietly reflective, nearly slipping into a cadence I heard as a bedtime story's, and listening, it was possible to forget that the characters in her memories were my parents and herself. The time seemed so long ago, the concerns unlike any I would have thought the three of them could have.

I'd finished the second root beer float and I shook my head when she asked if I wanted more.

She nodded. Then she said, "I'm madder at your mom than I am your dad," and it was the flatness of her statement, her tone of disinterest, that most surprised me. "Not to say he hasn't done some stupid things, your dad. He was only just back from the army and overnight he turned into an undertaker. I don't know where he got the idea that you had to be a grim old man to farm, but it wasn't from his father, I can tell you that for sure."

She reached for a towel and dabbed the sweat from her neck. The air felt as if the heat of all the world had found its way up to the cramped space of her kitchen. I wiped my own neck and forehead, surprised at how wet I was.

"But she had the run of the big kitchen, and their privacy, and they *didn't* get my misery. I stayed out of their way and I suspect there aren't too many who'd know that was the thing to do. But I did, I stayed up here, out of sight . . . the old bat in the attic." She grimaced hard and it collapsed her face; she looked toothless for a moment. And though she was speaking with a wounded self-righteousness, what impressed me now was hearing that she felt a terrible hurt being dealt to *her*, since all day I'd been carrying the assumption of a child: that the only injustice was being done to me.

Then, abruptly, she seemed finished and said nothing more until she looked at me and asked, "Are you tired? You must be tired."

I lied and said I wasn't, though my limbs were painful with the thrum of fatigue.

She nodded, her expression again dispersed. I heard a car moving down the road toward us but for the moment I'd lost the hopeful reflex to get up and look out.

Finally she said, "You should take a bath before you go to bed." But when I protested she let me have my way, saying that at least I must scrub my face and hands.

As I filled her bathroom sink I could hear through the wall her cupboard doors slamming with the force of farce, plates and pans rattling from the quake she was creating. When I'd finished washing, I moved into her living room and sat close to her big turning fan. We hadn't discussed where I'd sleep, but the thought of going down to my own bed was dreadful. The empty rooms below had felt cavernous whenever I'd had to scurry through to get upstairs. Sitting in the dark on my grandmother's couch, I felt the haunting fact of them.

My mind was now hectic with the history my grandmother had been offering and it made me remember the day I'd learned my birth was scandalous, having been confronted by a group of first-grade boys who, confused, teased me for being adopted. I'd denied I was adopted and then that night asked my mother if I were and, if so, what it meant. This led to a contorted explanation that I felt I somehow got the gist of, my mother and father conspiring to tell me that they'd been so eager for me they hadn't been able to wait as long as people normally did.

In truth, only rarely did some classmate, reaching for an easy meanness, bring the subject up. But of late I'd been bringing it up to myself whenever I dwelt on my chances with God. Sitting there that night, stupid with sadness, I couldn't resist doing so again. And when my grandmother joined me in the living room and turned on her floor lamp, I blurted out, "I don't care what you say, I think it's God. He's punishing us for not believing in Him."

I was ready for her to give me one of her scowls, but she didn't. She said, "Well, *you* believe in Him these days, don't you?"

"Yes," I said loudly, with the thought that you never knew when He might be listening.

She'd not yet sat down. "So why's He punishing you, too?"

"Because I don't do a good job showing Him. I keep telling Him you're going to take me to church, but I know He doesn't think you will."

She plopped down in her padded armchair. Her card table was beside her, her scrapbook of famous Iowans resting on top of it. There appeared to be no new clippings waiting to be entered. Her face was harshly lit beneath the floor lamp. She rubbed her brow and shook her head at something she was thinking. She said, "Think whatever you want," and even I, in that moment, could hear how tired and defeated she felt.

"Why don't *you* think that could be the reason?"

"Well," she said, "it's hard to think like that if you've got a working brain, and in a town where the Dutch act like God is, I don't know, the truant officer."

"Why's it hard to believe in God if you have a working brain?" I'd asked her several versions of this question in the past few months and she'd always dismissed them with an annoyed flippancy. But this time she seemed to gather herself and think her words through carefully. It was as if she wanted to make certain she'd never have to answer me again.

Then she said, "Mother, my mother, had been a fairly regular churchgoer before Harris died. But after, I think she felt any God who'd take her son that way was nobody she wanted to have to make chitchat with in heaven. And I don't think she thought much of the argument that since we killed *His* son, we had no grounds to complain. That sounded like someone holding a grudge, and she figured if He could, so could she."

Though my grandmother never said it, I've come to suspect that her problem with God was in thinking He tried every day to be a big shot.

She'd gone quiet again and then said, "Maybe *that's* part of it; it's hard to believe if you're the sort to hold a grudge. Mother was, and I've always been one that was, too. There are those in this town I've held a grudge against for years and I've enjoyed every minute of it. It's an underrated pleasure as far as I'm concerned."

We sat in silence in her heat, in the country's burnished quiet. And then she added, "I know you didn't ask, but if you want to know what I think, I think your mother is a woman who needs to feel unsafe from time to time. And she hasn't felt that way for a long while now."

"Why would she want to feel unsafe?"

"Some people just do." She required several seconds to shift her body in her chair. "Remember the morning I caught you jumping off the chicken house onto hay bales? And you tried to tell me how exciting it felt, to be so scared?"

"It *did*," I said, ready to explain myself again.

She said, "I know. I know it did. And I believe your mother thinks so, too."

———

In my dreams, I was hosting the *Will Vaughn Show*, waiting backstage while the orchestra played my opening theme. Emerging from the wings, I waved to the audience and said that that night we were lucky to have a special guest, Miss Jean Seberg. I looked offstage and she came toward me. She was beautiful but thin and boyish, her hair brutally shorn like a Trappist's for her role of Joan of Arc. She appeared to be floating, even though she was dressed in the chain mail and armor she wore in photographs I'd seen of the making of the film. I shook her tiny hand and told her that I, a fellow Iowan, was especially proud of her. She looked at me and begged permission to ask if I could still detect the sound of the Midwest in her voice.

I thought the compliment would be to say, of *course* I could, but when she heard this her eyes grew wide with alarm. Trying to recover, I said I'd been teasing, that her accent sounded British. Hearing this, she looked relieved.

I could sense that the pace of my show was lagging, but all I wanted was to talk with her. I asked if she were worried about catching polio in France, since it was crowded and filthy and the plumbing was so old, and she said no and, besides, polio was quite fashionable in France. Then I realized all at once what I desired and I asked her to take me back to France with her. She looked startled and said that wouldn't be possible because she was going back to France with the famous pitcher, Bobby Markum. I tried to keep calm, but there was a sudden hysteria where my heart had been. I asked her please to reconsider, but this time she refused me with a crisp efficiency. She turned to leave and I tried to stop her, but she was moving away with her particular floating ease. I heard people in the audience hissing and stomping their feet. I reached for her. My arms were elastic, I could stretch them limitlessly, but she somehow stayed just beyond my grasp and I shouted after her, and that's when my grandmother woke me.

"It's all right. It's all right." Her voice was not fully awake and had the weak scratch of an ancient's. I was lying beside her and I scanned the darkness to see where we were. "You were having a bad dream." I could make out the tall posters, shaped black stalks, of her huge bed.

I lay still, my eyes blinking, waiting to return from the dream, and when I had I whispered, "Are they back?"

"Not yet."

"Mom's not here?"

"No."

"Or Dad?"

"Not yet."

———

I came downstairs the next morning, feeling again the astonishing heat, which I took to be the sign that all else was unchanged too. Weather was the day's palpable humor and it was sovereign. In this way, at least, I thought like a farmer.

I hurried through the kitchen in search of my grandmother and when I stepped out onto the porch, I saw my father sitting on the old blue couch beneath the screened windows.

13

My father smiled as he put down his coffee cup, the meek smile of a good child who's been waiting to be dealt with for his misbehavior. His shirt and pants were wrinkled and splotched with sweat, his face swollen from exhaustion and whatever else he'd been through. He sat forward on the couch to receive me and, relieved as I was to see him, I also felt a fearful shyness toward my father. The sense of him in all his vibrant drunkenness was still strong in my mind. As he took me in his arms I stiffened in the way some infants do when you try to hold them. He rubbed my spine as if to ply it and pulled me closer. I was shocked by the strength with which he held me.

"How you doing?" he whispered in my ear. "You doing okay?"

I nodded, my face moving against his chest and stirring the fetid dampness of his shirt. I smelled his new sweat mixing with what had settled in his pores, and more than anything this told me how far he was from who he was. As I've said, he always scrubbed himself immaculate after a day's work. And though I'm certainly mistaken in remembering a vagrant's stench about him, it is what I remember and perhaps it means that I was looking for signs he was still that brutish stranger, that I was waiting to be shown he was my father again.

He released me and sat back, slouched in the worn pillows.

I asked, "Where have you *been*? Did you come home last night?"

"Yes," he said.

"I didn't hear you."

"It was late."

"*How* late?"

"I don't know," he said. "Too late for you to hear me."

"I was sleeping upstairs or I would have heard you." I needed for some reason to win this point and he smiled and said nothing, letting me. "But where *were* you, Dad? Where have you been?"

He frowned.

"Where's *Mom*?" My voice was rising. I looked over his shoulder and through the screen out to the acreage as if I might actually spot her out there. "Were you looking for her? Is that where you've—"

"Whoa, Willie," he said and touched my shoulder. "Just slow down a little and take it easy. Okay?"

I felt furious with people telling me to slow down and take it easy. I knew they were wrong to ask me to; knew I was entitled to know everything immediately. "Were you looking for Mom?"

He let a thought cross his face. "Yes," he said.

"Where did you look?"

He shifted on the couch and loosely waved his hand. "Every-where," he said.

As the story of his search would grow over time, I learned that this was barely an exaggeration. People living in all directions from the village would speak of seeing his pickup moving slowly over the dirt and gravel roads, crisscrossing the countryside, meticulous and methodical, the uncompromising ethic of tending finely to a field. They would speculate that he slept for a few minutes at a time in the broiling truck, then started out again, moving helplessly to the adrenaline of rage, hotter and more exhausted and no doubt more fanatical as he recognized the incremental folly of his behavior. He must have figured the only way to justify it was to find her, until by nightfall, fairly mad with his need and humiliated but unable to quit, he was knocking on doors. And then, past midnight and all reason, rousing neighbors from their sleep.

That's the general version that would come to take its place in the lore of New Holland. Years later I once would overhear it referred to as the "midnight ride of Lewis Vaughn."

Again I looked past him through the screen and saw my grandmother stepping from behind the granary. She was working in her garden. Head down, she leaned on her hoe, then nimbly flicked it, cane and wand, toward a weed, and my need for heroes flew out toward her.

I said to my father, "But where *is* she?" There was now accusation, a note of daring in my voice, and it suddenly seemed that the work of waiting out my ruined life might just as well start with blaming him. I tried to hate him at that moment, first for having left and now, as much, for coming back. For as he'd held me and talked to me I'd begun to sense that his return marked a deepening of my troubles, not their end.

He shifted on the couch and looked in the direction of my grandmother. She was straddling rows, then straightened up and removed her straw hat and wiped her forehead with the back of her hand. She held a bouquet of weeds in her fist. When he faced me again he said, "I'm not sure where she is."

I strained to hear what wasn't in his answer. "But you *maybe* know?" I asked.

He picked at the stuffing that sprouted from the frayed arm of the couch. "No," he said. "I don't know where she is."

I thought, *She's taken up with Bobby Markum,* and I wanted to ask what I sensed I couldn't: if he'd looked for her with Bobby, if he'd looked where Bobby was. It didn't occur to me that Bobby might have varied his routine, even if he and my mother were together.

I said, "Maybe she's hurt or something. Maybe we should call the highway patrol."

My father said, "I wouldn't worry about that."

"Why not?" I asked, pressing further. "How do you know for sure she isn't hurt?"

"I don't know for sure."

"Then you should *call*."

He said, "We'd've heard if she was hurt. Don't you think?"

"What are you going to do now?" I asked.

He squinted hard, holding his eyes shut. "I don't know," he said, then opened them. "Before I do anything else, I have to try to get some sleep."

"Then you're going to look for her again after that?"

"I—"

"Maybe you won't have to," I said. "Maybe she'll be back when you wake up."

His mouth was a tight line. "Yes," he said. "Maybe." Our glances met and caromed and I realized what mattered was that I not start to cry again; something told me I would lose a great deal if I cried. It seemed the terms of survival in this world of adults, the idiotic world I was being forced to live in. So to take my mind away as I stood before my father, I thought to picture Jean Seberg's face, which I could almost make myself believe I'd touched the night before. And I tried to imagine living in Paris and catching polio in some world-headline-making way, prompting an outpouring of love and consolation. Then I worked up a sense of my appendix, a feature of the body designed by God in His own image, blithely churning its poison, like snake venom. I imagined the appendix to be a rattlesnake in each of us. Of course all these thoughts came in flashes far quicker than the time it takes to describe them.

My father slowly stood and placed his hands on my shoulders. He said, "I know none of this makes any sense. But I'm so tired right now I can barely remember my name. So I'm going to try to lie down for a bit." He hugged me and let go and then thought to add, "I'm not going anywhere else, just to bed for a little while."

"Then will you call the highway patrol?" I asked.

He paused and said, "If it seems like we should."

He moved past me into the house, then turned to ask, "You want to keep me company? I know you just got up, but if you want to come in and lie down with me, you sure can."

I shook my head. "That's okay." I watched him walk through the kitchen toward their bedroom. Seeing him going off to sleep alone where they slept together somehow startled me. I turned and looked outside and saw that my grandmother was walking in from her garden. I could hear her talking to herself as she often did, remarking on the look and conditions of the morning. She held her wicker basket filled with lettuces, behaving as she might have on any other day of her life.

———

From my place beneath the evergreens, I saw Dale Van Zant walking out into their field to meet his father. He was close enough that I could see him struggling to carry a huge red plastic water jug and a large brown paper bag. I heard Orie's tractor backfire, then go quiet, and he stepped down from the seat to wait for Dale to reach him. When he did, Orie took the bag and thermos and together they walked to an island of high grass and shade beneath a single ancient maple in the middle of the field. Orie sat down and leaned back against the tree trunk and took off his railroad engineer's cap. Dale dropped to his knees and waited for his father to open the bag and distribute their lunch. Watching them, I had a sense I couldn't then have named, that they were moving suspended in the medium of fable.

Beneath the trees, I was not now trying to hide from anyone, but from the sun and from its opposite—the mortuarial darkness that had settled in our house. When she'd come in from her garden, my grandmother had told me we should try to be quiet so my father could sleep. She'd taken off her shoes and, as well as her body would let her, walked on tiptoe up to her apartment, an effort that made her footsteps percussive and even heavier than usual.

I'd headed outside, feeling miserable and slothful in the heat. I thought about pitching my rubber baseball against the garage door where my father had painted a rectangular strike zone for me, but I knew that would have been unacceptably noisy.

Wandering about the yard, I pictured him deeply asleep in their airless bedroom, still filthy and dressed in his sweat-stained clothes, and my attempt at hating him slipped away completely. This seemed perilous; it had briefly felt so justified, that possibility of hatred, and I wanted nothing of the bottomless sorrow I sensed was moving in to replace it.

When Orie and Dale had finished eating, they stood and Orie put his cap back on. Then they retraced their steps across the rows to the tractor. Orie climbed up and, in a moment, set off. Dale again held the water jug, but instead of heading toward his house, he started down a row in my direction. Seeing him, I understood that he was carrying the jug to the end of the field, where he'd place it under bean leaves for his father to drink from later.

Dale was small for his age but strong, and he had an imp's pinwheeling energy. I watched him coming down a corridor of beans toward me, his body leaning less extremely against the weight of the now lighter jug. Reaching the end of their field, where a hem of end rows paralleled their fence, he stopped and put down the jug and looked up and down the road before turning his back to take a piss.

"Dale!" I called.

He jumped, fumbling frantically.

"Over here!"

He looked around and squinted across the road in my direction. He knew my hiding place well. We sometimes sat in it together. He shouted, "Jesus Christ! You scared the shit out of me!" A codpiece of white underwear showed through his still opened fly.

I crawled out, down the slope of the ditch, and sat on the bank looking across the road at him. "What're you doing?"

He turned sideways to me and said, "What's it look like I'm doing, Sherlock?" Momentarily he began to direct his penis left and right, watering bean leaves. He said casually over his shoulder, "We're not supposed to be talking."

I said, "We're not supposed to come *over*."

"Same diff," he said.

"Not really," I said.

"Yeah it is."

"No it's not."

As he finished he said, "I'll be right back." He reached down and picked up the jug, again tipping his body radically and extending his free arm for balance, a show of great strength now that he knew I was watching. "I gotta take this heavy son of a bitch over there." Grunting and cursing, he headed off.

Away from anyone who might inform on him, Dale swore constantly and it's hard to imagine he never slipped in front of his sister or his parents, but if he had, he'd have received some combination of beating and banishment from which he would not have soon recovered.

Still, I wouldn't call Dale cynical, for he believed all he heard and read about the Lord's omnipotence and was reminded every day, in some way or other, that God preferred his congregation. To Dale this meant, simply enough, that he was saved while others were not and there was no use wondering why; it was simply God and Satan divvying up the workload.

He came back and climbed up and sat on a fence rail. "See your dad's pickup," he said.

"Yeah."

"Your mom come with him?" he asked.

I flushed and looked away. "No."

"She home?"

My stomach tightened. "Not yet."

"Son of a bitch," he said, shaking his head. But there was sheer appreciation in the tone of his response, a student of sin admiring sin on such a scale and true to Dale's interest in my family, particularly in my mother, so beautiful and with such a lurid history.

I looked across at Dale and asked him, "How'd you know my mom was gone?"

"Right," he said and shook his head, dismayed at my ignorance. "What else do you think the whole town's been talking about?"

Yes. What else? This should not have been a surprise. And now, added to my grieving and my fear, I felt humiliated at the thought of everything we Vaughns had provided the town since my father had set it all in motion. I was suddenly hot, then cold, my shame malarial, and I tried again to find a hatred for him, but it simply wasn't there.

Instead I said, "It's your dad's fault."

"What?"

"Him coming over to tell my dad—"

"Ha! That's rich!" He bent forward and slapped his knee, his wiry body wiggling merrily on the fence rail. Then he stopped and, quite serious, said, " 'Whoever slanders his neighbour, I'll cut him off.' " He made a throat-slitting motion with the edge of his hand. "That's a Bible verse, in case you'd like to know. Dad read it to me and Mom and my sister before he came over to talk to your dad. He said he'd decided it wouldn't be slandering his neighbor if he talked to your dad, since God kept telling him he had to do something. And Dad kept saying, 'Well, what should I do?' and God kept saying, 'Get your ass over there.' Dad said, if it was the wrong thing to do, God wouldn't've kept telling him to do it."

Dale opened his palms and shrugged his shoulders, as if to ask what other evidence I could possibly need.

I said to Dale, "What do you think I should I do?"

"About what?"

"My mom."

"I told you before, there's a pretty much curse on you."

I nodded. "I tried to tell my grandma that last night."

He jumped off the fence rail and crawled down the ditch, then maneuvered and lay on his back, partially covered by weeds. The bank was steep enough so that he was lying almost vertically and from that position, looking over at me, he said, "If you belonged to our church then she could confess and repent."

I said, "She'd be okay if she did that?"

"*Hell,* yes," Dale said. "But since it's *your* mom, she might have to do something extra."

"Like what?"

He picked a weed and sucked on it. "Haul a bunch of burnt offerings around to all the elders. Men like my dad's one. Maybe both of you together. Or maybe your dad, too. Yeah, all three of you. That would do it."

"What would we burn?"

"Lambs or goats."

"God *likes* people to do that?"

"Are you shitting me? He *loves* it."

"You burn up a lamb in front of someone like your dad?"

"Your mom would have to offer more than one. Plus if you and your dad went with her. All of you, you'd have to offer a dozen. Four apiece."

"Really?"

"Yeah. But you don't belong to our church so what difference does it make?"

I was fixed on the procedure, the practical steps. "How do you kill it?"

"Shoot it. Blow its brains out. Or knock it out with a club and cut its throat. The Bible lists all the steps for you."

"We don't have a Bible," I said.

"Tough titty. If you belonged to our church you'd have one for every member of your family."

"I don't know," I said.

"You don't believe *me*?"

"It just doesn't sound like something God would like."

"And you know what He likes?"

"What about doing good deeds?" I asked. "You don't have to go to church for those."

"Your mom's too big a sinner for good deeds."

"I could do something really amazing that would take God by surprise."

"Surprise *God*? Are you shitting me?"

"*Amaze* Him."

"I already said, it's dumb to even talk about it." Then, sounding genuinely more offended than angry, he said, "I can tell you think it's just bullshit about the burnt offerings, don't you."

We stood up again. "Yeah," I said. "I do."

"Well that's *double* tough titty," he said. "Even if they wouldn't save your mom, it's too bad for you that you think I'm bull-shitting."

"It doesn't make any sense."

"Well you know what?"

"I'm going to talk to my grand—"

"Well you know what?"

"What?"

"I was just trying to make you *feel* better. But you know what?"

"*What?*"

"There's *noth*ing you can do. Your mom's really screwed, and so are you, and your dad and grandma."

"Well, screw *you* then," I said. I felt my tears returning.

"No. Screw *you* then."

"No, screw *you* then!" In trying to hold them back, my voice was a squeak.

Struggling to keep his balance, Dale slowly turned around. "Kiss my rosy red ass," he said and wiggled it at me. Then he started up the bank and as he did scrambled forward. Through a blur I gathered a handful of roadside gravel and threw it at him. "Ow!" he shouted. "Hey!"

I scooped up more gravel and tossed it broadcast, spraying him. "Shit!" he cried. At the top of the ditch, he squirmed through the fence and stood up and faced me. "You ever come over here, I'll beat the shit out of you!"

I was sobbing, making high inhuman sounds, and clawing wildly at the gravel with both hands.

Dale shouted, "I hate you, Vaughn!"

I ran up onto the road and flung gravel blindly and I heard it ricocheting off the boards of the fence.

"You bastard!"

"You goddamn Dutchman!" I screamed and tried to say more while I threw gravel at him.

"Bastard, bastard, bastard!" And scurrying away, he gave a

nursery rhyme's sing-songy lilt to it—"Willy's a bastard, a willy little bastard!"—until his voice faded and was gone.

———

The sun was so strong that second day that it appeared to tint the humid air, giving it in places, from certain angles, an uneven yellow wash, the streaked sky of a watercolor. Maybe something in science explains this illusion: the water in the air holding the phenomenal light.

At the far border of the field east of our house, I was moving in this heat through the shin-high rows of soy beans, using my grandmother's hoe to chop away button weeds and volunteer corn. I'd first walked the width of the field to get as distant from our house as possible, so I could move along undetected and surprise my father with the work I'd done while he slept. I'd walked until I'd reached the fence that separated our land from Nell and Carl Beal's farm and I could see their house easily, had seen Nell coming in and out with baskets of clothes to hang on her line.

I'd completed one round-trip: north to south, where the field met a busy two-lane highway, then back north to our gravel road. Now I was again more than halfway to the highway and could hear the speeding traffic's distant alto hum. I know roughly how long it took me to walk that field as a boy, so I can say I'd been at it for a couple of hours. Though I was used to some manual labor most summer days, I held the heavy hoe in an awkward way and blisters had already formed on my hands. Also, I'd brought nothing to drink and was starting to think about little else but water, the image of Orie's huge red insulated jug persisting. Luckily, I'd drunk glass after glass of iced tea at noon and though I still had little appetite I had forced myself, in a mood of bleak defiance, to eat the portions of one of my grandmother's stevedores.

And all the while, to my astonishment, my father slept downstairs. The simple fact of this made it seem as though my life, our life, had given over even more to a maddening inactivity. The sense of hours passing while we waited and slept had made me wild with the truth that my mother was still gone. As I ate and tried to think how I could take revenge on Dale, my mind flitted among fears for her safety. I imagined her dead in a ditch, thrown from her car. I heard in my head, *taken up with Bobby Markum,* and, unable to rid myself fully of what I'd imagined that might mean, I pictured her gagged and tied to a chair, Bobby inexplicably holding her hostage.

When I felt myself beginning to sob again, I got up from the table and hurried outside. I determined to do something, anything, since my father was apparently going to let the awful calm continue.

This weeding of the beans was the deed I'd come up with to offer to God for his amazement. I was skeptical that it was enough, but it was the best I could think of, and as I'd walked the field I'd begun to have a small bit of hope that the painful blisters and my great thirst would help me make my case. Also, I'd tried to hold myself to extraordinary standards, at least through the first hour or so. With one hand, I'd separated the weeds from the bean vines, then cut them low and laid them on the ground so they wouldn't sprawl, dead-brown, across the row. I hoped that this neatness, accomplished while in pain, might go some distance toward amazing Him.

In the spring, in this same field, I'd tried to learn the work of plowing. I'd asked my father if I could, and before he'd even had a chance to respond, my mother said, "He won't know how if you don't teach him, Lewis." Then, while continuing to clear plates from the noon meal, she began to recall her life as a girl when, at my age, or maybe even younger, she was mining quartz with Lean Dean McQueen. She claimed she was working with him on the day of his most memorable strike. She said it was raining and had been for a week, and they were standing in mud to their ankles when they struck a rock face and the rain rinsed its surface and a ribbon of quartz gleamed up at them.

She said the strike had paid enough for them to live on for the next three months. And my father had shaken his head and said, "That's a good one, Leanne. I've never heard that one before. Tell us some more about how you and your dad used to go mining together." His attitude, his tone, was newly exasperated, a voice I don't remember hearing again until the night they argued about Specs, the bandleader, in the darkness of the porch.

I now recognize that on those few occasions when my mother described the mining life, she seemed to betray her ignorance of it. It was as if she'd gleaned some sentimental images from reading a couple of Bret Harte stories. And though, that day, she held her smile as my father spoke, her voice was softer when she said, sounding chastened, "Oh, you're right, you're right." And I wonder if my father thought she might say then that she'd made the whole thing up. But she continued, "I know the only reason he let me stand out there with him was he was too drunk to even notice it was raining." She sighed. "He was a louse. But what's that got to do with your helping Will?" Then she'd walked into the living room and turned on the television and sat, smoking a cigarette, watching her favorite soap opera.

After leaving the kitchen my father and I had driven his tractor, with the plow, directly to the field. He sat behind me and leaned into me as we started forward, his big hands hovering, sun-browned birds, just touching mine, while I tried to keep the tractor's rear wheel in the rough narrow trench of the furrow. And even as I struggled to hold us on course, I was conscious of this intimacy, his body surrounding me, the air of his voice on my neck.

As I've said, one of my problems as a farmer was that, no matter what the task, I couldn't make myself see it as anything other than a heightened act of play. Besides that, I had not shown my father—as most boys with a gift for farming had, by my age, shown theirs—any ability to read a field as I passed through it; to see in its slope and gradient textures, in the way the light breaks the earth into informative shades of blackness, how it needed to be treated and what it would need up ahead.

I'd already had some minor mishaps with the Case and had driven my father's tractor only a few times, over untilled ground, pulling no implement. So I hadn't imagined there existed such a thing as the strength I needed to steer it that day. Again and again, for half the length of the field, it leapt from the furrow, the plow obedient behind it, drunkenly carving the earth. All the while my father kept urging me to hold it steady, "*Hold* it, Will," his twitching fingers eager as an addict's for the wheel, until at last he lost his patience and fiercely grabbed it, cursing through a growl as he steered us back on course.

I stopped the tractor and climbed down, squirming past him, and stalked off in a fit back toward the house. Over the noise of the engine I heard him calling me to come back, but I ignored him, trudging through the loosened soil, much too slowly and awkwardly for the high drama I was trying to enact.

"God*damn* you!" he'd said as he'd suddenly seized the wheel.

Now on foot in this same field, as though it were my fate, I'd begun without really realizing it to grow careless in my weeding. Weariness and the heat were undermining my resolve and I was starting almost to flail my hoe at the weeds.

I squinted ahead. The weeds were as individual as children among the tight rows of beans. I was near enough to the highway now to also hear its silence. I closed my eyes and felt water in my throat, ice cubes against my mouth.

Hurrying away from my father that day, I'd made my way to the house and burst into the kitchen and found my mother sitting at the table. She'd asked me what was wrong.

I said nothing was wrong; I said I'd learned I hated plowing.

"What *happened*?" she asked.

At the end of my brief account I'd told her he'd cursed me, had said, "God*damn* you!" and she'd said, "Oh, honey." She'd frowned and shaken her head. "He wasn't talking to you."

Now I moved past the spot where I had scrambled down from the tractor that afternoon. I was getting weak and a little dizzy in the heat and I remember feeling that I was being punished still further. The fact that I'd devised this chore to amaze God was getting lost in my anger, my anger at simply everything. I was conscious of my blisters and my thirst, but they had lost their appeal as evidence I might show Him.

As I stumbled along, I asked myself, How would you rather die? From a burst appendix? Or being burned alive, like an offered lamb? I thought perhaps that hell was being burned alive, except that the burning went on forever, and I wondered again why my family didn't believe in God if there was even the slightest chance you'd go to hell if you didn't?

Still sitting at the table, my mother had held me in her arms that day and then she'd leaned back and looked at me and said, "Come on." She'd stood and reached for the keys to the blue Dodge.

I'd asked her where we were going.

"For a drive," she'd said.

At the car, she'd stopped me as I'd started around to the passenger side. "You're driving," she'd said, smiling, and handed me the keys.

I'd looked at them and then at her. "I don't know how," I'd said stupidly.

In response she'd simply gotten into the car and rolled down her window. From her seat, she'd said, "Let's go, I'm a busy woman with things to do." She'd tapped her fingers on the roof, syncopated riffs.

I'd opened my door and edged in and closed it. "We might get arrested."

"There aren't any highway patrolmen in the pasture," she'd

said. "Just don't run over more than twenty chickens or I'll have to make a citizen's arrest." She'd suggested I just think of the car as a tractor with a roof and windshield. Then she'd smiled and said, "Well, maybe that's not such hot advice, come to think of it."

I'd been ready for any insult, but she'd laughed, poking me in the shoulder. "Come on, Gloomy Gus, can't you take a joke?"

I'd turned the key and gripped the wheel; it felt like the world, huge as hope in my hands.

How would you rather die? By freezing to death, or having your head axed like a chicken?

Walking the field, hacking at button weeds, I decided that freezing seemed a far from torturous death: buried up to your neck in ice, watching the smoke of your breath slowly thinning, was a death I thought I might trade some years of life to get to.

On the other hand, my grandmother had told me that a headless chicken felt nothing, the length of its pain the time the axe took.

Then why does it go crazy afterward, I'd asked.

It's just the nerves, she'd said.

Aren't the nerves in pain?

If they were, she'd said, there's no brain left to tell it to. Not that there was any brain *before*.

With my mother alongside, I'd steered the Dodge at inching speed through the gate into the barnyard. Then I'd headed down a path made by decades of tractors leaving and returning, toward a small west pasture, land my father was letting lie fallow. After the tractor, I was amazed at how smoothly the car handled and gathered speed without any sense of strain.

"Give it a little gas," my mother said, and when I did the Dodge lurched and surged up a shallow rise. "I said a *little*." She laughed. "Lead Foot Willie at the wheel!"

"Sorry," I said. The car was again crawling.

"You're your mother's son," she said. "Speed's in your genes."

Where the pasture flattened out, she told me to stop and she said that I should hold the wheel attentively but lightly because the car would tend to go straight on its own. She said I mostly needed just to correct it from time to time, not muscle it, as I had to do when steering a tractor.

Then we commenced a series of pasture-length trips, as I tried to get a feel for the touch and play of things. I was sitting forward in the seat and could barely see above the steering wheel, my angle of vision yielding through the windshield a world of vast sky with pasture threading its base. All the while she kept up a patter of encouragement and made a show of leaning back and lighting a cigarette, the very posture of trust and relaxation.

After a time, she began to give me directions—"Turn right at the intersection, just before that grocery store. . . . Left at the stoplight, be sure to signal, and let that truck come past before you start your turn"—and I maneuvered the car with riskless grace through the busy city streets she brought to the pasture. She seemed to be enjoying herself immensely and it's true that a powerful aspect of her charm was in giving you a sense of her involvement in your life, a feeling that she wanted just your company, wanted nothing but to do what the two of you were doing.

In the bean field, the sounds of the highway I was nearing were becoming those of that pasture traffic. And my blistered hands seemed now to hold the steering wheel, not the hoe, and I was passing slower-moving semis, then braking alertly for darting children and their dogs.

"You're still steering too much," my mother had said. "Take your hands off the wheel and see what happens."

I looked skeptically at her.

She laughed. "Go ahead." She reached over and pried my hands loose and put them in my lap. I held the speed at twenty as the car glided along, then hit a slight bump and began to veer left. "Okay," she said, "*now* guide it back and take your hands off the wheel again."

I did.

"Now close your eyes."

"No!" I said and grabbed the wheel.

She laughed. "What could you hit?"

"Mom!"

"What? There's nothing but grass."

With great fear, I took my hands away and closed my eyes.

"Keep them closed."

Crossing the flatness of the pasture, willing my eyes shut, the car felt to be plummeting and my heart moved up into my throat.

"Don't open them," she said. "You're doing great, straight as an arrow."

"I need to open them, Mom."

"See how long you can keep them closed."

"Mom!"

"Sing the *Will Vaughn* theme song before you open them."

"Mom, I'm scared!" I laughed.

"Oh, come on! Start the verse and I'll come in on the tag. Whoa, slow down a bit. See what I mean? You just *correct* it."

At the wheel of the Dodge, my terror was something sublime, my stomach wild with the thrill of what she was insisting that I do. Eyes closed, I began to sing my theme and my voice was nearly yodeling with sweet fear. And when I'd finished the chorus, she joined me for a verse we'd written together—*nothing delights me like seeing moonlight and you*—while I felt the Dodge moving through the pasture on its own intelligence, heard its bumpers softly, steadily rustling the high grass, and we laughed hysterically and then she let me open my eyes.

After that day, she asked me several times to drive her through the pasture.

"Will!" I'd hear her call and when I came she'd say, "You know, I feel like taking a ride. Would you mind driving?" And each time we returned she'd say, "This is our secret, okay?"

Recalling it now, I doubt that my father would have been anything but pleased and grateful. Neither do I believe she'd have thought of us, before that spring and summer, as having secrets from him.

"Will! Will, it's me!" And in the bean field, I heard my name and realized I wasn't hearing it in memory. "Will!" I wiped the stinging sweat from my eyes.

"Will, it's *me*," my mother repeated and I saw her hurrying toward me, having stepped over the low wire fence between the Beals' farm and our own.

14

She reached me and hugged me and rocked me in her arms and when I knew I was not just imagining the feel of her, a warmth like the descent of grace filled me. She seemed to be laughing and crying at once and I, pressed against her, could follow the sounds moving up through her chest and into her throat. She said, her voice tremoring, "I didn't know how I was going to get to see you again." And hearing these words, which should have been mine, I felt the hauntedness and anger of the last two days come free.

"It's okay," she said in response. "It's okay." She kissed the top of my head as I cried. "It's okay." I was pliant in her arms, letting her voice and her body hold me up, until I could feel myself taking strength from my deep sobbing and then my fingers began to rake her back and hips as if I were searching for a way to open her. She only held me as she had, whispering, "There," whispering, "Yes," then saying, "Willie, you're so *hot*. You'll have a sunstroke out here."

When I was able to let go of her, she held me at arm's length and wiped my face and nose with her skirt. "I brought you some Kool-Aid," she said, motioning toward the fence.

"What flavor?" I asked. The shock of her, suddenly here, had made me stupid.

She laughed. "I don't know. Red. Beggars can't be choosers."

"Where'd you get it?"

She put her arm around me and directed me along an end row. "From Nell's refrigerator."

"That's where you were? At Nell's?"

"Mmm," she said.

"Is that where you've been?"

She hesitated before saying, "Yes."

"Since you left? You've just been *there*?" I nodded toward the Beals' house.

"Yes," she said.

"Were you watching me?"

We'd reached the fence and she'd bent down to pick up a thermos before she said, "I couldn't stand it, seeing you out here."

"Why didn't you come out sooner?"

Again she paused. "I was afraid your father would show up to help you."

"He's sleeping," I said. "Why don't you want to see him?"

She didn't answer.

"Why'd you say you didn't know how you'd get to see me? Mom, why have you been hiding at Nell's?"

She said nervously, "Too many questions, too fast." I recognized yet another version of this maddening complaint and as we walked I felt the anger I'd tried to have for my father that morning. It was a sense that for the moment both pleased and frightened me, and I was held by the idea that all this was her fault.

She led me down the fencerow away from the highway to a

line of mulberry bushes that were nearly trees. We knelt in their shade. She removed the thermos cap and filled it for herself and then handed the bottle to me. For an instant my resentment made me think I could refuse it.

"Don't gulp it," she said, oblivious. "You'll get sick."

My thirst for something liquid and for her favor was too great. I took it and swallowed. "It's cherry," I said.

I watched her take a drink. "Quite delicious," she said.

She leaned back against the fence post and slipped her sandals off. Her slender feet were patterned with dirt from her walk across the fields. There were bands of cleaner skin where her sandal straps had been. She gave an elaborate dreamy-seeming sigh, as though to show me that these days, for all their tumult, were ones in which a person could still sigh dreamily. Then she reached into her pocket for her cigarettes and, lighting one, exhaled as deeply.

From my sitting height, the beans and bordering brush seemed to surround us. I felt us occupying an exclusive brimming life within this space we'd made. I looked at my mother. She'd lifted her chin to get the day's first small breeze, which barely moved her hair off her neck. And something—maybe the sense that the two of us, as we had so often, were again fashioning our private world—distilled my curiosity into the only question.

But before I could ask it, she abruptly sat up, away from the fence post. "Willie, listen to me," she said. "I can't imagine how awful this is for you and I wish it had worked out . . ." She shook her head. "I don't mean it *is* worked out. What I mean is, I'm confused, too, Will, but I know that doesn't help you." As she'd spoken, she'd rearranged herself until she sat, alert, perched with her legs beneath her. She was looking at me directly, her eyes seeming not even to blink, and I had to look away from their intensity.

She described her sorrow for what she'd done to me and there was no chance of interrupting her. Her words were coming headlong, and she smoked as furiously. She seemed to be taking enormous energy from reliving both those first hours and the emotions of those since. I wasn't listening so much to what she was saying as to this giddy flow, something the opposite of a song's measured recitation.

The thing that stopped her was the rich rippling roar of a motorcycle accelerating on the highway. Hearing it, we both looked up over our field of cover, straining our necks like hiding children. I saw the rider dip his cycle in that low sweep of adieu as he came back into his lane after passing a semi.

And then I turned back to her and finally got to ask, "When are you coming home, Mom? I want you to come *home*."

She blurted, "Oh, honey, I—" then looked again at me even more intently, as if the answer might be hidden somewhere in my face.

Her eyes searched me until I said, "What?"

She shook her head. "It's harder than I thought."

"What is?"

She reached and squeezed my shoulder. "I missed you even more than I thought I did."

I couldn't make sense of this but it sounded at the same time both hopeful and ominous. "So come *home*."

She was quiet for some seconds. "I have to know how to talk to your father first."

"Just tell him you're sorry, like you told me. I'm pretty sure that would work."

She smiled at me and reached over to wipe my forehead with her palm. "My sweaty Will," she said, then thought to ask me why I'd come out here in such heat. I was sure the truth would sound absurd to her and I mumbled something moronic, saying I didn't know why, I'd just wanted to.

"Will." She cleared her throat. "I know how embarrassed you must have been." Again I didn't know what she meant and my face must have shown it. She explained, "The other night. At the game."

I reddened, then nodded and said, "I wasn't that embarrassed."

She shook her head. "Of course you were. And I apologize."

"I was pretty surprised." This was the most I would concede.

She raised her eyebrows. "Well I was pretty surprised myself. Your father put on quite a show, didn't he?" Then I thought she nearly smiled and it seemed the nature of her voice was not what it should be. Remembering it now I hear an eagerness that tells me how thrilled she was by these events. Thrilled, I mean, in all its definitions: delighted and excited and terrified to her core. And toward my father and his display, she may have felt within it all a pleasure at being paid so grandly staged a compliment.

She shifted her legs out from under her and her manner shifted as well, her loose and merciless energy returning. "This is stupid. I know. I feel like an escaped convict." She looked at me and her face made a quick caricature of distress. "Another fine mess I've gotten myself into, right, Ollie?" She waited for me to respond and when I didn't she said, "Willie, honey, it's going to be fine. We just have to wait until I get over feeling afraid."

"When will that be?"

She didn't say anything.

"What are you afraid of?"

She took a sip of the Kool-Aid, then gave the rest of hers to me. "It scared me," she said, "to see your father so angry."

I heard my father saying, *You're a whore, Leanne. You're just a whore.* I suspect it was only vaguely clear to me what he'd accused her of. In any case, the words made no sense to me as any he would speak, as words meant for my mother, and briefly in my mind my father was again someone she was right to be afraid of. And yet I'd seen, I knew, that he'd become himself again; even more, I knew I had to persuade her of it. "Mom, don't be scared of Dad. He was just—"

"I know about him driving all over, banging on doors. Nell heard in town he just shoved people out of the way and walked right into their houses. He knocked Buel Van Wyck down when Buel told him to cool off and go home and get some sleep."

"He was worried about you. This morning, he wasn't like that. He wasn't mad anymore. Really. He was just real tired." I said, "You could come home and talk to him when he wakes up. He probably has by now. He won't yell at you or anything. I know he won't."

"My brave Willie. My brave man. Will you protect me if you're wrong?"

"Sure," I said and it seemed to me I'd done it, that we were going to get up and gather ourselves and march across the field to our house and our life. I said eagerly, "But I'm sure he'll be glad to see you." The nervousness that seized me held everything I'd ever wanted.

Then she lit another cigarette and said, "I want to explain to you where I've been." And my heart fell, for this told me that we weren't going anywhere right away.

"Why?" I protested. "What difference does it make?"

She drew on her cigarette, seeming not to have heard me. "I had no idea what I was doing that night. I took some clothes with me, but . . . I just did that. I guess that's what you see people doing in the movies, so that's what you do too." She softly smirked, as at her bumbling amateurishness. "Then I just drove for hours. I think I drove all the way down to Grinnell and back up to Marshalltown. I really don't remember. But everywhere I thought I might go I was afraid your father would've figured it out and be there waiting for me. That's what I mean, that I feel like an escaped convict. And then all I could think to do—I was exhausted, you could hardly call it *thinking*—was drive to Nell and Carl's and ask if I could stay." She looked at me and gave me a sheepish shrug of her shoulders. "I threw myself on the kindness of friends. Carl's away, buying cattle, until tomorrow, and I don't think he'll be real pleased to find me there. But that's my sad story for now, my Will." She smiled with mock self-pity, the helpless coquette. "I'm like the man without a country, aren't I."

I wouldn't learn for some time that she'd also seen Bobby that night, that she'd gone to his apartment very late, the sky near dawn, and that, to her surprise, he'd been furious with her and she'd driven then from town to Nell and Carl's.

"Where's your car?" I asked.

"In their barn," she said.

In my mind I went through it all, her driving in and knocking on Nell's door and hurrying the Dodge to its hiding place.

She gave another breath of embarrassment. "It all sounds ridiculous, and childish." She looked at me. "Don't you think?"

I shrugged my shoulders. "I don't know," I said, and I didn't, though neither *ridiculous* nor *childish* seemed right. I again imagined her driving through the night, roaming the back roads with a hunted recklessness. I said, "Dad might've yelled at you, if he'd've found you, but I bet that's all."

In answer, she looked away and lifted her gaze again, striking her breathtaking profile that was surely not the conscious pose I see in my memory's eye. I raised the thermos to my lips and drank more of the Kool-Aid and I heard her laugh, but lightly. She put her cigarette out and said, "When I heard he was driving like a maniac all over the country, the same way I was, I pictured us running into each other." She looked at me. "I mean *actually* running into each other at some dirt intersection out in the middle of nowhere. Wouldn't that have been something?" Once more she laughed.

I watched her sit straight up and run her fingers through her hair, and it was this new laughter that infuriated me. Whatever prompted it, I heard it as too close to sounding pleased, and for a moment it made me suspect she was enjoying this, and had been. I said, "You shouldn't've taken up with Bobby. You shouldn't have done that. Why *did* you?" Of course, I wanted to know her answer, but mostly I'd asked the question to upset her, retaliation of a kind. And I remember assuming—seeing her again, learning she'd been at Nell's—that whatever she and Bobby had done was finished.

Her face went blank. Not knowing I'd borrowed my words from my grandmother, she may have thought the quaintness of my phrasing bizarre. After a moment, she got to her feet and moved away toward the highway, brushing the back of her skirt as she walked. And as I watched it seemed possible to me that she would just continue on, *hurrying smoothly* her exit, not her entrance, over the fence and through the ditch to signal a car, which would instantly stop for her, a beautiful woman alone. I imagined her then, climbing into the back and leaning forward to thank the driver, and in my mind it was Bobby and the car his wondrous Ford, and as they pulled away she looked back in my direction and gave me an almost formal wave.

I can't say why I didn't jump up and run after her. Maybe something in me was satisfied that I'd seemed to unnerve her and I wanted to savor my small revenge. Or maybe I was tempted by the scene I'd just imagined. Not because I wanted her to leave, but because a part of me that came from her was keen to the drama, enough to want to see what might happen. The first of these at least seems plausible. In any case, I drank the last of the Kool-Aid while I watched her standing with her back to me, holding her arms behind her and looking out at the highway.

I saw that she'd left her sandals behind. I reached for them and smelled their intimate malodor, then slipped my hands into them. It felt wonderfully illicit, and comforting, to sense that I was inside some piece of her. She continued to stand there for a while longer, appearing to watch the traffic, her languid posture suggesting the composure of a penitent.

At last she turned and when she'd come back and knelt down next to me again, she said, "Promise me something." Her voice was unsteady and her eyes looked red from crying. Hearing her, seeing her, I was surprised, for nothing in the way she'd stood calmly by the highway suggested she'd been lost in anything but a daydream.

"What?" I asked.

"That you won't tell your father where I am."

"Why?" I asked. "Aren't you—"

"I need another day," she said.

"*No*, Mom!"

She nodded.

"But why?"

"Because I do. I just do. One more day."

"No."

"Willie."

"No. I want you to come home."

"Will, help me here."

"They're going to ask me where I've been."

She said nothing, but smiled slightly and again wiped my forehead with the back of her hand. "Watching the cars just now," she said, "I saw me coming back and getting you and the two of us hitching a ride to wherever. Just doing that until we got somewhere we wanted to be."

"Where would you want to go?" I asked. The sound of her fantasy was so familiar to me and, in voicing it, she was too. I felt myself following her in.

"I don't know where," she said.

"Wyoming?"

She thought. "No. Probably not. Where would *you*?"

I shrugged again. "Des Moines has always seemed pretty interesting."

"Not nearly far enough," she said.

"We have to go a long way?"

"You can't take the trouble of running away if you're just going to Des Moines."

"St. Louis?"

"Why St. Louis?"

Having suggested it, I found I didn't want to speak of Bobby. I said, "I read something that made it sound neat."

"I think their summers are too hot. Like *this*, but every day."

"Paris, France?" I said.

She laughed. "Well, I guess that's far enough. So we'd hitch-hike to Paris?"

"I didn't know we had to hitchhike all the way."

"I'm afraid so. Our funds are limited."

"Well, I don't care," I said stubbornly. "That's where I want to go."

"Do you speak French?"

"No. You know that."

"Well, neither do I. So how do you expect us to survive in France, *monsieur*?" She arched an eyebrow.

I thought, then said I was sure we could learn French quickly if we made ourselves believe we *were* French. I didn't know where I'd gotten this idea. Perhaps it had come from last night's dream. But I warmed to the absurdity of it, explaining to her that the approach was like an actor's. Then I thought to say that even if we didn't ever learn to speak French well, we could just mumble, relaxed, the way Perry Como sang and it would sound as if we knew what we were saying.

I was speaking with the free exuberance both of us brought to the feeding of fantasies. But when I paused to take her in I saw that my mother was again looking out over the fields. Her face had that particular expression that told me she was far away inside herself, somewhat bored, somehow wounded, palpably impatient to get to her next mood. Absently, she began to clean her dusty feet, spitting on her fingers and rubbing at the dirt.

At last she said, "I'm afraid I wouldn't fare too well in Paris, France, no matter what you say." She spoke this as though it were her rueful decision, as though she'd been seriously weighing my argument. She moved the hem of her skirt back and forth over one foot, then the other, a caressive gesture that merely streaked the dirt.

Then I asked her, "Do you feel unsafe?"

She frowned. "What?"

"Grandma says you did all this because you need to feel unsafe."

She chuckled hollowly. "Ah, Dorothy. God love her."

I said, "She wasn't really criticizing you."

"No?"

"We were just trying to figure out why you left."

She nodded. "I see." She was quiet and seemed embarrassed. Then she turned to look at me and smiled. "Do you think anyone needs to feel unsafe?"

"No," I said. "That's what I said to Grandma. But she said some people just do."

She gazed into the frank, unblemished distance. "I guess I *feel* unsafe, right now, anyway. But I don't know about *needing* to."

She cleared her throat and breathed and, sitting, brought her knees to her chest and wrapped her arms around them. "For a long time now," she said, "I've been trying to find out how to feel . . . *safe*, I think, not unsafe. I think your grandma's wrong. I want to feel safe, but, just . . . *surprised* sometimes, I guess. Not every day, but some days, maybe even a *lot* of days." She paused. "Maybe too many days."

I said, "I don't know what you mean." I thought of my grandmother reminding me of the day she'd caught me jumping from the roof onto hay bales, but that didn't seem to be what my mother had in mind.

She sighed and shifted her weight. "I don't really know either. You deserve a better explanation." She looked at me. "I'm sorry. I wish I could say it better."

"Maybe sometime you'll be able to," I said.

She smiled. "Maybe," she said. She reached for a cigarette, lit it, and exhaled. "Well, you know what I mean about feeling *safe*, surely?"

"Yeah."

"But don't you like it when you don't know for sure how something's going to turn out?"

I tried to think if this was true. "I don't think so," I said.

"I think so," she said. "What if you knew the team would win or lose before the game started? You wouldn't care so much then, would you?"

Now I felt I knew at least what she was trying to say, though the idea of knowing the team would win seemed a gift.

She said, "Before the game starts, aren't you a little bit scared they won't win?"

I nodded. "I guess."

"I think that's what I'd like too. To feel safe, but surprised, and a little scared sometimes."

"You said you ran away because you were scared of Dad."

"Not that kind of scared," she said. "That's scared and *un*safe. I don't want that, no matter what your grandma says."

She smoked and flicked her ashes and straightened her legs out in front of her again. "Okay," she said, "how about when you play and change around the way things are? Scare the devil out of the hens with your bicycle game? Huh? Or throw some eggs against the wall because they're 'really' baseballs? You like being able to do that, I *know*." Her smile was teasing. She said, "That's what I don't know how to do—change the way things are, or the way things seem, so they're more interesting. I think I used to know how to do that, but I haven't for a long time."

She cleared her throat again and I wanted to ask, *How* long? but I saw her wiping at some tears with the back of her hand, leaving a streak of field dirt on her cheek. When she spoke next it was with emphasis, giving her words the even banality of a pledge. "It's hard to be surprised here, Will. Hard for *me*. So that's my task, that's the assignment I'm giving myself. Everybody else knows how, so why can't I? I think your father does, and your grandma's the expert at it." She turned again and looked at me. "And *you* do, certainly. Don't you?"

I shrugged.

"Of course you do. You know you do. Think about what I've just been saying." Her eyes held me. "Right?" she said.

"Okay. Right," I said.

"Okay," she said. She worked to smile and to make me smile. She nodded and I did, too.

Then I watched her begin to screw the cap back on the thermos and slip her smudged feet into her sandals. "You've got to go now, sweetie," she said.

"No I don't," I said.

She said, "It's almost supper. They'll be worried where you are."

"No they won't. They'll be—"

"Will, please don't argue."

"Mom—"

"Please."

We got up together. I couldn't speak. Her tight, rocking hug, the same embrace she'd greeted me with, reminded me of what she'd said. Wrapped in her arms, I swallowed hard and was able to ask, "Why'd you say you didn't know how you'd see me again?"

I could feel her shrug before she said without affect, "Because. I didn't." As if she'd heard the inadequacy of that, she squeezed me harder. When she released me, she lifted my chin. "Now this is our secret, okay? Don't *worry*, Willie, I'll see you soon."

"When?"

"In the morning." She smiled. "I'll come and talk to your father. Now that I know you'll be there to protect me." She rubbed the top of my head. "Okay?"

"No. Come *now*."

She shook her head.

I said, "Shouldn't I tell Dad he'd better not get mad?"

"Not a word," she whispered. "Our secret."

I wiped my eyes and watched her move away, over the fence and back into the Beals' field. She turned to me and waved and hurried off toward the house. I watched her go, blinking and rubbing my eyes, but there was nothing left in me I could have used to help me cry. I stood inside a delirious calm; it was as though I were watching myself leaving me.

Only when I could see no trace of her did I look around, and then at the highway. In a daze, I began to walk toward it. I climbed the fence and moved through the shallow ditch, idly listening to the traffic but not really seeing it. Reaching the road's edge, I stopped and watched while a pickup and a line of cars whooshed pneumatically past, after which there was the country's entire silence. I could see the next cluster of traffic, not yet close, and I shut my eyes and listened.

With my eyes still closed, I found myself stepping forward and starting to walk across the blacktop. I took three, four steps, and felt about to lose my balance.

Keep them closed! I heard her say. *Sing your theme before you open them.*

I sensed the highway's narrow breadth to be a desert's. I wanted desperately to see, and to counter this urge I stopped dead in my tracks and waited, waited, for the sound of something coming. I thought to sing my theme song's chorus but knew I needed soundlessness. And then, still hearing nothing, I couldn't wait a moment more and I opened my eyes just as a semi's bleating sounded. I saw that it was some safe distance from me, but I hurried across to the opposite ditch, wondering as I ran what I had touched, whether fear or surprise or some need to feel unsafe.

15

From my bedroom window, I looked out across the fields. I'd climbed out of bed, thinking, almost expecting, that I would find a light on at the Beals'. And there it had been, a bright pin, low in the night, which meant, I was sure, that my mother was awake. Seeing it, I felt uniquely wise, the sense I'd been carrying ever since she'd come to visit me in the field that afternoon.

All evening long, glancing at my father, I'd had to fight the urge to tell him not to worry; that she was safe and nearby and would be back in the morning; that she was still afraid of him, but I'd assured her there was nothing for her to be afraid of.

Several times, I'd felt I was being cruel not to ease my father's distress and I'd had to get up and go outside and wait until I seemed to have hold of the secret again. I'd briefly tried to talk to God about it, but what I heard when I began was my mother's admonition.

I'd wandered restlessly, walking out to where the lawn met the crops, filled with a heady recognition of myself at the vital center of everything. I was the only one who understood that our lives were moving at last toward reunion. All there was, and all I wanted, was to worry my lovely impatience for the morning.

For her part, my grandmother had watched me hurrying in and out, barely taking her eyes off me all night. "What's the matter with you?" she'd asked, much irritated, when she'd seen me moving toward the screen door for the third or fourth time. "You're the dog who can't decide where to hide the bone." She'd stayed downstairs with my father and me that evening; it was as if she'd determined not to let either of us out of her sight again.

Her temper was prickly, the quiet in the house seeming to annoy her as much as my edgy energy did. My father had dozed off in his chair before supper and when her call to him from the kitchen had gone unanswered, she'd walked into the living room and, shaking her head, made a loud *tsk* of disgust, as though wondering why he'd even bothered to come home if *that* was all he planned to do.

Still, her humor had softened from the way she'd greeted me when I'd returned from seeing my mother.

"Where have *you* been?" she'd demanded as I'd walked into the kitchen. She'd come around a corner of the stove toward me. "Answer me!"

I couldn't think what to say. I'd rehearsed my story on the walk back to the house, believing she and my father would be pleased when I told them I'd been weeding the beans. I looked to my father, who'd come into the kitchen, cleaned up and holding a coffee cup. His eyes made it obvious he'd slept little if at all.

He said, "Mom, take it easy."

She'd immediately turned to him. "Maybe it hasn't occurred to you, but I'm the one who's had to sit here waiting for people to show up when it pleased them. And I'm tired of it." Her face was flushed, a tearful hitch was in her voice. I stood ignored in the doorway while she continued. "These couple of days have not been all that pleasant, and frankly I'm not the least bit interested in the next one. I'm telling the both of you right now, I don't plan to get out of bed tomorrow."

Finally my father had set his cup on the table and said to me, "Where've you been, Will? Your grandma called you three or four times."

I'd come on into the kitchen and sat down.

She said, "Your father finally gave up and gathered the eggs himself."

"I'm sorry," I said.

"That wasn't the problem," he said.

"It was *one* of them," she snapped.

"Mom," he said, "please." Then he turned back to me. "We didn't know where you were."

"I'm sorry," I repeated. His spiritless voice sounded like his old calm. I'm sure I needed to believe he was calm. So I didn't hear that, like my grandmother, he too had to be beyond impatience with not knowing where people were. Then I told him that I'd been weeding the field.

He looked perplexed. "Why?"

I said I'd wanted to help.

"But that field's still low enough to cultivate."

I pouted instantly. "I thought it'd be a help."

He studied me for a moment. "Well, thank you," he said. "It is. That *is* a help."

He was quiet through supper; we all were for our reasons, I with my secret, my grandmother with her anger, he with a shifting and intricate bewilderment beyond anything I could ever hope to apprehend. He didn't say much through the evening, either, seeming to concentrate on the newspaper, noticing neither my restlessness nor my grandmother's.

I'd remembered his words from the morning, that we'd try to talk sensibly after he'd gotten some sleep, and I watched nervously for some sign he was about to begin. Having come to know everything he didn't, I had no need to talk and I worried that if we did, I might say something that would give away the secret. I wanted, above anything else, to hold the secret. It was the thing *I* had; the gift for all of us I'd been asked to keep.

Then the day had descended on me and I'd fallen asleep on the living room couch and when my grandmother had waked me to send me off to my room, I'd seen that my father's chair was empty. As casually as I could I asked her where he was and she said he was outside in his workshop. I looked out, enormously relieved to see that his light was lit.

She said, "He tried to rouse you to tuck you in, but you were dead." I've always assumed that while I slept on the couch, the two of them had moved to the kitchen to talk about my mother and he'd gone out to think about whatever had been said.

And now, standing at my window, held by the light from the Beals', I was living in the details of the morning to come: my mother's rich and summoning voice and my father's astonishment at her return and my grandmother's benedictory hovering in the background.

Watching the Beals' house was like watching a star that had fallen to Earth and sat still beaconing. Its steady light was mesmerizing as a star's, inviting you, as a star did, to imagine its life. So I looked at the light and my thoughts ran across the fields toward it. I saw my mother and Nell sitting at the table as they smoked and talked. I knew she was there, knew that's what she was doing, and without thinking I reached for the clothes I'd thrown on my chair.

In a few moments I was dressed. Carrying my shoes, I tiptoed out and past my father's door, looking up the stairwell to make sure my grandmother's lights were out. I moved through the kitchen and saw by the clock above the refrigerator that it was half past midnight. Outside, I sat on the steps to put my shoes on.

As I started down the walk toward my bicycle, a weak push of air moved over me, much of the heat of the day still in it. I peered up at the muggy night sky that seemed to mute the stars, their light a lesser phenomenon than the Beals'.

I wheeled my bike from the garage and headed down the driveway to the road. The sounds were my pedaling and the bike's tires over gravel. I rode past the Van Zants' house and pictured Dale in his bed, sleeping smugly, sure of salvation. On the other side of the road, the field I'd walked that afternoon ran away toward the spot where my mother had surprised me. Pedaling, I turned and looked back at our house, its ghostly shape something massive, like an improbably beached ship.

As I rode I felt the breeze I was making. I rose up in the seat and raced the bike to make more of it. I pedaled as fast as I could, never taking my eyes from the Beals' house up ahead. The desire to be closer was a pull, not an idea, its current the thing that had drawn me from my bedroom. She was awake and so was I and that's the extent of what I knew.

In a minute or so I reached the house, turned in, and dismounted. I walked my bike up their potholed driveway past a scattering of implements—a disc, a planter, a low wagon—that in Carl's casual style stayed wherever he uncoupled them. Beyond, behind the night, the smell and then the stirring from the feed lots was apparent.

As I came alongside the house, I could hear my mother's voice carrying very faintly through the window screens. Instinctively, I veered away and only then realized that I wasn't going inside. I felt as I remember a delicious mischief, coming upon her and seizing the chance to watch her. Also I suspect a part of me was enthralled with the great dreamy tease of not having her back quite yet—a lovely torture now that I knew I would.

I laid my bike in the grass and, crouching low, moved ahead, keeping a strip of lawn and the driveway between the house and me. I stepped past another wagon, stopped in front of the tall windows at the back of the house, and I believe I noticed the outline of his car just before I rose up and looked inside to see Bobby sitting in the kitchen with my mother.

He was wearing a white T-shirt, his long arms bare and muscle-corded. He sat slouched in a chair, picking at the label of a beer bottle, as my mother leaned toward him, a compensatory posture. Her eyes were fixed on Bobby and I could tell by her expression and the fluid movement of her hands that she was speaking intently. But her voice was measured and sure, and soft enough so that I got none of her words. I knew from experience that she often spoke with this kind of charged calm as she was rising to or falling from a peak of temperament.

Bobby was listening, at times nodding or shaking his head slightly, adding afterward a word or phrase like punctuation. His eyes would meet hers and hold them briefly and fall again to watch his own hands peel the label.

Then he shifted in his chair and raised his arms above his head. He stretched through a series of feline movements before he began to speak. His voice, like hers, came indistinctly to me. The words that rose enough for me to hear were *crazy* and *makes no sense at all*. He continued—I heard the word *damn* with high emphasis—and I thought I saw him smile as I stood there in the dark, watching them as I'd watched and listened to my parents quarreling on the porch that earlier evening, though I did not think of that night now.

When my mother tried to interrupt him, he sat forward in his chair with all the athlete's torpid elegance and touched the palm of his hand to her cheek. Then he drew his fingers slowly down the line of her jaw. She sat back in her chair and looked away. His gesture seemed to me astonishing in its power, and I ran my fingertips down the side of my own face, as though I could experience how it had felt both to touch and be touched in such a way. As she sat, looking shy, my mother appeared briefly transformed. The closest I can come to describing it now is to say that she looked small and suddenly weakened, but not at all unhappy or afraid. I believe that her response was to having glimpsed something vast and humbling, an enormous clarity that Bobby's touch had summoned.

He got up from the table, and she did too and followed after him as he moved to the door. Then he turned, leaning back against the wall, and she stepped forward into him and though I knew that I was watching something truly dangerous, I somehow felt reassured, odd as that sounds. For seeing them, I saw that the depth of my sadness, the pitch and drama of my fear, had been legitimate. My mother and Bobby's long and eager kiss was at least an explanation, however stunning.

Bobby cocked his head and looked closely at my mother. He smiled and said something, and she nodded. Then he opened the door and they moved outside to his car. My mother's arms were folded as she walked beside him, looking down at the ground. She stepped lightly in her bare feet. She was wearing the same sundress she'd had on that afternoon. I ducked around behind Carl's wagon and dropped to the wet grass, hidden by one of its tires.

Bobby said, "So I'll see you there."

My mother said, "And wouldn't you be sorry if you did?"

"The hell I *would*," Bobby said. "I'm expecting it. You owe it to me." His voice was light and smiling.

My mother giggled. "On the contrary, mister. You owe *me*." She sounded as he did, deliberately silly, with a false *dare me* toughness in her voice.

"After I drove out here in the middle of the night?"

"And that makes everything all right?"

"Absolutely," he said.

"What a scene, if I *did* show up." I'd realized that they must be speaking of the next afternoon's game, the first round of a tournament New Holland hosted every year, an important event in my life and one I'd completely forgotten about.

"What would happen?"

"They'd probably stone me. Tar and feather me, at least."

"Yeah," Bobby said. "Probably they would. But you might get to see me pitch an inning first."

She laughed. "Oh God. Go home."

"I'll figure to see you."

"Go *home*."

"Say you're coming."

"Stop it," she said, suddenly serious. "You're being absurd."

He said, "For Christ's sake, I'm kidding. That's not what I'm asking."

"What are you asking?"

"When I'll see you."

She was quiet before saying, "I don't know."

"Why not?"

"I have to think."

"What's there to think about?"

She laughed quickly. "What *isn't* there?"

There was a longer silence—I imagined them kissing again—before I heard the Ford's door open and then its engine start. It sat idling, maybe covering their voices. Then he put the car in gear and made a loop and crawled out the rough driveway. He turned onto the road and, as he had the night he'd brought me home for the last time, drove some distance in darkness before switching his lights on.

Still propped against the wagon tire, I watched the Ford head toward our house. Crazily, I imagined Bobby pulling in the driveway. To confront my father? To spirit me away? I followed his taillights as he continued past our farm. I pictured the two of us driving together, as we had. I felt myself wanting with everything in me to be in the front seat of the wondrous Ford again. It seemed, for a moment, sublimely a solution: to ride with Bobby through the countryside forever, whether or not she'd decide to come along.

But as I watched the lights of the Ford disappear, I dimly understood that what I really desired were those nights when he'd been Bobby and I'd been me. Sitting in the grass, propped against the wagon wheel, I held the picture in my mind of the way his touch had changed her. I saw the ease with which my mother had moved into his arms. I heard the charged frivolity of their talk outside just now. And all of it told me that I understood nothing; that I was in exile from what was going on, stupid to the world of adults and what they wanted.

I heard the screen door close and then the scrape of a chair against linoleum. My mother, I saw as I came around to look, was sitting at the table smoking a cigarette. She was in partial profile to me, and whatever expression was on her face was too subtle to read from where I stood. But her posture in the chair was dramatically erect and she smoked with what seemed an elaborate affectation, the way a child holds a twig and pretends to smoke.

I see her sitting there and I think that, even alone, she was imagining an audience, or had settled at such moments for being her own. But on the other hand, there I was: an audience peering in, shaken to have learned I had no voice in the lives of those who had made and mattered to me.

She studied the smoke braiding upward, then crushed her cigarette and lowered her eyes. I don't know how long she sat there, maybe five minutes more, but her posture never noticeably relaxed. She remained so still that when she once shook her head, then shifted in her chair and recrossed her legs, it seemed a virtual seizure of movement.

The night around me sounded. A semi, far away, could begin to be heard. A dog barked and waited and answered itself. Finally she got up and pulled the light cord overhead and the Beals' kitchen was instantly black. I blinked, surprised at the abruptness with which the scene had gone away. And I sometimes see it now, that surprise, as symbolic of my ignorance of the power my mother had to light her world, then disappear, while I stood outside it, watching, at her mercy.

I thought I could hear her footsteps leaving the kitchen and when they stopped I stayed where I was, staring at the darkened windows, willing her return. I held my breath to stop its noise, thinking it might cover some slight sound from inside. I waited for a light to come on. I needed keenly to locate her. I waited a while longer, but there was no new light and I sensed she had somehow slipped out of the house. I knew this was impossible, but what had that to do with feeling it?

I crept toward the kitchen windows and put my ear to a screen. The darkness inside made its quiet a pure thing. In response I moved to the door and opened it and tiptoed toward the table. The floor creaked very slightly.

I eased into the chair she'd sat in and listened. Despite the open windows, the air felt close and warm even at this hour. I couldn't believe our house, or any other, had ever been this quiet at night. People sleeping could not make such a silence. It seemed further evidence that she had left.

There was an ashtray filled with her cigarette butts, and I picked one out and straightened it. I thought I could see her lipstick on its filter. I put it in my mouth and, sitting up in the chair, mimicked the exaggerated style with which she'd smoked, looking out through the screens into the darkness where I'd stood.

I pretended to smoke a while more, then pressed the cigarette into the ashtray again. I'd begun to forget about listening to the silence, instead hearing something like conversation in my mind. I got up from the table and slowly circled it, then walked back toward the door and turned around. From where I stood, I could look through the kitchen and down the hall where stairs led up to the bedrooms. I couldn't see any more than darkened shapes, but I knew the Beals' house well.

I turned again and leaned against the door frame as Bobby had, and whispered, "I love you." I opened my arms to take her in and fashioned an embrace that closed across my chest. I shut my eyes and whispered, "I love you," and whispered in reply, "I know. I love you, too." My eyes were closed, my crossed arms squeezed tightly, holding her and holding myself and holding the need to know her life again.

There was a noise overhead, footsteps crossing the floor, and I hesitated, urgent with the thought that I should walk up the stairs and into her room, and surely she would see me and say, "I love you." Then a light came on. Its vague cast in the hallway was strange to me, which somehow reemphasized my knowing nothing; it seemed as likely that if she saw me she would say I had broken the promise I'd made that afternoon.

I hurried out the door and found my bike in the wet grass and pedaled wildly down the drive, careless of my noise. I was on the road, fifty yards toward home, before I looked back to see a light, which wasn't coming from Nell and Carl's bedroom. I felt relief to think that I knew one thing after all, and that I would again have to try to sleep, while she lay in a bed half a mile away from me.

16

The next morning I walked into the machine shed to find my grandmother perched atop the massive Case. She was talking to herself, as she often did, but her raspy whisper was unusually sustained and animated. I'd come in behind her, she didn't know I was there, and I heard her before my eyes could adjust to the darkness.

When they did, I could see her sitting sidesaddle, her left leg angling stiffly and resting on an axle. At some point in the days after she died, my father, reminiscing, would recall coming upon her in the Case's high seat maybe half a dozen times, forever struggling, he was sure, though he said she once denied it, to envision and accept my grandfather's accident.

"Gram?" I said.

She jumped and turned to me. "Judas, Will!"

"I couldn't find you." I walked to the tractor and looked up to where she sat.

"Well, now you have."

"I remembered what you said."

"What did I say?"

"That you weren't getting out of bed today."

"You looked for me in bed?"

"You weren't there." I peered around the shed, tried to see into its corners. "What are you doing?"

"I was talking to your grandfather," she said matter-of-factly. She began to shift her leg in order to climb down.

After bicycling home from the Beals' the night before, I'd returned to my bed and, alive as my mind was after what I'd seen, I'd slept fitfully. I'd listened to the early morning noises of my father and of my grandmother overhead, then scrambled out of bed. In the first few seconds as I'd hurried to dress, I was pushed by the certainty that I'd somehow slept through my mother's return.

My grandmother was making her way down from the tractor seat, and as I watched her I was trying to think of how to ask it. "Gram," I said finally, "has anything . . . happened?"

She waited until she'd reached the ground, grunting as she stepped down, then stretched her back before saying, "Did you leave your brain in the sun too long yesterday?"

"What do you mean?"

"What I mean is, yes, I'd say a few things have happened. You don't think so?"

I shook my head. "This morning, I mean. Anything . . . *surprising?*" I heard the word as my mother had spoken it, her wishing she could learn how to be surprised again.

My grandmother put her hand on the back of my neck and we emerged into the day's much cooler air. She looked up into the overcast sky and shook her head, as if to note that this wasn't the sky she had ordered. "Anything surprising," she said. "Well, let's see. Your father's out there." She flung her hand in the general direction of the fields. "He's cultivating beans like it was just another morning in paradise. He announced to me this morning he was going to go to work. He said he'd already lost two days and he wasn't about to . . ." She stopped herself from telling me what more he'd said he'd lost. "And meanwhile, I've been sitting on a tractor talking to a dead man. But otherwise, I'd say, no, there's nothing surprising going on."

We headed for the chicken coop. It was unusual for her to kill two hens in a week, but she'd decided to make creamed chicken and biscuits, my father's favorite dish, for supper. And as we walked along I found that, eager as I was to think my mother was returning, I was feeling both protective and ashamed of her and, most of all, again outside of knowing anything.

I said, "Has anybody *been* here?" and I sensed my grand-mother's quick, hard glance at me. But when she spoke, the exasperated edge had left her voice. "No," she said quietly. "Nobody's been here."

My grandmother put her arm around me while we walked and I adjusted my step to hers. She said, "You think I'm a sour old coot."

"No, I don't."

"Yes, you do, because you're not a fool. Only a fool would think I wasn't. I've been mean as a Dutchman who gets stuck with the check."

"Not really."

She laughed, a single bark. " 'Not *really*,' he says."

At the door of the chicken coop, she looked down at me. "You can act like such a big boy, it's easy to forget you aren't."

I said, "I'm not *little*, you know, Gram."

"Okay." She smiled and nodded. "You're not little and I'm not old. And we can both of us act like that's the truth. We can both pretend we matter in all this."

"What do you mean?" What she'd said sounded close to the exclusion I was feeling.

"Oh, I don't know." She flipped her hand and gave a sigh, one deep enough to fill a room if we'd been in one. "I'll try not to be so mean," she said. "But I can't guarantee it."

"Okay," I said.

She opened the door and we stepped inside. Some of the hens shifted and sent up their spinster whines. We both stood there for a moment while our eyes got used to the darkness, then she took down the long-handled hook and reached for the axe hanging next to it. As always, she gave the axe to me to hold, but then said, nodding at it, "You want to do the honors?"

"What honors?"

"With the axe."

"On the hen?"

"Well I don't mean on me."

"I never have," I said.

"I know. But you're not little anymore." She reached down and, with her usual economy, immediately hooked a hen around the neck.

When we got to the stump, she said, "Take a practice swing, why don't you?"

I nodded grimly and raised the axe, aware of the blisters I'd made yesterday, then brought it down and felt the satisfaction of the blade sinking into the gray face of the stump. A fluid strength ran up the handle and into my hands.

"Good," she said. "Don't take it back so far."

"What if I miss?"

She was holding the hen by its legs. She said, "Pretend it's one of those contests you're always dreaming up. The Iowa Hen Neck Chopping Championship or something." Upside down, the hen flapped intermittently but otherwise appeared nearly contemplative.

I nodded again.

"You're Will Vaughn, the defending champion."

"Right."

"Of course, I was the champion until I retired."

"Okay."

"I'd still *be* the champion if I hadn't."

"O-*kay.*"

"I'd won so many years in a row I decided to let someone else have a chance."

"Okay, o-*kay.*"

With her free hand, she grabbed the hen just under its beak and placed it on the stump, wedging its head between the two nails.

I swung and the blade barely nicked the hen's red comb, sending it into a mania of panic.

My grandmother put her foot on top of the hen to keep it still. "Don't aim it," she said calmly. She took her foot away and resumed her hold. "Keep your eye on the neck. The blade'll go where you're looking."

I paused to picture her instruction, *Don't aim it,* a central piece of Bobby's pitching advice. Again I took the axe back and brought it down.

"Good!" she said. "The winner and champion, for the second year in a row, Will Vaughn." The hen had begun its madcap route around the yard. We watched it crash into the base of an elm, spattering blood on the bark, watched its wings flap with such frenzy that it briefly left the ground. She asked, "Aren't you going to chase it? You'd better get going, it's already running out of gas."

I shook my head. I was working as I stood there to feel grave and responsible and I didn't see how you could be the boy who played tag with headless hens if you were also the one whose job it was to chop their heads off. Most of all, what I wanted was not to be a child, someone who didn't matter in all this.

My grandmother picked up a bucket and went off to get the chicken. I looked down at the head and its small blot of blood. It lay intact on the stump, appearing, as always, more alive than when alive. Severed from its body, it had acquired an expression, one almost heroic in its absence of complaint.

———

My father said, "I saw how far you got. You made a real dent out there yesterday." He was sitting across from me pouring milk into his coffee and speaking of the weeding I had done the day before. I'd waited hours after killing the hen for him to come in for the noon meal.

"I got pretty hot," I said, "or I would've done more." I reasoned that this was partially true.

"You did a lot," he said. "It gave me a good head start."

"I messed up some," I said.

He smiled. "I noticed." His voice was warm but weak, maybe from the strain of trying to make these minutes seem so ordinary.

"What'd you do?" my grandmother asked me.

"Oh, nothing," my father said for me. "Just chopped a few beans with the weeds here and there." It was rare for him to understate a mistake, his own or anyone else's.

She gave me a suspicious look, of which there were, like her scowls, perhaps a dozen subtle variations.

My father said that if the skies were as full of rain as they appeared to be, it might be a week or more, after it had quit, before the fields were dry again. By that time, he said, the beans would be too tall for the cultivator to pass through. As he spoke his voice was changing, becoming almost chatty, the way some people ramble when they're feeling afraid. He said he'd likely need my help to finish the work by hand and he asked me what I thought about that.

What I thought was, *Did you see her?*, for as I'd waited those hours for him to come in, I'd watched him working the same field I'd walked yesterday, watched his impeccable labor move, a patient narrative, along the Beals' fence line, and I'd begun to imagine she'd come out to see him there.

He said, "That's if it rains like it's supposed to."

I thought, *Did she call your name and take you by surprise?* I felt the stirrings of an excited sympathy with him, each of us able to describe for the other just how it had felt to suddenly see her. I thought, *Didn't it seem like a dream at first, the way she just appeared?* I imagined telling him that she'd said she thought we might never see each other again, then asking my father if she'd said the same thing to him.

"Sure," I said. "I'll help."

"Wear gloves if you do," my grandmother said. She told my father that I had killed the hen that morning, swinging the axe like a practiced executioner.

"Well, good for you," he enthused too strongly.

I said without thinking, "It's a lot like pitching, the swing."

A long moment passed before he recovered his false cheer. "Did you want to try it?" he asked. "Whose idea was it?"

Waiting, simply waiting, for my father to come in, I'd walked out into the road, meandering slow as a streetwalker past the Van Zants' house, then back through our ditch to the edge of the lawn. From there I could see him uninterruptedly and, in the way that distance flattens perspective, it appeared he was working just a few feet from the Beals'. I closed one eye and squinted, lining him up, placing him on my upturned palm. He was a toy farmer on a toy tractor moving across the flat of my hand.

I'd sat on the grass and felt the morning's damp gray coolness, so complete it seemed that the previous days' heat was something I had only heard about. I'd thought for the first time of the game that afternoon and wondered if the rain would wait for it. I'd tried to place myself there in my uniform, but the life in which I'd done that seemed, like the heat, a rumor.

At the table, my father was saying that I might, if I wished, add the killing of hens to my list of routine chores.

"Not by himself, not right away," my grandmother said.

"I didn't say right away," he said. "I didn't necessarily mean right away."

It sounded to me as if they'd determined to speak of some already changed future—the roles I'd need to play, the way things would need to be. But I wasn't at all ready to move from where things were, not until I felt I might influence them again.

My grandmother rose to pour more coffee and he held up his hand to refuse a second cup, saying he had to hurry back out and get as much done as he could before the rain began. I imagined that my mother had brought a thermos of coffee and asked him to come with her and sit while they talked. I was sure they'd sat in the place where she and I had. I tried to hear what she was telling my father and the words that came were these: it was not that she loved no one, but rather that she now loved Bobby too and was worried that she didn't have enough to give us all.

My grandmother and my father were still talking, then my father pushed back his chair and was saying something to me. But I was wondering if, that morning, he'd touched her face as Bobby had and if he'd risen and leaned back against the tall stand of bushes and, like Bobby, invited her into his arms. I had the thought that it would help so much if I could ask him this. I could tell him what I'd seen and tell him what to do: to lay his palm against her cheek and feel her flow into his hand. If I helped him in this way, it would mean I mattered greatly.

He stood and spoke, his voice sounding as if it was working even harder to find a normal tone. "I'll see you in an hour or so, if it rains," he said, and then I stood too and asked him, "Did you see Mom this morning?"

His head snapped back slightly. "What are you talking about?"

"Did she come out and talk to you?"

"Come out where?" he asked.

"To the field."

As I remember his face, it was choosing among fears.

"Why would you think such a thing?" my grandmother demanded.

I looked at her, then dropped my eyes.

"Will," my father said.

"What?"

"Look at me." I was slow to lift my head and my father waited to speak to me until I did. "Will, I'm sorry," he said. His voice was now too soft to be anything but genuine.

"Why?"

"Because I promised you we'd talk. But there's nothing . . . I couldn't say anything that would make you feel better. I wish I could."

"When are you going to start looking for her again?"

He glanced at my grandmother, a quick pain changed his face, and maybe I was asking him much the same thing she had asked him that morning. He rubbed his eyes with the bases of his palms. He said, "You know she can come back whenever she wants. You know that, don't you?"

I dropped my head again. "Maybe she's afraid you'll yell at her."

I looked up to see that my father was frowning. He exhaled bitterness, and when he spoke his anger sounded simple. "If she's ready to come back, that doesn't seem a reason not to."

Hearing this, I felt the threat that it sounded true. I said weakly, "Yeah, but still."

He said, "Your mother knows you want her here. Okay?" Again, he held his eyes on me until I had to meet them. "Okay?"

I nodded and he did too, and he looked past me to my grandmother, as though to get the three of us to agree. Then he started for the door and I took a step toward him and said, "Mom's at Nell and Carl's."

He turned around. "What?"

"Will?" my grandmother said.

"Mom's staying with Nell."

He looked at me and at my grandmother and asked, "Why would you think that?"

"I saw her," I said.

He'd come back and was standing by the table. "When?"

"Yesterday," I said.

"You were here all day yesterday," my grandmother said.

I described the way she'd come to talk to me in the field.

My father glanced out the kitchen window toward that same field and when he looked back he appeared most of all embarrassed, as though thinking of her nearness as a mocking of him. I hurried to say, "She didn't want me to say anything. She said she was coming to talk to you this morning, but she's afraid you'll yell at her, Dad."

"Son of a bitch," he said, his tone a prayer's.

My grandmother said, "You knew this yesterday?"

I felt my lower lip quivering. "I said I wouldn't tell."

"Oh, Will, good God," she said.

He stood utterly still, looking past us, maybe waiting for his emotions to order themselves so he would know what to feel. My grandmother struggled up out of her chair and went to the window and stood looking out toward the Beals', her back to us. I wanted badly to tell them what I'd seen the night before, perhaps to push the moment more certainly toward action, maybe in the hope that I could find out what it meant. Then I heard my grandmother at the window mumbling something. I turned to see her shaking her head. It was as if she were watching the performance of weather.

My father moved again toward the door. "I'll be back," he said.

"Dad?"

"Stay with your grandmother," he said.

"I want to come with you."

"No," she said, turning away from the window. She came to me and put her arm around my shoulder and there was a strength in her hug that wasn't affection.

"Dad, please?"

"Will," my father said, "we don't even know if she's there."

"She is!" I said. "I saw her! I want to come."

"No, Will."

"Yes! I should get to! I told you where she is."

"If she *is* there," he said, "I need to talk to her first." He looked down at me and started to say something else, then changed his mind.

"It's not fair." My grandmother's grip on me tightened even more.

He squinted his eyes and when he looked at me, I could see there was no chance of persuading him. "Don't yell at her," I said. "Whatever she says, don't yell at her."

He looked past me to my grandmother.

"Promise!" I said.

I could feel her shrugging her shoulders. "For all I know," she said to him, "it's good advice. I've got no better for you."

Improbably, he laughed, breathing out a bleak amusement, then said, "This is so goddamn crazy."

"Don't tell her I told you!" I demanded.

"All right," he said.

"What're you going to say?"

"Will," he shook his head. "Please."

"Yes," said my grandmother.

"Say you thought you saw her when you were working by the Beals'."

He nodded. Then he turned and left the house.

I moved frantically, as dogs do, from window to window, watching him walk to his pickup and get into it and head out and at the end of the driveway turn right onto the gravel. Finally I left the house and hurried down the sloping lawn and watched the pickup disappear, the road's gray dust behind it like a tail of loosened sky.

The porch door slammed and I turned to see my grandmother. I expected her to come on out to where I stood, but she simply lowered herself to sit on the steps and leaned back against the door. Her head was lifted slightly, her eyes closed I assumed, and I remember the world seeming to pause.

I watched her for a brief time and then looked back toward the Beals', knowing he was there by now. I hesitated before starting back up the lawn toward my grandmother. I looked up at the sky. The clouds were finicky, continuously rearranging their grays. I thought, *He's up there*. But that was all. I was merely, dumbly, placing Him and He seemed to me able to pose no threat, to offer no help; seemed in regard to the world He supervised a mere clerk with standards, like my grandmother with her scrapbook.

As I sat down next to her she opened one eye and fixed it on me, then after a moment closed it again. I panned the horizon and in the northern distance I saw a cluster of lights, blossoming ice-white at the bottom of the sky. There were only flat grain fields between our house and New Holland, so from the porch steps it was possible to spot the lights of the baseball field suddenly coming on. Seeing them, I knew that Bobby was warming up on the sideline, beginning to throw to Burl Starkenburg, ignoring the dark skies. I heard the two of them trading teasing insults; it was their habit to toss them back and forth with the ball.

It did not occur to me that Bobby might be distracted. I thought of him, among us all, as remaining unperturbed, his fragility reserved for games and those who watched them. I pictured him touching my mother's face and with his smile asking her a question I could not begin to understand; one I now think of as his wondering how much he could have, or maybe how much of herself she didn't want.

Without shifting or opening her eyes, my grandmother said, "I should've followed up my threat and stayed in bed all day. I talk so much I don't pay attention to myself when I should. I forget to take my own advice, which is usually damn good." She finally opened her eyes and looked at me. "Why didn't I stay in bed?"

"You'd've found out everything anyway," I said.

She squirmed to face me more directly. "I cannot believe this business of your mother camping out just down the road." She shook her head. "As far as what's going to happen next, I have not got a clue. Not a blessed clue. Until this latest I thought I did, but I do not."

"I don't care," I snapped, but she didn't respond to my rudeness.

I stood and walked away from her. I looked first east, then north; my parents in one direction, Bobby in another.

She said, "If you told all this to somebody they'd think you made it up. And anyway, where would you start? How far—"

"Gram, *stop* it."

"What?"

"Stop *talking!*" I shouted.

She sat up and narrowed her eyes. "Listen here, young man!"

"Shut up, Gram! Shut up!" I turned from her and her calls for me to stop made me run faster toward the garage.

"Will! Come here!"

When I emerged with my bike, I saw she'd gotten to her feet and was doing her best to hurry down to intercept me. Her heavy body was all flapping, spastic movement, her legs and her arms working individually.

"Will!" she shouted. I mounted and moved past her. My tears made the driveway roll and shimmer. I blinked to clear them and heard my father saying, *This is so goddamn crazy,* and I shouted a ragged sound of agreement and then I saw his pickup turning in.

He braked and I pedaled out to meet him. When I reached the truck I saw two faces in the cab and my body was my heart as I gazed, astonished, thinking that my father must have said what she'd needed to hear. I pictured his hand lifting to her face. Then both the pickup's doors opened, my father climbing out from his side and Nell Beal from the other.

Nell stepped back to let him reach me first. He bent down to me and said, "Your mother's not there," but I was looking past him, watching Nell's face become her own, nothing like my mother's, the lines and squint that work had made saving it from plainness.

I blinked to clear my eyes and turned to him. "I saw her!"

He said, "She's not there now is what I'm telling you." He squeezed my arm, then held and clumsily stroked it. I hated his touch as if it were a violation. It stopped the last hitch of weeping in my breathing. He said, "She left last night."

"No! I saw her!" At last I was confessing that *I* had seen her last night. I didn't care that he'd be angry as long as he knew he was wrong about her leaving Nell's.

But what he heard was his frantic son, simply and wildly repeating himself. "Listen to me, Will," he said. "I know you saw her, but she's *not* there *now.*"

I glanced back toward the house. My grandmother was still standing on the sidewalk. Then I turned and looked up at him. There was field dust in the early creases of his face; it looked like stage makeup, a crude penciling of age. He nodded at Nell, as if to say, *You see? This is why I asked you to come with me.*

He finally let go of my arm.

"Willie," Nell said, stepping forward, "your mom was at our house when I went to bed and she was gone when I got up." She went on to tell me what I mostly knew, describing my mother's knocking on their door the night she left us; she seemed to feel obliged to give me an idea of what my mother had been doing since she'd been gone. Or maybe my father had requested her to. As Nell spoke, I saw my mother with Bobby, waving formally to me from the back seat of his Ford.

I heard Nell say, "I told your dad, I probably caused her to go."

"How?" I asked.

"I said she had to let your dad know where she was. I said she could stay if she thought that's what she had to do, but she couldn't just use our place to hide."

I remembered my mother saying she felt like an escaped convict.

Then Nell said to my father, "Carl's back sometime today and I know he'd think the whole thing was pretty crazy."

"Mom's not crazy," I said to Nell.

Nell shook her head. "No. She's not. But it wasn't right of her to make you keep a secret."

I wanted to say, But I loved keeping it. It was the last thing I'd been sure of. Until I'd seen her with Bobby, it had been the thing I knew.

I looked at them both and said, "What are you going to do?"

The silence caused Nell to glance nervously at my father. "You're a sweetie boy," she said. She looked at me. Her face from habit was a glare, as if it were receiving winter weather, and she said, "You *mustn't* think any of this is your fault."

I nodded blankly. It had not occurred to me that any of it was.

Nell told my father she needed to get back in case her children had awakened from their naps.

My father nodded and said to me, "When I get back we'll talk about wh—"

"No you won't," I snapped.

"Yes, I—"

"You said yesterday we would." I wanted badly to provoke him.

He took a deep breath. It seemed he might be losing his calm again, and I waited for him to shout and curse so I could be reminded he was someone you could fear enough to hide from. "I know," he said, disappointing me. "And when I get back we will."

"I'll see you soon, Willie," Nell said.

My father said, "I won't be long."

I watched them get in. He backed the truck out onto the gravel and then it pulled away. I waited until I couldn't hear his truck and as I turned to pedal back up to the house I felt certain my father was finished trying to find her. Hearing in my mind the way he'd just talked to me, I felt a sense of something closing, shutting down; his kind, firm tone, his patience, even Nell's report seemed acknowledgment of it.

I pushed off on my bike.

I heard the quiet in his voice as the relief of surrender. And though I did believe he meant for us to talk, I imagined it would be in a mood that depended on both of us seeing that this part of it was over. I thought of his words as his way of crying, so he would talk to me and that way we would cry and miss her for as long as I wanted to sustain such avid gloom. I believed we'd talk about why she'd left us, and he might ask me to look back and help him search for reasons; but not for her; no longer for her.

Without thinking to, I continued past our house and once I had I suddenly knew I couldn't stand the thought of the future that would start when I turned into our drive, having given up on finding my mother.

I hadn't looked to see if my grandmother was still outside, but I assumed she was and I waited for her voice. It didn't come. But imagining her eyes on my back, I pedaled lazily in the direction opposite my father's. I steered the bike through soft zigzags. If she were watching me, I couldn't give her a reason to suspect where I might be going. I didn't know myself.

I headed up the road, the picture of aimlessness, until I sensed I was beyond the range of her weak eyes. And then I stood and pumped the bike with all my strength, pulling crazily on the handle bars, the tires taking hold and gravel spitting. I felt the effort of the muscles in my thighs and I pedaled even harder, gladly giving over to the frantic work of it. I raced along the ends of fields—there were no other houses on our road in this direction—until I met the first crossroads and slowed enough to turn, then rose again and worked the bike. I felt my heart and its blood moving once more, now that I knew I was going to find my mother.

After a minute I heard a tractor coming up behind me. When it was close enough I looked back, relieved to see that I didn't know the driver. He waved as he passed, pulling a small wagon, and I watched a pale yellow powder—feed or fertilizer of some kind—leaking from its tailgate. It drew a loose line on the road, as though to mark the way for me.

I followed it for a mile until the next intersection, then instinctively turned again and started down another road. I'd gone a hundred yards when I recognized that I was tracing the back route we sometimes took into town; in the absence of a plan, habit had directed me.

I slowed and focused on the horizon. I saw the field lights in the distance, more luminous against the darkening sky. It was then that I felt the rain's first steady sprinkles, and as I rode, watching the lights, the thought came to me that that is where she was. It was as if I'd suddenly broken the code to her behavior: if she'd not come home that morning as she had said she would, then she must be doing what she'd said she wouldn't. If she hadn't returned and she wasn't at Nell's, then she had to be sitting in the bleachers watching Bobby.

I knew that in another mile I'd need to turn right if I were going to take the last stretch of gravel into town. As I started down a long hint of hill, I saw her sitting in the stands behind home plate, wearing the same sundress she'd worn yesterday, her sandaled feet resting on the bleacher below. I saw her huddled and curled into herself against the chilly dampness and I hoped she'd taken a coat with her.

I tried to picture how I might walk up and sit beside her. As ever, she was with me as I thought of how to enter, and I imagined myself, serene with self-assurance, hurrying smoothly to sit down next to her.

Coasting, I saw the crossroads coming nearer and I was sure she was feeling frightened and alone. I'd heard her say as much to Bobby the night before. The crowd was ignoring her; no one was sitting near her. I ached to tell her not to feel lonely, just to stay where she was.

I spotted a car moving along the intersecting road ahead. I thought of cars and how she'd walked to the traffic on the highway while I imagined her stepping into the back of Bobby's Ford. I remembered her turning and coming back to me and saying she'd seen the *two* of us leaving. In neither her dreams nor mine had she wished to flee alone. I knew I had to get to her before the rain sent people home.

And it *was* rain now, angling across my vision. I peered toward the field lights. The sky of rain was smudging them. Picturing my arrival, I wondered what I would say to her first and how long I would wait after hearing her great joy to ask her why she hadn't come home to us that morning. I tried to think how I would get her to tell me what she'd felt when Bobby's hand had touched her face. Had his touch surprised her, or had it made her feel safe?

The car I'd noticed reached the intersection and turned in my direction. As it neared, I recognized the driver, an eccentric bachelor who lived and farmed with his unmarried sister a few miles beyond us on the same gravel road. He looked at me and shook his head as he passed, as though unsure if he should stop and offer me a ride. Then I was at the crossroads and I turned toward New Holland, moving now with the rain and the light wind carrying it.

17

There were puddles dotting the baseball field, a huge one spreading near the fence in deep right center. The dirt parking lot was also troughed and rain-pocked and, struggling to pedal through the thickening mud, I headed for the empty bleachers behind home plate. When I reached them, I got off my bike and climbed up to the spot where I'd pictured my mother and me sitting. I was too soaked and too chilled to feel more of either, but looking out over the wet, deserted field, a mourner's full thickness came into my throat. There was the sound of the rain, though I didn't hear it; it had become as uninsistent as still air. But a sorrow, sure as sentences, filled the quiet.

As I wept, I peered through the screen behind home plate to the place by the bat racks where I always knelt. I tried to imagine how I should act, who to mimic, but I couldn't think of anyone else I might be.

I realized I was shivering, and had been. I heard my mother and me asking each other where we would go if we ran away; if not Wyoming or Des Moines or St. Louis or Paris, where? I looked out to the field and watched my father charge toward Bobby, seeing it all from the bleachers as my mother had.

Then I pictured Bobby, walking away from my father and standing with the posture of a grazed matador. I sat there for some while and gradually the idea came to me that Bobby was directing all our lives; that, more than my mother or my father or my grandmother, he could tell me what had happened and what would happen next. I scrambled down from the stands and got my bike and, once out of the parking lot, I headed for the town square, three blocks away.

The street from the field became the north side of the square and I rode past the grocery store, the drugstore, and the granary. A few cars and then a pickup met and passed me. A couple of women in raincoats and men's overshoes were hurrying along the sidewalk. I knew them both—they sometimes drove out to play canasta with my grandmother—and I feared they'd look up and recognize me. I wanted to hide from anyone who knew what was happening to us and it seemed to me this meant everybody in New Holland.

I turned left and coasted past the stores that lined the west side of the block, passing the Hungry Dutchman and continuing to the end, then made a right turn away from the square. I rode for another block and another and, reaching the bank, I saw that Bobby's Ford was not parked next to the stairs leading up to his apartment.

I don't remember what this signaled to me. I probably imagined that he and my mother had gone off somewhere once the game had been canceled. I may have thought that she was up there waiting for him, having hidden the Dodge somewhere as she had at Nell and Carl's. In any event, I got off my bike and leaned it against the wall under Bobby's steps and, only then becoming frightened, began to climb them.

When I reached the top, I peered through the window in the

door. I saw no lights, no sign of anyone. I tried through the rain to hear a sound from the front room. However long I waited, I found the courage to knock, forcefully I hoped, the *rap-rap-rap!* of an arrest.

Finally I opened the door to Bobby's kitchen. A wooden table and two chairs, the room's only furniture, were pushed against one wall. A window above the sink let in a little light. Looking through the kitchen door and down the hallway, I could see two tall windows in a front room giving to the street. The dark of the day made it nearly night inside, and I had to keep myself from turning on a light.

For a second I just stood there, listening to the rain and the quiet of the apartment, and then I took off my shoes and put them by the door and reached for a towel draped over the sink. I placed the towel on the floor and stepped onto it and began to shuffle forward to keep from dripping on Bobby's worn linoleum. I don't know whether I was trying to be considerate or stealthy, but I made my way in this fashion down the hall toward the front room. As I moved along I considered calling out a bold hello of warning. It seemed just possible—anything seemed possible— that they were waiting in a stillness only my mother could dictate.

I reached the front room and peeked in. On one side there was a narrow bed, its brown blanket tightly tucked in at the corners, on the other a pale green armchair lined up to face a television set. I imagined Bobby sitting there on Saturday afternoon, watching Dizzy Dean broadcast the baseball game. There was a large wardrobe in the far corner opposite the bed. The walls were bare, the floor a continuation of the kitchen's yellowed linoleum, the space altogether as spare as a novitiate's cell—a novitiate allowed a television set.

I stood a moment more, then walked to the wardrobe and opened it. It was empty except for a sweatshirt and a pair of jeans on a hook and his baseball uniform on the bottom shelf. I made nothing of the fact that it was washed and folded. Closing the door, I looked around again. I was neither surprised nor disappointed by the room. In fact, its clean and made-smooth surfaces seemed to me exactly Bobby's personality, that splendid tidiness he valued and seemed able to protect against everything but his temper. Odd as it sounds, I felt at ease in Bobby's room, maybe because I felt Bobby powerfully, and sensed my mother in it not at all.

Turning, I walked back down the hallway and into the bathroom, where two large towels lay neatly folded on a shelf. I took one of them and dried my hair and face, then roughly ran the towel up and down each arm. I'd thought I'd stop then, but instead found myself peeling off my sopping shirt. And when I'd dried my shoulders and chest and back I struggled out of my jeans, my underwear, and socks and dropped them all, with my shirt, into Bobby's tub. As vigorously, I dried my legs and feet, wrapped the towel around my waist and sat on the edge of the tub. I felt myself dry but still too cold to sense the sting of wakened blood. Sitting there, I knew I should immediately put my wet clothes on again and leave, but I couldn't imagine doing so. Taking the other towel from the shelf, I caped it around my shoulders and walked out into the hallway and back into the kitchen.

His shelves held only a box of cereal and a bottle of bourbon. Without thinking, I took down the cereal and stood scooping handfuls of cornflakes into my mouth. The more I ate, the hungrier I felt, and I finished the box, then closed it and put it back on the shelf exactly where it had sat.

Next I reached for the bourbon, unscrewed its cap, and took a sip. Its long raw fire made me gasp. When I'd put it back, I looked around the kitchen, trying to picture my mother here with Bobby, the two of them moving about the room in a minuet of domesticity. But I couldn't imagine so homely a scene, maybe because it didn't seem one that would allow my mother to feel surprised or safely afraid. Instead I pictured them at the table, as they'd sat at Nell's, then Bobby reaching languidly to touch my mother's face.

I swept up the cornflakes that had spilled from my cupped hands and dropped them into the wastebasket, then walked back into the bathroom.

Fingers of water, colored palely from my socks and jeans and shirt, had spread out over the bottom of the tub. I withdrew my shirt and underwear and braced myself for the shock of their wetness. Groaning, I struggled into them, then stumbled like a drunk as I pulled my jeans back on. I'd just wedged my feet into my socks when I heard the door flying open and banging shut again. I was too stunned to think or move.

A sheath of light came into the hallway, then I heard his footsteps crossing the kitchen, and in the next moment he was standing in the doorway and, seeing me, cried, "Jesus!"

"What are you doing?" Bobby demanded. His voice was harsh. He was wearing an old leather jacket and a merely damp fedora.

I looked away from him, my mind too wild to find any words.

He said, still more agitated, "What's up, Will? How'd you get here?"

"On my bike," I said weakly.

He glanced to the front and back of his apartment.

"I left it outside."

He was looking toward the kitchen. He must have spotted my shoes because he turned and squinted down at my stockinged feet. "You're soaked," he said, at last taking me in.

I nodded. He stepped back into the bathroom. "Did . . ." He looked around suspiciously. "Who told you to come here?"

"No one."

He appeared to be deciding whether or not he believed me, then looked at his watch and repeated, *"Why are you here?"*

I was silent again and he let me be, until I finally blurted, "I was looking for my mom. I thought she'd be here, or you'd know." Then I managed to ask with more defiance, "*Do* you? Where is she? Do you know?"

"Ah, *God!*" Bobby said. He smacked the door frame with his palm and I flinched. He said, "You rode here from *your* place?"

"It wasn't raining when I started. I thought she'd be at the game."

He blinked. "*Where?*"

"At the game. *Was* she? Was she there?"

His eyes dropped and he stepped back into the hallway and looked again to the front room, then the kitchen. He showed no interest in answering me. His fingertips drummed the door frame, the nailless one requiring a beat of dexterous effort. I faintly heard, from below his front windows, girls' voices squealing in the pleasure of the rain. Bobby took off his hat and ran his fingers through his hair. Then he looked back at me and said, "You'll catch pneumonia in those clothes."

I shrugged and something made me say, "Or polio."

"Come here," he said. He hurried from the hall and, still fearful, I followed him into the front room.

He opened his wardrobe and tossed me the jeans I'd seen hanging from the hook. His movements were quick and jerky, those of someone extremely anxious to leave. "Roll the cuffs up," he said. I held the jeans to my waist. Their long legs came down over my feet and ran along the floor to make a denim boulevard. He looked in again and then threw me a sweatshirt, which I held to my chest with my chin.

We'd both seen I could manage to bunch the sweatshirt's sleeves, but that the jeans were hopeless. He reached into the wardrobe again and tossed me his baseball pants. "Wear these," he said. "They come just below my knees."

"They're your uniform."

"They're dry."

"But—"

"Hey," he said, "this isn't a department store. Get your young butt in gear."

"That's not what I meant." I took them and the sweatshirt and headed toward the bathroom.

He called after me, "Shake a leg. I'm leaving in two minutes and I want you out of here."

When I came back into the room, the sweatshirt to my knees, the flannel baseball pants like grain sacks around my ankles, he was standing at one of the tall windows. His hat and coat lay on his chair. Outside, the rainy sky was a fabric seamed to the horizon.

He turned and tossed me a pair of his sweatsocks. "I found these," he said.

I bent down and began to pull the huge socks on.

It was while in Bobby's bathroom, listening to him pace back and forth before his windows, that I understood he was leaving to meet my mother. Now, as I pulled the legs of the pants down over the socks, I was trying to think through what to do with that knowledge.

I stood, dressed head to toe in dry, warm clothes, and I felt the luxury of them working against my chilly skin.

"How are you getting home?" he asked. "I can't take you."

I shrugged. "My bike, I guess."

"Don't be an idiot," he said. "It's pouring. Can't your . . . somebody meet you?"

"Not really," I said.

I watched him. Nervousness moved like an idea across his face. "How're you gonna carry your clothes?" he asked.

I shrugged again. "I don't know."

He'd picked up his hat and begun to flick its brim. "Go to one of your friends in town till it stops."

"I don't want to."

"Just till it stops."

I shook my head.

"Go to the Dutchman. Buy yourself a bottle of pop and a doughnut." He reached into a pocket and held a palmful of coins out to me. I looked at them in his hand and perhaps they seemed a bribe, for they convinced me even more that he was meeting my mother. Again I shook my head. My sole idea was not to cooperate with him.

"Be that way," he said. "Come on and get your shoes on." He clapped his hands. "Let's go, I'm late." He snatched up his jacket and hurried out of the room.

In the kitchen, he paced while I stalled for time, forcing my feet into my soggy shoes. Then, straightening up, I looked past him and said as strongly as I could, "Where is it you're going?"

His jaw muscle pulsed, a skin-blink of violence. "I've gotta meet someone," he managed. "In Marshalltown."

"I could ride with you. You could take the blacktop. That goes almost by our place."

He shook his head. "It's six miles longer. I'm late already."

"You could just pull over at our road and let me out."

"That doesn't make it any shorter for me."

"You could—"

"Hey, cut the shit, Will! I can't take you."

Then I said, "You're going to see her!"

"What're you talking about?"

"I'm going with you! You're going to see my mom, and I'm going with you!" I was retreating as I said this and my back smacked against the door.

He started toward me and, to stop him, I shouted, "She doesn't love you! I know she doesn't love you!" Turning, I flung the door open and fled down the rain-slick stairs, listening for Bobby behind me as I ran, but when I reached the bottom and glanced over my shoulder I saw that he'd come down only two or three steps. I paused to look up at him. Looming above me, he was monstrously tall and appeared somehow to be standing in front of the rain. I'm sure he thought I was going to mount my bike and ride away. Instead, he watched me hurry to his car, open the door, and climb in.

I locked the driver's side and scooted across the seats to the other door, my knee brushing his keys dangling from the ignition. I was sitting in the middle, straddling the hump, when he reached the car and looked in through the windshield. His long face was mostly hidden by his hat brim and the turned-up collar of his jacket.

"Get out of there, Will!" His voice came muted through the glass.

"I'm going with you!"

He shook his head and shouted, "I'm not going to see your mom!"

I stared at him. I don't know if he could see my face. I don't know what it might've shown him.

He moved to the driver's-side door. "I'm going to Marshalltown. I don't know where she is!"

"Yes you do!"

"The hell!"

"I saw you at Nell's!"

Hearing this made him appear to sag for just a moment. He looked around as if sensing someone sneaking up behind him, then, more angered, he pulled on the door handle with a wild pumping strength, enough to rock the Ford. "Open it, you little shit!"

I frantically shook my head.

He cupped his hands to the side of his face and peered in through the window. Rain guttered from his hat brim and spilled against the window. He was looking for his keys and when he saw them he cried, "Shit!" He pounded on the roof; it boomed tympanically. He drew his fist back and I braced, prepared for him to smash the window, but he pounded the roof again, then started to circle the car. He was moving in a kind of loping crouch, as though hoping he might find a new way to get inside. I turned in the seat, watching him through the windows. Behind the Ford, he beat on the lid of the trunk, before coming up along the passenger side. He pulled on that door less fiercely, spread his arms pulpit-width, and leaned against it, peering in.

He said something I couldn't hear, but I shook my head again and shouted, "I have to see my mom!"

He didn't move or speak, which emphasized the rain, and then he surprised me by straightening up and stepping away from the car, christening it with a slap of his hand to the hood. He turned his back to me and bunched the collar of his jacket and started up the steps, almost moseying it seemed. Darkness was beginning and it looked as if he were ascending into a thick pool of it at the top of his stairs.

He opened his door and went inside and turned a light on in his kitchen. After a few seconds, I heard a muffled commotion, a banging of some sort that went on for a minute. Then everything was quiet.

As I'd headed toward Bobby's apartment on my bike, I'd thought how it would be to hear him explain things to me, how he would offer me, because it was what I had to have, the same wisdom he brought to teaching me to pitch. But now I sat with the sense that he was as lost in all of this as the rest of us were. Alone in the Ford, the dark of rain around me, I felt the flush of outsmarting Bobby leaving me. As the minutes passed, I began to wonder why he hadn't come back out and agreed to my demand.

I imagined then my mother waiting somewhere for him, and I started to think about her worrying where he was and that he might not be coming to see her after all. I saw her parting the drapes of some featureless room, looking out and sighing noisily and smoking cigarettes. This was as close as I came during those days to feeling I had caused anyone's unhappiness.

I ran my hand over the dashboard of the Ford, then along the backs of the seats, thinking of the times I'd ridden in this car and, watching it move past, the times I'd wanted to. I remembered my fantasy of riding out of my life in it, and then of Bobby and my mother driving away. And I add to it now a picture of them nakedly entwined in his cramped backseat. There were so few places in that world for them to hide that they must have sometimes stopped on back country roads and, like libidinous teenagers, pushed contortedly against one another for their pleasure.

Bobby's head and shoulders appeared in his kitchen window. He looked out toward his car for several seconds, seeming to scan the parking space with interest. Then he nodded and stepped back out of sight. Forgetting the fact that there was no food up there, I pictured him casually fixing his supper and carrying it in to eat before his television, having chosen just to leave me out here until I got bored or afraid or cold.

I was beginning in fact to be all three. I tucked my hands up into the sweatshirt's sleeves and folded my arms against my chest. As if prompted, a serious chill passed through me.

I moved over to sit behind the wheel and held the chrome-bright steering knob, gripping it as Bobby did, as I was sure no one else ever had, like a safecracker feeling for the combination. I felt suddenly tempted to start the car, in small part to get the heater going, but mostly with the thought of driving off. I wasn't sure I could work its manual transmission and tried to argue myself into the conviction that if I found a low gear I could coast away at a slow trolling speed, my grandmother's speed before she gave up driving. Then I realized there was only one place I wanted to drive to, and I had no idea where that—where she—was.

I looked up at the lighted kitchen window, just then recognizing that the rain had almost stopped. There was still no sign of Bobby and I wondered if this meant he'd decided not to see my mother, if he'd concluded I was too much trouble to deal with. I thought of her growing frantic as she feared he wasn't coming.

I felt still chillier. I turned and peered into the back for something to wrap myself in, then thought of the army blanket he kept in his trunk, the one I'd watched him use the day the Ford had overheated. I opened the door and hurried around behind the car. I unlocked the trunk and raised the lid to see two suitcases, one an average size, the other a sort of fat briefcase. Both were made of the same badly worn imitation leather. Three small cardboard boxes sat snugly next to them, their overlapping flaps obsessively taped. I looked at the tags on the handles of the suitcases. On each of them was written in nearly faded letters, "Robert George Markum, West Alton, Missouri." *George*, I thought, *Robert George*, and couldn't help but feel a brief rascal pleasure, as if I'd stumbled on a secret he wouldn't wish known. I'm sure it didn't truly come to me that I was looking at everything Bobby owned, except for three worn towels, the sweatshirt and socks I was wearing, and the pair of jeans hanging in his closet.

I spotted his glove, which lay like a pet, tucked with care into a corner of the trunk. Its fingers, closed around a baseball, were held with two thick rubber bands. I picked up the glove, wanting to slip my hand into it, but it seemed a violation to remove the rubber bands, so I put it back and scanned the trunk a moment more. Even with all I knew about my mother and Bobby, I gave no importance to the fact that he'd arranged what he'd packed in a way that left quite a lot of space.

Rather I remembered his words to me the last time he'd driven me home from a game. Drunk and uncommonly modest that night, asking with a lovesick boy's beseeching clumsiness whether I thought my mother was happy in New Holland, he'd said he'd been thinking of moving away. And that is what I thought I was looking at: the evidence that Bobby was packed and poised to go. Reaching up for the lid, I felt an elation that, with Bobby gone, we could all again be who we'd been; that like people who'd been hypnotized, we would hold no memory of this time.

I slammed the trunk to close it. Worried that the sound might draw Bobby's attention, I looked up to his window and saw him leaning casually against the railing, halfway down his stairs. I jumped, startled, but he simply stood there watching me. Above him, his door was open and the kitchen light came out to cleave the darkness barely. His arms were folded. There was an ease in his stance that had the authority of the way he stood between pitches when the ball was moving as if alive and obedient.

We looked at each other through the chilly mist. He'd taken off his hat and jacket. I watched him unfold his arms and raise a bottle to his lips, the tilt of his head like a dog's to the moon. My instinct was to scramble back into the car, but I didn't think I could beat him to its door, and besides, to my surprise, I felt the effect of the light from his kitchen; it had a force, a kind of calling warmth, and I found myself starting toward the stairs.

Again I looked at him and waited for him to move or speak. He did neither until I'd reached the bottom step. Then he said, "You'd better come on up, don't you think?" There was no menace in his voice; there was perhaps a tone of asking in it, as if he were hoping for the favor of my company.

18

He stood at the sink in the bright, hot room, both the light and the heat like welcome weather to me. I walked past him to a chair and sat down at the table. I was shivering again.

Bobby came over and joined me. "Well, here we are," he said as he sat, then placed the whiskey bottle on the table with an emphasis that made me think for a moment he was offering it to me.

I looked away from him, my eyes searching the room for anything at all, and saw the empty cereal box I'd put back on the shelf now sticking up out of his trash can. In the silence, I heard the sound of Bobby taking a swallow of whiskey and his show of calm left me at a loss. It was as if something fundamental had changed during the time I'd been sitting in his car and I wondered what it was, what he'd let go free, that had left his face with an expression no more violent than a slack vague sadness. I had felt that we were moving through the same clamorous life and now his manner made it seem that his had nothing in common with mine.

But I still suspected he knew where my mother was. And though I couldn't understand why he appeared no longer desperate to see her, I realized the question didn't really matter. My impatience now was for him just to go, to get into the Ford and drive away from New Holland.

"So," he said, "you got a look at my stuff."

"Not really. I didn't open anything up."

He raised the bottle to his lips again and when he wiped his mouth I noticed that the knuckles on his right hand were raw and had been bleeding. He sighed. "It doesn't make a shit to me now what you know."

"I al*ready* know."

"What?"

"That you're moving away."

Bobby's smile lifted his face a bit. "That doesn't take a genius. You saw I was packed."

"Where are you going?"

"You tell *me*. You said you knew everything."

"I don't know *that* part."

"It's a kick in the butt, isn't it? You think you know and then you don't."

"I never said I knew that."

"Oh. I thought you said you did."

This sounded to me like our old dialogues, when he'd refused to give me his opinion or advice, and I heard in it the mockery I'd sometimes feared was there. But now, with so much changed, I was only angry. I said, "I'll get on my bike and go if you'll tell me where my mom is."

"What?" He sat up a bit in his chair and leaned toward me.

I asked, "Do you know why she didn't come home this morning?" And I had the thought that she might be home now.

Bobby's frown was so complete there was a kind of wisdom in

it. But before he could speak I said, from somewhere, "It's rotten you were going to leave without saying good-bye to her. I bet Dizzy Dean wouldn't do that to somebody he's taken up with. I bet—"

"Whoa," Bobby said. "Listen up a minute."

Bizarrely, my anger was feeling like indignation on my mother's account. I said, "Maybe you don't know how it is, but—"

"Shut up." He slammed his palm on the table and though I went quiet, my body couldn't be. All I felt was moving in me, powerfully as ardor. I sat on my hands and my legs began to jiggle.

Bobby shook his head. He took a sip of whiskey, then crossed his legs. I caught the polished sheen of the black shoes he was wearing—in memory there's no trace of rain or mud on them—and for the first time I took in the fact that he was dressed for an occasion in neatly pressed gray slacks and a maroon silk shirt.

"She was coming here."

I sensed everything this meant while understanding nothing. I waited through a moment. "Mom was coming here?" I said. "My *mom*?"

"None other," he said.

"When?"

In answer, he looked at his watch, then took another drink. The whiskey was noticeably lower in its bottle, but he didn't seem the least bit drunk.

I said, "Sometimes she forgets to watch what time it is."

"Yeah, you could say that," Bobby said.

"She forgets that a lot, actually," I said. In defending her, it was as if I were also summoning her and I felt her being drawn back to where we all were waiting for her. I stood, my body had to, and I walked the edges of the kitchen and then came back and sat down again. I looked at Bobby and said, "I'm waiting here with you."

"And tell me again, what is it we're waiting for?"

I heard this as him trying to trick me one last time. I said, "You can go ahead and go. I'll wait here till she comes." I gripped the seat of my chair in case he tried to pry me from it.

He fingered the lip of the whiskey bottle, his knuckles evident, a blood-red row. "She's not coming," he said, and to his credit, he turned as he did and looked into my eyes.

"You're lying."

He said nothing.

"You said she *was*."

"It hit me while you were sitting out there. Bing! All of a sudden, clear as a bell."

"How do you know?" I demanded. "How do you know she was even coming here? You don't know *where* she's going, do you?"

"I sure don't," he said and his almost cheerful admission stopped me. He started to take a drink but didn't. Then he said, really to himself, "She'd never come here in broad daylight. Not even now." He shook his head and snorted. "Hell, I knew that."

He looked at me and I don't remember if I asked him something or if he just began to describe my mother calling him late the night before from a motel room at the edge of Marshalltown, waking him to say she'd left Nell's house and asking him to come for her the next afternoon. She'd told him that she wanted them to leave and that it didn't matter where they went; *leaving* was what mattered.

Roused from his sleep, Bobby was slow to hear what my mother was asking and his first blunt thought, which he kept to himself, was that he couldn't go with her that next afternoon because he was pitching a baseball game. But as he grew more alert and listened to her, he realized she'd decided what hadn't even been discussed. They'd never spoken of leaving New Holland, only of ways to remain hidden in it. He voiced his surprise at her eagerness to go. My mother said simply he must tell her yes or no. Did he love her, as he'd said? And if he did, would he meet her at the motel at three o'clock tomorrow?

Sitting with Bobby, trying not to listen to him, I heard only a phrase here or there that somehow got past the violent shrillness in my head. I heard nothing in particular of his arriving at the motel, only to be handed a note from the clerk, who told him my mother had left an hour before. I heard nothing that caused me to wonder what his mind was as he read her note and made himself believe she would meet him, as she'd written, back at his apartment.

But having heard him say she was eager to leave, having gotten the detail of her asking if he loved her, I lunged at Bobby, screaming as primitively as my father had screamed, trying to strike him as my father had tried.

"Hey!" he said. He grabbed my wrists and held them to his chest. He scrambled up out of his chair, still holding me, so that I had to stand with him, struggling madly to get free.

"You son of a bitch! You bastard son of a bitch!"

"Take it easy."

I screamed again and kicked at him and caught a shin, which made him buckle. "I hate you, you bastard! I hate you and so does my mom! She told me she hates you! She told me she did!"

He slightly loosened his grip on my wrists and I beat against his chest—weak, silly punches he was allowing me. I growled in frustration with each feeble blow and then I kicked at him again and missed, his dodging step a folk-dance curtsy.

"Okay, that's enough," he said. He turned me around and, with his hand gripping me by the back of the neck, marched me down the hallway. He stopped me in front of his bathroom door and roughly squared me to face it. "Here," he said. "You wanna hit something, hit this."

I was sniffling and panting and, looking at his door, saw that it was badly battered. At my eye level there were three deep craters, one of which had broken all the way through the wood, cracks and toothy splinterings spreading out from them.

"Go ahead," Bobby said and then he demonstrated, an overhand delivery, his fist grazing the wood on its follow-through. He said, "Use the side of your hand unless you want to wreck it," and he held out his own for me to see the line of bloody knuckles.

I looked at Bobby and then again at the door. But I didn't want to hit it; I wanted still to hit him. So I halfheartedly positioned myself and took a swing that was little more than a knock.

Bobby asked if that had made me feel any better.

I shook my head.

"Then hit it harder," he said.

Resentfully, I swung again.

He shook his head and said I should aim just below one of the ragged dents he'd already made. He tapped a spot. "Make your hand like it's a hammer."

"What for? This is stupid."

In answer, he merely nodded at the door, and so to prove to him his idea was idiotic, I took aim and swung hard, bringing the side of my fist forward and, to my reluctant delight, sending a few small cracks and new splinters running.

"*There* you go," Bobby said. "Go on."

So I swung again and then again, and despite myself found that I was giving over to it, stepping back and striding forward with each blow until finally I broke the panel cleanly, my hand plunging through to my wrist.

"That's the way!" Bobby said. He told me to withdraw my hand slowly and when I had he nodded toward the door again and I went to work even more eagerly. The weakened wood was ideal, both resisting and cushioning my punches, and I let a laugh escape when I broke through to make a second hole.

"All right!" Bobby said.

Newly expert, I eased my hand back through. He turned around, his back to the door, and kicked it hard with the heel of his shoe. I watched, the waiting pugilist, while he started two new lower holes for me.

"There you go," he said, stepping back, and I went at it, feeling looser still. I was sweating, sounding blunt feral grunts each time I struck the door, and for the time it took I was now purely inside my chore, oblivious to anything but it and Bobby's encouragement.

When at last I was done, my hand pulsing and numb, he stepped forward, gave the door two fierce kicks, and punched it once more himself with the side of his hand, causing it to collapse, leaving a dangling ragged semblance of a frame.

We both leaned back against the wall and began to laugh. Inspecting his hand, he said, "I think it's busted," but he was smiling. We were goofy vandals, our laughter a language, and I was exhausted and proud of my wrongdoing. I let my back slide down the wall until I sat on the floor. For just a moment I felt purged, beatified, and then I heard a noise coming from the kitchen and looked to see my father standing in the doorway.

"Dad." I glanced back to see that Bobby had turned to face my father and instinctively I sneaked a look at Bobby's other hand, his glove hand, for the flicking motion against his thigh that was his temper building. But it was still and, in comparison to the bloodied, swelling right, looked pampered.

I was on my feet and hurrying toward my father, who'd moved into the kitchen and closed the door behind him. I reached him and looked up into his eyes. They showed a spiritless amusement as he studied my costume. I felt suddenly awkward, and very small, my body lost in the folds of Bobby's sweatshirt and pants.

"Dad," I hurried to say, "I was coming home right now." And saying this brought the only question back. "Is Mom home?" I blurted. "Is she there?"

My father frowned in response, then a faint smile crossed his face. And maybe it's hindsight that makes me believe he saw me in that instant as something returned to him from a larger thing he'd lost, a piece that he'd begun to fear was lost as well. I believe gratitude was in his expression, and a sense of alliance; that he and I were the ones who knew how it felt to search for her. It was as though I had at last performed, and well, the same delicate and difficult work he had.

He put his hand on my shoulder, then looking past me, said, "What, are you trying to take my son, too?" I whirled around to see Bobby just behind me and as my father moved me aside I expected him to take a step or a swing or just hurl himself at Bobby, as I had tried to do, as he had done three nights before.

"He's the one found me," Bobby said to my father. "I'm not trying to take anybody anywhere."

I saw that this was the resumption of what had started at the field and I felt the adrenaline of my wish for it. My father's eyes were fixed on Bobby. "If you're waiting for a ride," he said to him, "she isn't coming." I glanced up at my father, thrilled to hear that he knew something of my mother. He looked cruelly pleased to be saying this to Bobby.

"Tell me something I don't know," Bobby said.

But my father persisted. He'd moved a step closer to him. "You're not the reason," he said. His voice was perversely triumphant and becoming again one I didn't know. He said, "You're not the reason for any of it. You're just what she found."

Bobby looked weary and careless and sick of it all. He was surely drunk, if he didn't seem to be, and his broken hand must have been draining his strength. He breathed deeply and I suspect he was trying to think of something that would push my father so they could get it over with. "Sometimes," Bobby said, "you find the thing you're looking for. But you're right that I wasn't the reason." He paused. "*You* were, Vaughn. She made that clear as—"

My father's swing was low and sweeping, a discus thrower's, and Bobby instinctively threw up his broken hand. "Ahh!" he shouted from the pain as it blocked my father's arm. I watched my father's other hand fly up and he grabbed Bobby by the throat, the two of them stumbling backward into the kitchen table. Bobby tried to grip my father by the neck in the same way, forgetting his hand made it impossible, but he managed, with his left, to grab his shirt front and hold on. Coupled, their faces bright with hate, they staggered about the room, crashing into the stove, against the sink, and the sounds they made beneath this were oddly contemplative, the aggravated mumbles of furniture movers. Their bodies dipped viciously to the left, to the right, a frenzied choreography that was nothing like wrestling's. Then they toppled, hit the linoleum, and the room boomed and shook. They wiggled wildly over the floor like spilled animals, kicking at each other and scrambling for advantage.

My father threw himself at Bobby and as they scuffled he struck him, a blow to Bobby's stomach that made him wheeze unremarkably. He hit him a second time and a third, and then Bobby rolled over onto his side, protecting his hand, and, nearly whispering, said, "It's busted." My father, on his knees, paused as Bobby raised his hand. "Go on," he said. "Kick the shit out of me." Then he lowered his hand and, still lying on his side on the cold linoleum, made finicky adjustments in the positioning of his body, like a man getting comfortable for a long night of sleep.

My father got up slowly and then bent over, his hands on his knees, looking down at Bobby. He appeared not to know what he should do, confused by the nature of Bobby's surrender. He looked at me then and, panting, said we were leaving. And I sensed as I watched him straighten up and come to me that I was once again an equal, that my chaotic grief was my father's grief as well, and that his and Bobby's world was the world I lived in too.

19

When my father had returned from Nell's and heard that I was gone, he and my grandmother argued briefly. She'd insisted he set out to find me right away, but he'd said, more to calm her than because he believed it, that I'd be back soon and that I had every right to act up a little, given everything I'd been living with.

My grandmother's outburst was immediate. She told my father she was fed up with it all and that included him, and that she too had every right to be. Then she caught herself and apologized, but said he had to realize that she was an old woman and I was a child and we'd both been going crazy because we couldn't do a thing about any of this. She said *she* understood that, but I did not. And now she was sure I'd ridden off to find my mother. She said that, given the state I was in, my father could not just leave me out there, wandering around the countryside. He simply could not do that to me.

My father knew she was right. He went to the porch, saw that it had started to rain, and took down from a hook the coat he wore when he was working in wet weather. Then he pulled on his overshoes and left the house for his pickup.

I imagine the loose buckles of his overshoes making small spur-jingling sounds as he hurries down the sidewalk and that he's nearly reached the truck when he hears a car approaching. I imagine him looking out toward the road and seeing the blue Dodge turning in.

He slows his step, but continues on while he watches, and comes around behind the pickup. He folds his arms and rests his back against the tailgate, while my mother pulls up and comes to a stop and looks out through the windshield, her wipers working.

My father stands in the rain; my mother looks out past the fanning wipers at him. Neither of them seems able or willing to move, until my father pushes himself away from the truck and walks around to the passenger side and gets in beside her.

The rain begins to fall harder, drumming the roof, and my mother continues to stare out at it. Her hands are wringing the steering wheel so that her knuckles appear about to burst through their skin and she says, not yet able to look at my father, "I'm sorry, Lewis."

With this, my father sighs and seems to relax into the seat. He says nothing, but his head starts to nod almost imperceptibly. He's also looking straight ahead at the rain. And surely my grandmother, inside the house, scurries furtively for a view, from the porch to the living room and back again.

"*Are* you now?" my father says. "Well, that's just great, it really is. You coming home like this to say you're sorry."

My mother's mouth tightens. She reaches for a cigarette, lights it, and opens her window vent. She says, "Take whatever tone you need to, Lewis. I know I don't have a right to ask for anything, but—"

"You bet your ass you don't. Not a single goddamn thing!"

"*But,*" my mother persists, "if that's the way you're going to speak to me, it'll only make this that much harder."

"Making things hard for you doesn't bother me much right now."

Rain gusts in through my mother's vent, hissing out her cigarette. She reaches for and lights another and when she exhales her voice is in the smoke as she says to my father, "I'm leaving here, Lewis." She clears her throat. "I have to. I've thought about it and I have to. I'm going and I'm taking Will with me."

My father wearily massages his forehead, then begins again his barely perceptible nod. "No," he says at last. "You're not doing either one. You're not leaving and you're not taking Will anywhere." He reaches over and turns the engine off and takes the keys.

Watching this, she says, "I don't need a car to leave, Lewis. I can walk if I have to, if that will make you feel better."

He looks at her. "Why are you doing this? What in God's name are you doing? Will you please just tell me that?"

There's another silence as she lets him hold the keys. More quietly she says, "I don't expect you to see how things are for me, but I can't help wishing you could."

"So how *are* things for you, Leanne? Tell me how things are. I've been trying to figure that out for twelve years now."

"Oh," she says, not really bitterly, "I'm not so sure about that. Maybe when we first got here, maybe then you did. But not for—"

My father groans. "Is that all this is about?"

" '*All*' this is about?" Her voice is quicker. " '*All*' means the *whole* thing, Lewis. Every bit of everything."

"My God," my father says. "My *God*! I can't believe it. Tell me we aren't having this same fight *again*: I've turned into a farmer, and where's the man you married who said he'd never—"

"Lewis—"

"So you decided to fuck that Ozark hillbilly, because I don't

222

drop everything and take us to Chicago like you thought I would when we first came home? Screwing him's what you came up with to substitute? Are you *that* miserable, Leanne?"

"If that's the way you see it, then I guess I must be."

"You're that desperate?"

"If that's the word that pleases you, apparently I am."

"Ah, *Jesus!*"

This outburst leaves them momentarily speechless. My mother puts out her cigarette and wipes at her first tears. She waits, the rain flurries as if obliged to fill their silence, and then she says softly, "That's one of the things I've been thinking about."

"What is?"

"That I'm wrong saying you'd 'turned into' someone else after you came back here. You couldn't have. When we met you weren't *anyone* yet. And I wasn't either, neither one of us were."

"If you see that, why would you leave? What would that do? You don't fix anything that way. You only make it worse."

She nearly smiles. "I *do* remember that damned determination. You already had *that* in Cheyenne." She flicks her ash. "It was something, I didn't even know what to call it. It seemed . . . exotic. I'd only known men who couldn't hold a hope in their brain from one beer to the next."

My father says, "You didn't answer me."

After a moment she says, "You haven't changed. You've just become who you are. But I haven't. I don't think I've done that yet." She clears her throat.

"You're not making any sense."

"Yes, I am. You know I am."

"No, I don't."

"I'm lost here, Lewis. I have been. I kept waiting for you to see I was. I was even waiting for you to see *you* were lost too. That's what I mean." She paused. "For the longest time, I remembered how unhappy you were when you decided we had to come back.

I kept waiting to see that unhappiness again. I kept thinking, some day you'd finally have to show it. I've been so angry with you sometimes thinking about it; I've felt like you were *lying* to me, that just your getting up in the morning and pretending not to mind your life was telling me a lie every day."

He says, "God, that's such nonsense. You *know* it is. We've talked about this over and over and it comes back every time to the same thing, Leanne. You can't live in the past."

"I don't think that's what I've been doing. Maybe some, but that's not all of it. It's not that simple, Lewis."

"Yes, it *is* that simple. You say it isn't because you don't want it to be."

She smokes. "No. Some of it is what I said. Finally seeing that you *weren't* lost, you aren't, so how could you help me? I mean, how could I *expect* you to?"

My father shakes his head. "What are you talking about, 'you're lost'? I don't know what you're saying. Just talk to me plainly for once. What do you want? What should I have done?" The momentum of his questions is leading him away from the meanness he's been clinging to. "What *is* it you want me to do?"

She rests her chin in her hand, ignoring her wet cheeks, and says, "Be someone you aren't. Make me someone completely different than I am."

"Oh, for Christ's sake."

"It's not you, Lewis, it's me. There's nothing you can do."

This brings my father's anger back. He bangs the dashboard with his fist, while the rain falls like the assaultive world and sprays in again through my mother's open vent. "This is stupid!" he shouts. "This is all so goddamned stupid."

"No, it's not," she says. "It's awful, and I hate it, but it's not stupid. That might be the only thing I know it isn't."

"Bullshit! Don't tell me what it is and what it isn't."

"All right," my mother says. "I won't."

My father is stopped, and he visibly suffers through a long

quiet. When he speaks again he says he can't believe she could hide for two days, just half a mile away, and not give in to the pull of her home.

If he wants her to respond, she doesn't at first, then says softly, "I couldn't believe it either."

This only makes him angrier. He returns to the idea of Bobby Markum, wanting her to tell him when it began, tell him where, and how, and again, "Why *him*, Leanne? He's a drifter, for God's sake, and they say he's a drunk."

My mother can't keep from smiling bitterly. "Ah, yes," she says. "The great, all-knowing 'they.' I always hoped I could find out just who 'they' were and how 'they' managed to have so much information." Then her voice and her expression change, become strained, and she says, "I don't think . . . I don't see how you knowing any of that, how it would help either one of us now."

He doesn't answer. He studies the rain. Beyond the drive, a hen, escaped from the coop, has settled among puddles and waits to see if it will drown.

"I guess," my mother says, "it's what I said before. He's so exactly someone you aren't. So maybe I thought that meant I could be completely different than I am." She looks at my father. "And whatever I am, despite what you think, I am not a whore."

My father grimaces and closes his eyes. When he opens them again they are glistening. "Don't do this," he says. "Stop doing this, Leanne."

In answer, my mother very slightly nods. She might be agreeing to stay after all; she might be saying she's sorry but, yes, she has to leave. She reaches for my father's hand, opens it, and strokes his palm. He merely lets her, having turned back to stare out again through the windshield.

"Do you love him?" he asks.

She waits. "I'm . . . grateful to him. I don't know when I'd've seen things if I hadn't . . ." She says, "It helped me see how I was, I *am*. But I'm leaving alone, if that's what you mean."

"Do you love me?" he asks.

She waits longer. "I don't know if I love anyone right now." She watches him slowly shake his head in response, watches his face alter, begin to set and harden, the pleading sadness going smoothly out of it.

"I have to go," he says.

"I need to see Will."

"He's not here."

"Where is he?"

"He rode off on his bike, I suspect to look for you."

"In *this?*"

"He got pretty tired of waiting for you to show up. I don't think the weather mattered a hell of a lot to him." He nods toward his pickup. "If you want to come, I'm going out to look for him."

"Lewis, I—"

"Listen to me." He pulls his hand away from hers and turns toward her. "If you leave, you're not taking him with you."

"I—"

"*Hear* that, Leanne. You're not taking him with you." He holds his eyes on her, a look that proves unanswerable, and she finally turns away.

"We'll see," she says, a primness in her voice, and each of them has sensed some valedictory hostility. She reaches for the keys he's placed between them on the seat.

She starts the car and he climbs out into the rain, then leans back in. "If you find him before I do, bring him home, Leanne. You'll be sorry if you don't. I'll make sure you're very sorry if you don't bring him home. I don't know how, but I will." When she glances up and meets his eyes, she sees in them a more composed and knowing bitterness and he appears distinguished by the perfect burden of it.

Then he shuts the door and walks to his pickup. He doesn't turn around as he hears her put the car in gear and back out of the drive and speed away, the gravel sloshing.

20

My father lived in New Holland for fifty years after his return from Cheyenne, thirty-eight of them after my mother left. As if he'd been waiting for me to depart, he began, soon after I left for college, to buy additional land, year after year seeking ever more seriously the rigorous cadences of the farming life. Over time, he would acquire nearly twelve hundred acres and the necessary implements and hired hands to work them. He would, in other words, exemplify a version of ambition and dream that my mother could not have understood.

Gradually, then, with all his acquisitions, he built for himself a kind of enormous moat of land and labor around his life. And while I don't mean to say he became reclusive, it's true that he had, with so much farm surrounding him, the reason and excuse not to leave it very often.

About four years ago, after his first mild stroke, he began to experience fits of paranoia. They grew gradually more frequent until, toward the end of his days on the farm, he often called the

Van Zants to say that men bent on murdering him were hiding in his fields. One night he became hysterical in this conviction and drove his pickup out into a cornfield in search of his killers. Back and forth he roamed, the pickup's headlights on high beam, ruining several acres of his crop, as harvest-ready stalks snapped like cane beneath the axles. Shortly after this, I flew from Chicago and spent several days arranging for his move to the nursing home in New Holland. During the months he lived there, he became more and more convinced of plots against him.

At his funeral, Anna and I spoke to a woman I'd known when growing up. After several minutes of polite conversation full of the condolences such talk requires, the woman told me, to my great surprise, that she and my father had dated for a few years. She said they'd begun to see each other some even while I was still at home, but I can say that they'd done so with such secrecy that I, at least, hadn't known.

Timid as a schoolgirl, she smiled and confessed she had fallen deeply in love with my father. Her blue eyes widened behind her glasses as she admitted this to me. She said, though, that she'd seen soon enough there was no chance that my father would ever love her. She said she believed he lived all too keenly with a notion of how he'd been viewed during the time of my mother's affair and in the first years after she had left. He had, my father's friend believed, in some measure accepted the role he felt the town had given him, and a share of his mind was forever occupied with the sense that people were waiting to see if he would somehow lose control of his life again.

"I kept telling him," she said, touching her tightly curled gray hair, "I kept telling him, Lewis, forget the past. But he couldn't." Then, as she prepared to leave the funeral home, she told Anna it was a pleasure to have met her, though she wished the circumstances could have been different. She kissed me on the cheek and summoned a memory of some clever thing I'd said to her when I was eight, and told me my father had been a kind, good man.

———

When I think about the months, the first year or more after my mother left us, I remember almost nothing particularly. I don't recall—a small example—if my mother's Aunt Marla Jo, not knowing she was gone, sent any letters to Iowa. I don't even know when or how my parents' divorce got done. I retain instead a feeling, profound and immutable as the air's shifting heat, that moved from numbness to expectation and through intensities of emptiness. And threaded through all that there are also the words—my memory has reduced them to a litany I came quickly to despise—of my father and my grandmother offering me the message that they loved me, and that my mother was not coming back.

I was often in trouble during that time. I picked fights with classmates. I stole from the stores on the square—it hardly mattered what—becoming a blatant and reckless little thief. Which meant I usually got caught, the merchant lecturing me and informing my father I'd been at it again. Obviously, I'd lost all concern with what God might think of my behavior.

I do remember that at some point early on in my delinquency—my sense is that less than a year had passed—my father sat me down and struggled to tell me in some detail of my mother coming to the farm that rainy day. He was doubtless growing desperate with my antics and hoping such a talk might somehow help to quiet them, would perhaps answer questions I didn't realize I was trying to ask. Though I know I already understood some broadly stroked version of her leaving, again I don't remember how any of the story got to me.

When he began to talk to me, my father started oddly, saying,

"I don't want you to worry." I recall a vow, the sound of resolve in his voice.

"About what?" I asked.

"About . . . anything." I sensed then what he was referring to.

I looked at him. His curly hair was wild, as it often was from his habit of running his hands through it. My mother sometimes teased him when it got this way, calling him "Snookie," after a similarly curly-haired singer on television whose dull and range-less voice she loved to be offended by. In response to her, my father would smile; as I've said, he always seemed to like it when she teased him.

As I recall, I responded with ugly impudence to my father's effort to explain things in detail. I accused him—I don't know what words I used—of betraying me by not telling me all this sooner. Angrily, I demanded to know why he hadn't.

"Because it seemed too soon," he said. "Because . . . I couldn't see what good it would do."

Hearing this, I became even more insolent. I asked him why he'd bothered then to tell me at all. What good, I wondered, did he think it would do now? He looked at me and answered, his voice quiet, but with a sudden coldness in his calm that gave him frightening strength. He said, "None at all, apparently."

Late that same night, I was awake in my bed when I saw a flicker of light move across my window. After a moment it repeated, patterning the shade like a hectic dawn. For a while I simply lay there, but the flitting light persisted until I grew curious enough to gather myself up and get out of bed. I walked to the window and raised the shade and that is when I saw the fire.

It was coming from the corner of the barnyard where I nor-mally burned the trash in an old fifty-gallon barrel. I could see my father standing behind the barrel, lit by the fire. I wondered why he'd thought the chore couldn't wait till morning.

He was tending the fire with great care, bending down and adding to it at regular intervals, never wandering away or even looking out into the night. I continued to watch him for a short time, then started to turn back toward my bed when whatever he gave the flames at just that moment caused them to pennant fiercely. For an instant, the whole low sky was fire and I realized he wasn't merely burning trash.

I found my slippers and put them on and shuffled through the kitchen out onto the porch. I stopped for a moment to watch the fire, then opened the door and stepped outside. As I began to walk the thirty yards toward my father, I glanced up to see that my grandmother was looking down from her lighted window.

I opened the gate and entered the barnyard, walking past her garden and past the stump where we killed hens. I could feel my slippers, squishing-wet in the grass. After a few more steps I was close enough to call to him. I looked up again and saw that my grandmother had left her window.

He'd moved to get away from a tail of shifted smoke and his back was to me now. "Dad," I whispered, because the pure, speechless business of his work made it seem to me I should. "Dad, what are you doing?" I was ten feet behind him but he gave no sign of having heard me. He bent down, and I stopped to watch. He was in the darkness, the fire above him in the barrel growing smaller as it waited. I could barely make him out, but he appeared to hold his pose, perhaps sensing something near, perhaps reaching for the can of gasoline, perhaps only pausing to gather more of my mother's clothes from the pile beside him.

Standing, he turned enough for me to see that he was holding some blouses and dresses. A blue wool winter coat I'd forgotten her wearing was draped over his arm like something slain. He dropped the clothes in his hands into the flames. The coat slithered off his arm to join them.

"Dad?" I said more loudly. He jerked around to face me.

"Why are you out of bed?" he asked.

"I couldn't tell what you were doing." I walked up and stood next to him.

"Never mind what I'm doing. Why are you up?" His voice was irritated. He stepped to place himself between the fire and me, as if to try to hide the evidence. The fire had furled to take everything he'd given it and now it snapped and leapt.

Burned offerings, I thought.

When he turned away from the flames I glimpsed the fury—it was stunning—distorting his face.

From the house I heard the porch door slamming and I didn't glance away to see my grandmother hurrying toward us, for my eyes could not leave my father's face.

"Get back inside," he said. He took a step toward me and began to usher me away.

"What's going on?" my grandmother demanded, reaching us.

"Nothing," my father said. "We're coming in now." As we walked toward the house, I squirmed in his grasp so that I could still look up at him. I was determined to hold my eyes on his face.

For some time afterward, when I remembered the way my father looked that night, I was strangely grateful, as cruel toward him as that sounds. Seeing his face in my mind, I felt a flickering, as if from the flames, of how new his anger must have seemed to my mother and, so, how newly frightening to her. And this allowed me for a while to cling to the belief that she'd told me the truth when she said she'd feared his anger; that his anger had caused her to leave their quarrel and not return.

———

By the time I reached high school, I was regularly getting into more serious fistfights and I was drinking beer whenever I could find someone to buy it for me. I'd begun to grow into myself physically, becoming the broad-backed muscular copy of my father, and because I didn't any longer play a sport—had gradually dropped out of all school activities—I must have found fighting the best way to use my restless strength.

I liked the taunt, the foreplay, the exhilaration of the thing about to begin, better than the fights themselves. But I liked them, too, well enough at least to want to put myself in places where there might be one. I was suspended from school for a week two or three times after starting fights behind the bleachers at football and basketball games. I broke my arm in one of my most memorable fights, when a group of us had gotten brave after several beers and driven in two cars to Dunbar, New Holland's most hated rival. There, we'd cruised its deserted square, rolling down our windows and loudly cursing the place and anyone sorry enough to live there until we'd flushed out a number of our counterparts, the would-be hoodlums of Dunbar. We'd all scrambled out of our cars and quickly matched up according to size and gone at each other beneath a cone of street light that illuminated us like performers on a spotlit stage, until Dunbar's night policeman arrived and broke things up.

Sheer hormonal excess, and to a real extent my drinking, explained some of the desire for this sloppy and craftless violence (and that *is* what it was; I simply launched my body toward my adversaries, mauling them like an uncoordinated cub. If there were a chance I might hurt someone, or get hurt, in the process, this seemed only so much the bonus). But it was also true that in the eye of a fight I felt the adrenal rush of reflex and frenzy. I felt weightless as I flailed away, sensing I was free inside an instant that demanded a fury of near-panic; demanded something anyway the opposite of thought.

Besides the periodic fistfights, what occupied me for quite some time were long solitary drives through the countryside. I drove the blue Dodge, which my father, without saying as much, had given to me when I'd gotten my driver's license. This was, of course, the car we'd thought of as my mother's and he'd driven it only a handful of times since the night, shortly after her disappearance, when a highway patrolman called to say it was sitting by the side of a gravel road near Grinnell, its keys under the floor mat on the driver's side. A farmer who worked the land next to the road had grown curious after seeing it there three days in a row.

My excursions in the Dodge were nothing I planned. I'd leave school at the end of the day, intent on driving straight home, and the next minute I'd find myself heading off somewhere.

Once I'd started out, I was instantly conscious of ignoring my chores at home and of causing my father and grandmother to feel a great, insulted anger, one that couldn't believe I was doing yet again what I'd been ordered not to do. As I drove, I would picture my father coming into the barnyard to discover that I hadn't gathered the eggs or fed the chickens. I would see his face flush and hear his burst of anger—spoken, alas, to the chickens sashaying stupidly at his feet. I'd see him rushing to the house to hear my grandmother confirm my absence, the two of them helping one another's agitation.

I never ventured more than twenty or thirty miles from New Holland. As twilight deepened, I continued to aimlessly crisscross the dirt and gravel roads, following their rigid grid, the surveyor's scheme, that served to section the prairie so precisely.

Hours and the black land passed and I'd have forgotten my father's and grandmother's fury, my mind fashioning instead a kind of undefended void that let everything come in. I smoked cigarette after cigarette, the flicking of my lighter as menacing as a switchblade in my imagination of who I was. And in the gathering momentum of night, I'd let myself feel rage; rage at the place and at my life and at all the real and exaggerated circumstances that kept me in them. Within it I'd feel a simple longing: to be entirely other than I was; to be the outlaw I was pretending to be.

Some nights, ravenous, I'd point the Dodge toward Marshalltown and pull into an A and W Root Beer drive-in on the out-skirts of town. I'd devour my food in minutes and, as soon as I'd finished, head back out of town on the same highway, past the gas stations, a few low-roofed factories, and past the three motels that then lined the highway, wondering always which one of them my mother had stayed in the night she left Nell Beal's; wondering from which room she'd called Bobby Markum to ask him if he meant it when he'd said he loved her.

Then, back in the country, passing farm after deeply sleeping farm, I'd begin to sense that unbroken country stillness that makes the landscape seem not just quiet but more drastically abandoned. The smell of stockyards, cow and pig shit, was the evidence it wasn't. I'd find that I was heading home and I'd start to sense myself being caught in what I think of as a kind of mel-ancholy equipoise: wishing to run while wishing to be found. As I drove, I would try to imagine the will required to flee; to choose any one of the straight gravel roads and simply stay on it, what-ever the direction, ignoring the crossroads' invitations to turn. Both the notion and the person who could do this seemed heroic. Just then, my mother seemed heroic to me.

I would hold that idea until I began to get within a few miles of our farm. Then, predictably, I'd sense it growing complicated. And by the time I'd reached the beginning of our land, I'd have decided to tell my father the next morning that I was sorry for my cruel and pathetic disappearances. I'd tell him I knew my behavior was stupid and that I wasn't trying to make his life more difficult. I felt sure I was sincere; I felt sure he'd hear I was.

But home again and inside the house, I'd usually meet my father coming out of his room. He'd be still dressed, his eyes weary, his voice exhausted as he icily informed me of the time. I remember him once saying, when I'd come in after one o'clock, "Your grandmother is worried sick about you. I wish she wasn't. You don't deserve her worry." Then he'd state the terms of my new curfew or the length of time he was taking the car away from me. And in so doing he would give me the gift of renewed anger and save me from feeling I had to tell him I'd been wrong.

———

One night in late winter on one of my drives, I lost control of the Dodge on an icy bridge seven miles from home and drove into a concrete guardrail. The car was crushed and, among my injuries, the worst was to my legs. I needed crutches for months. Both knees had badly damaged ligaments and neither had much cartilege left after surgery.

It was during the time of my recovery that my father and I reached a kind of truce. I'm not sure how or why—again I don't remember the details—but I recall a sense of moving modestly toward a patched but gamely reordered life. I remember being able to linger in my father and grandmother's company—at the table after supper, in the television room. I remember not being driven mad, for the first time since my mother had left, by periods of silence among the three of us; of being able, night after night, to live calmly through the ordinariness of evening.

Obviously the step toward reconciliation had to have come from me, since my father was not the one who'd been committed to hostility. I can't imagine what my first gestures might have been, but I do remember something in me just surrendering, as though I finally saw that the work of resentment was stupid and fruitless and simply too exhausting. And maybe, dependent as I was on my father for those weeks—to drive me, to see to it that I had what I needed—I was glad to regress, seizing on the chance to play out the end of childhood.

At the end of one such evening, I was sitting with my father drinking coffee in the kitchen and felt all of a sudden, maybe to my own surprise, sufficiently bold or curious. And so I turned to him and asked, "Did you ever look for her?"

Naturally enough, he shot a startled look at me. My question, as I remember the night, had come to him with no warning, breaking an easeful silence at the table. "What?" he asked.

"Mom, I mean," I said. "Did you ever look for Mom?"

He shook his head and said, "My God, Will, have you been thinking all this time I didn't?"

Almost with apology, I said yes, I guessed that's what I'd thought.

He shook his head a second time and I readied myself eagerly to hear the story of his long and maddening search. Again he voiced his surprise that I'd been holding this assumption all along.

And then he began to describe for me the day and night he'd combed the countryside in his pickup. Listening, I could tell that he was forcing himself to speak with candor and as he recalled the maniacal way he'd behaved that night, I could hear in his voice an embarrassment so full that it quivered once or twice. I couldn't bring myself to interrupt, but wished he would hurry past this part of the story that was causing him such discomfort. And when he'd finished telling me what I had and hadn't known, I thanked him and waited for him to continue.

But after some moments I began to realize that he was going to offer nothing more, that he was done, that that was all the story there was. And as I sat there, unable to meet my father's eyes, I felt something go out of me, some vestige of faint dream, as if a light I'd been watching across a deep night distance suddenly went dark for what I feared was the last time.

It was years later, during the time I was traveling from one magazine assignment to the next, that I began to check every new town's phonebook for the name McQueen. Sometimes, if the town was of any size at all, I'd look in the local newspaper to see if there were clubs that featured singers. Needless to say, this yielded nothing.

Once, I thought I saw my mother in a women's shoe store on

Fifth Avenue. Another time, I was certain for a moment I saw her leaving the Petrified Forest souvenir shop outside Calistoga, California. Without a thought I started toward the woman I had glimpsed, then understood that she was roughly the age my mother had been when she left and I realized, however tardily, that it was futile to think I could easily recognize her so many years later.

As I headed back to my car I suddenly thought of what my father had said that day at the dinner table just before I told him my mother was hiding at Nell's.

"Aren't you going to keep looking for her?" I'd asked.

"You know she can come back whenever she wants," he'd said. "You know that, don't you?"

———

One day when I was maybe eight or nine I spent a morning imagining a baseball game on a field I'd created at the edge of the acreage. I'd arranged bases of burlap sacks filled with soy beans and I was letting the picket fence separating the lawn from the barnyard serve as a homely outfield wall.

At some point, after I'd begun to pantomime the action, my mother came outside and sat on the back-porch steps, assuming the role of the crowd while I played. She wore, let's say, a lightweight housedress; sleeveless, blue-and-white checked. No doubt she was barefooted, she almost always was in summer.

Watching me, she applauded on cue each imaginary hit, each theatrical catch I made. As always, I was glad to have her there, but that day I kept hearing her cheers as too high-pitched, as lonely solo sounds, and I stopped to ask her if she could make her voice sound more like a crowd.

"Like you usually do," I said, "like this," and I reminded her with my airy O-mouthed exhalation: "Yeaaaaaa!"

She offered me her best impression, but I still felt it wasn't as good as it could be. "Pretend it's a *huge* stadium," I advised.

She shook her head and smiled and then her voice, as though a medium's, spoke the black dialect of whomever it was she was conjuring from her lounge-singing past. "Honey," she said, "it ain't how *big* the room; it's how enthusiastic." And when I started to play again she watched for a moment more, then got up and went inside, maybe just because she had to start the midday dinner.

———

I live in Chicago, as I said. Anna, a photographer, inherited at her parents' death a large brick townhouse on Chicago's North Side near the DePaul Seminary. We met in New York, when she came to my apartment to take my photograph for a book jacket. I now teach and write novels, and still a few articles and essays. I am childless. I hope I've finally found, with Anna, that I can be less than perfect in a marriage. But whatever else, Anna has shown me that a woman's emotional evenness and her daily generosity are not the symptoms of her dull imagination. For she is calm and generous, though not to a fault, and she is a woman of high imagination.

When I think of my mother now, I sometimes have the idea that she might not have left if she'd herself held onto that lovely piece of wisdom she relayed the day she watched me play my imaginary baseball game. *It ain't how big the room, it's how enthusiastic.* For at least in New Holland she had, in my father, someone who adored her; and in my grandmother, whatever else, she had an ardent spiritual ally. But as the years there passed, it was as if she came more and more to feel the confinements of the room, no matter how great the enthusiasm of those—my father, my grandmother, me, even her worshipful friend, Nell—she regularly played to.

When I think about her in the first days, the first weeks and months, after she left, at times I picture her waking up in some boardinghouse, some rented room, and telling herself this was the day she was coming back; but then, before the morning was out, finding a sign, divining an omen of some sort, that persuaded her to wait another day. *One more day,* she said to me the last time I saw her. *I need one more day.* And I imagine this pattern repeating itself morning after morning, her vow on waking growing weak and susceptible as she thought about the life she would face if she came back, until the very accumulation of time became an ever stronger reason for her to stay away.

It's easier for me to think of her as forever a vagabond, living out her days on some bare, corrupted margin; easier that than to think she might in time have found a way, a reason, to embrace again a settled and more conventional life, the life with us that she abandoned. And picturing her, alone, I see her on the day— a year after leaving? two years or three?—when she suddenly realizes the balance of sadness has shifted, that her guilt for having left is now no greater than the dread that descends when she thinks of going back.

I see her sitting at a table, or at the counter of a diner, finishing her second cup of coffee and lighting another cigarette and only then the awe of it coming to her, that she had not waked and lain for minutes in her bed and told herself she was going home that day. She'd not had that companionable bleakness waiting for her to open her eyes. And in that instant of recognition, relief and despair break over her equally, her crying oblivious and eruptive and more intricate than sorrow, and as she cries something harder than a thought comes through to her: that in ways she can't fathom she might begin to hurt less, or if not less, at least somehow differently.

But at other times, in other dispositions, I've thought that she didn't come back, not because she felt an overwhelming guilt and shame, but because she could never feel enough of either, and, so, could not imagine how she might rejoin us if she couldn't present us with a returning gift of guilt.

And there have also been times when I've told myself that she was, after all, her mother's daughter; that their histories of pregnancy and youthful marriage are eerily the same; and that I should try to dwell less on my mother's leaving and more on all the years she stayed. I've remembered again the drama she brought to each day on the farm and have assumed there was, in every mood that took her away while in my presence, in every great sweep of her ecstasy or anger, at least a glimmer of her deep impulse to flee. I've recalled what she said to Nell Beal when she spoke of her first uncertain weeks with Marla Jo: that it didn't seem strange to be living day to day. I can't imagine how it would be to sense life as so precariously discrete and I've thought that, for my mother, leaving was easy; it was staying that was hard. For more than a decade she refused the easier thing, working daily to find something that made her able to stay.

So I've thought in a hundred different ways about what my mother did and how she could have done it. Sometimes I've seen her manner of leaving to be a facile gesture in the end, one of the least inspired ways of rebellion. But then I've told myself that life is not so founded as the well-constructed tale. In life, people do things with a glib randomness; with an apparent illogic that's indeed just that—apparent.

Several times I've decided that in fact she'd gotten somewhat comfortable in her New Holland life—in her disappointment in it, her great frustration with it. That she was unconscious of her resignation, but it was there, though not so deeply through her that she was unresponsive to Bobby's arrival in her life, a thing she first saw as an instant that had visited itself—rapturous, a kind of tropism—but which was merely, as my father said, the thing her unhappiness found.

Then I've decided she was only able to see herself once she'd stepped out of her life—with Bobby, because of Bobby, whose appeal began and ended for her because he was, as she said, so exactly not my father. And once she'd managed to do that, to look from outside back into her life, she knew she couldn't resume it, but could not imagine either where she'd find the will to change it.

It was my overriding hope that in setting down these memories I would give the story a shape and a final shading, most of all so that I could say to myself that it was done. For it seems to me that everyone needs to arrive at a point of quieted interest in his past, after which it becomes, if still influential, nothing more absolving or provocative than that.

But I've not been able to do that very well. For still, when I come back to the astonishing fact that my mother was able to go away and not return, her actions remain no more fathomable to me than they were the day she left. In the fantasies of leaving we shared when I was a child, neither of us ever left alone. So regardless of the reasons I work to give her, however explicable the history I place her in, whatever empathies I'm briefly able to call up, a part of me asks—and I face the likelihood that I will always ask—how it was that she could leave. How she could have done that. How she could not have schemed to steal me, not pleaded and connived. Why she didn't love me more; love me enough to need, simply need, to take me with her.

21

At the close of my grandmother's life, she lost that glint of aggressive candor that had been the definition—I want to say the soul—of who she was. In her final months she was a giggly ingenue, convinced for example that every male who entered her room had come in the hope of making love to her. This wonderful presumption delighted her—and who wouldn't make it the senility of choice? But before that time, maybe a year before, while her mind had grown simpler it was not yet completely confused.

During that time, I visited her one day in the nursing home in New Holland, the same place my father would come to, his final delusions not so giddy as hers. When I walked into her room, I found her sitting at a rolltop desk she'd moved from the farm. She'd lost so much of her size by then that she needed pillows on her chair to sit high enough to work at it.

She didn't see me when I entered; her back was to the door and she was hunched over the desktop, attending to something or other. She'd grown nearly deaf, so I didn't call to her. As I approached I could see her struggling with a pair of scissors in her gnarled arthritic fingers. I came to stand beside her and she smiled up at me, seeming pleased but not at all surprised to see me, as if she'd known I was in the room all along.

I saw that she was working on her scrapbook of famous Iowans, which she'd again turned to with ferocious recommitment some months before. She slid the book toward me. It was by then a massive, bulging volume—clippings pasted down, others spilling out—and anyone ignorant of the organizing theme would have been hard-pressed to guess what those included had in common.

I got a chair and sat beside her. Leafing through the pages, I came across a story about the anniversary of the radio station in Shenandoah where the Everly Brothers first sang. There was a scandalized article on Johnny Carson, a native of Corning, reporting the breakup of one of his marriages. (My grandmother had long resented Carson for speaking on television of his boyhood in Nebraska. "But you were *born* in Iowa, Johnny," she would say to the screen. I noticed that she had scribbled in the margin of the article, "I hope he's learned a lesson," implying, I assumed, that Carson had gotten his comeuppance for trying to be a big shot.) In the scrapbook there was also an account of an old man from Anthon who'd been hiccuping nonstop for nearly sixty years and had recently appeared, hiccuping cheerfully, on the *Today Show*. There was a newspaper clipping, not yet pasted down, whose headline read, "Iowa Horse Places Third in Kentucky Derby."

But the article that caught my eye was a long and sober piece in the *Des Moines Register* detailing the apparent suicide of Jean Seberg in Paris. According to the story, Seberg had been found in the backseat of her car, dead from an overdose of barbiturates, her unclothed body wrapped in a white sheet. There were suspicions that the death was not a suicide. It was apparently well known that she couldn't drive without her glasses, which were nowhere to be found in the car. Still, she'd left a note to her teenaged son. She was forty years old.

This was in 1979—I've recently checked the date—which means my grandmother was eighty-three and would live not quite another year.

My grandmother waited while I read this story and when I'd finished she said, of Seberg's death, "I think it's just real sad." At that stage of her life she had settled into that common self-absorption of people who are old which makes it hard for them to be interested in anything beyond themselves. But that day she talked on and on about how sorrowful Seberg's death was, and it was clear that something about the story had caught and enlivened her imagination. At one point she declared irrefutably, "If she'd stayed in Marshalltown, her life would've been different." Until finally she said, her raspy voice a near shout, "I think of that poor boy, all of a sudden without a mother. We can't imagine what that must feel like."

Her words made me miss a breath. I knew very well that she hadn't perversely planned their effect, that for the brief time her mind could do such work she was considering the fate of *that boy* and nothing more. Still, I couldn't speak over the rawness of my thoughts, so I turned and again began to page through the scrapbook. She sat silently beside me, assuming my enjoyment, the pride in her project evident on her face.

It was then, after I'd begun to recover my emotional balance, that I asked her to remind me just how she determined who was a famous Iowan. And she answered me immediately, with great solemnity, reciting hoarsely like an oath her guidelines as I've described them: that the person's recognition be truly national; that it preferably be gained in some way, some place, outside of Iowa, making it virtually impossible for famous Iowans to be presently living in Iowa.

What sparked my curiosity was the discovery in the scrapbook of the New Holland weekly newspaper's stories of my grandfather's death and his funeral, which was held at the Presbyterian church in Dunbar. It was the most relaxed of the nearby denominations and, so, I presume it was decided, the church my grandfather would have had the least objection to being celebrated in.

His funeral drew so many people, the article reported, that most of the men rose to give their seats to women and stood in the outer aisles and at the back of the sanctuary. Others were forced to move outside. But the false-spring weather, an accomplice in his death, had continued unabated, so the stained glass windows were fully raised and the men stood beneath them and listened to the service. And along with the stories, there were several letters to the editor that paid tribute to my grandfather. They cited his family's New Holland founding roots and his example, no less impressive for having been cut short, of fidelity to the ordered life, the local place.